ATOMIC REX

THE CONQUEST OF CHIMERA

MATTHEW DENNION

SEVERED PRESS

HOBART TASMANIA

ATOMIC REX: THE CONQUEST OF CHIMERA

Copyright © 2017 Matthew Dennion

WWW.SEVEREDPRESS.COM

ISBN: 978-1-925711-48-6

This book is dedicated to my fans and to their love of Atomic Rex! Thank you all for making this book series such a success and for always pushing me for more Atomic Rex. I love you for it!

Author's Note – In addition to being the third novel in the Atomic Rex series, this book also follows the events of my novel Chimera Scourge of the Gods.

PROLOGUE

Three massive figures stood in the space outside of time and between worlds. One being appeared as a giant human adorned in robes and a loincloth. The giant had a muscular build and olive-colored skin. His face had the weathered appearance of old leather. The giant's beard was long and tangled. His eyes glowed with a blood-red color.

The second being had the appearance of a colossal gargoyle who was wreathed in flames. The creature had pitch-black skin and huge bat-like wings that protruded out of its back. In his right hand, the figure held a flaming sword.

The third creature was a large wingless four-legged dragon with the horned head of a goat. The combined power possessed by these three beings was comparable to that of the sun itself. They were conquerors of worlds. On countless planets, throughout numerous dimensions, they had conquered worlds and destroyed every form of life on those planets to absorb their life energy. Once they drained a world of its life force, they would move to the next world, leaving only an empty husk of rock in their wake.

The three figures stood before a swirling vortex that was between them. They were staring at a world that had once been theirs but had been lost to them. They had ruled over the world, letting its population grow so that they could one day absorb the life energy of its inhabitants. During their rule over the planet, they carelessly indulged in their baser instincts and produced offspring. Their own children would rise up against them and drive them from the planet that was rich with life and potential energy. For centuries, the offspring now calling themselves gods, ruled over the planet. The gods were able to absorb energy from the planet Earth without taking life. The gods became caretakers of the planet, doing all that they could to ensure its survival. As long as the Earth thrived, it would sustain the gods until the planet's sun reached the end of its existence. Much like their fathers and mothers before them, the gods had the native population of the planet worship them. Then, much like the gods did to their parents, the natives of the planet would turn on them. The natives, known as humans, would turn their backs on the gods for other gods that were less tangible and offered much more rewards than they could.

The gods accepted that they had been replaced as the deities of the humans and they moved on to dimensions where they could still access the life force of the planet and guard it against the coming of those who they overthrew to gain possession of it. During their absence, the humans had not only turned on them, but they had also turned on the planet itself. The humans were slowly draining the planet of its life force through their abuse of its resources in the same manner that the progenitors of the gods had. The gods decided that they needed to intercede on behalf of the planet that sustained them. They sought to wipe the humans off the face of the Earth with their army of mythical creatures. The mechanical weapons that the humans had created over the centuries were powerless before the gods. The arrogant gods thought that the destruction of the humans would be more of an extermination than a war.

The gods were quickly proven wrong. While the gods' mastery over electromagnetic pulses rendered the humans' technological weapons useless, mankind had created a biological weapon that was more powerful than anything the gods had ever encountered. The humans, led by the brilliant Dr. Jonathan Toombs, had created the kaiju known as Chimera. Chimera was a gigantic monster created from the combined genetic material of a sperm whale, a gorilla, and a lion. The monster had the rubber grey skin, thick face, and fluke tail of the sperm whale, the torso of a silverback gorilla, and the hind legs, teeth, claws, and mane of a lion. Chimera stood at a height of two hundred and fifty feet tall. In addition to his tremendous strength, near inexhaustible stamina, and extreme durability, the creature also possessed the power to emit a sonic blast that would temporarily disable an opponent's central nervous system. With their technology largely unavailable to them, the humans turned to Luke Davis, a teacher of students with autism, to instruct Chimera using Applied Behavior Analysis techniques. This approach helped Chimera to not only bond with Luke but with all humans. So that when the time came to battle the gods and their beasts, Chimera felt as if he was not only fighting an invading force but that he was fighting to protect his very family.

Chimera crushed the gods and their monsters. Olympus had been left in ruins and the gods who lived there had fled to another dimension. The gods that had ruled over ancient Mesopotamia had nearly been exterminated. The Norse gods had been defeated and the Rainbow Bridge between Earth and Asgard was destroyed. In addition to these losses, most of the mystical creatures that the gods had at their disposal had also been slain by Chimera. Cerberus, the Scylla, Fafnir, and countless other beasts had all fallen in battle against the hybrid monster.

The gods had also attempted to create a new race of demi-gods by having their nymphs Allison and Aiden seduce young men and women to use as breeders. This part of the gods' plans also crumbled when Allison seduced Dr. Toombs. With Toombs under her sway, Allison kidnapped all of the young women who were carrying demi-gods and disappeared with them.

It was the raspy voice of the dragon-like creature known as Tiamat who commented on these events. "The gods who opposed us millennia ago are at their weakest. The monster the humans created has scattered them and greatly depleted their forces. They will not be able to mount a defense against us if we attempt to reclaim this Earth."

The demonic Surtr shook his head and when he spoke, his voice sounded as if someone was talking through a pyre of burning wood. "The creature, Chimera, as the humans call him, represents a threat. We could take the planet with our forces, but a war against that monster would leave us depleted as well. The gods could seek to attack us at that point and reclaim the planet from both us and the humans."

The majestic and yet terrifying titan known as Cronus settled the matter for them. "We can negate the threat posed by Chimera through the use of our own monsters and by adding a new variable into the equation." Cronus waved his hand over the portal they were viewing, causing it to shimmer and then reveal a different version of planet Earth.

Tiamat hissed when he saw the version of Earth that Cronus had brought into view. "The Earth of that dimension is dying. Most of the life there has been exterminated. There is not even enough life energy left to warrant our attention."

Cronus shook his head. "There is one life there that is of extreme interest to us." The titan waved his hand over the portal and the view shifted along the top of what looked like a primordial jungle until some massive creature could be seen in the distance. Cronus closed his hand, forcing the view through the portal to condense on one creature. As the view condensed, a colossal theropod dinosaur came into view. The kaiju had long, powerful, primate-like arms and a thick crocodilian caprice on its back. The monster turned and roared at the portal as if he could sense that something was approaching him. Cronus pointed at the creature. "This is the kaiju known as Atomic Rex! He has killed millions of people on his world and destroyed over a dozen other monsters that had dared to challenge him. He is currently near a nexus where the walls between worlds are weak and that is why I have called you here. We shall take advantage of this monster's current position. We will use our combined might to transport him to Chimera's Earth. Atomic Rex is extremely aggressive and will typically attack any other creature that he sees. Still, we shall ensure that Atomic Rex sees Chimera as his enemy by making him think that the god-destroyer has attacked him. I have watched this Atomic Rex as he laid waste to his homeworld. At first glance, the monster seems to be an agent of pure chaos, but he clearly remembers those creatures that he perceives as enemies and will stop at nothing to destroy them. By tapping into the monster's thirst for vengeance and directing it at Chimera, we will leave nothing to chance as to the outcome of placing Atomic Rex on Chimera's world. At some point, he and Chimera will battle to the death. In addition to Atomic Rex, we shall also unleash the monsters under our command on Chimera's Earth and specifically into the country where Chimera lives. As Atomic Rex and our other monsters slay the population of this Earth, we shall absorb their life energy. Chimera will battle our forces which will weaken and exhaust him. Then when he is wounded and near death, Chimera will face Atomic Rex. Chimera has never faced a creature as powerful as Atomic Rex. The nuclear dinosaur is nearly invincible. After he slays Chimera, Atomic Rex will walk across this Earth, killing everything as he did on his Earth but this time, we shall be there to absorb that life force. Atomic Rex will be our most powerful weapon in conquering and ending this world!"

Atomic Rex was engaged in battle with a large horned kaiju when he felt something pulling at him from behind. The nuclear theropod turned around to see a large green vortex moving toward him. The monster roared at the vortex as it approached him and he saw a glimpse of what he thought was Chimera reaching for him. A second later, Atomic Rex found himself surrounded by a green light and seemingly falling through nothingness. His mind was experiencing a sense of confusion and disorientation while his body felt as if it was being ripped apart on a molecular level. Atomic Rex saw a quick flash of three strange figures staring at him and then he saw a flash of bright yellow light.

Sahara Desert, Africa

The kaiju blinked his eyes several times to adjust to the light. When his vision finally cleared, he was able to ascertain that he was no longer in the rainforest but rather in the middle of a desert. The intelligent monster was well aware that he had moved much farther than simply from one place to the next. He fully understood that he was on another Earth. The nuclear theropod's body could detect the slightest amount of radiation in the air. If he was on his own heavily irradiated world, the monster's body would have detected a much higher amount of ambient radiation than he currently was.

Atomic Rex lifted his head and roared a challenge to this new world. He then began walking across the desert, intent on returning to this Earth's version of the Americas and what he perceived as his territory.

Through a portal, Cronus, Tiamat, and Surtr watched as Atomic Rex began walking across the desert. Surtr shook his demonic head as he stared at Atomic Rex. "As the beast passed by us, I could sense his power. He is truly a force to be reckoned with. Atomic Rex may even present a threat to us should we find ourselves engaged with the monster."

Cronus smiled. "The beast poses no threat to us. I am more than capable of influencing the monster's actions if need be. Even without me directing him, Atomic Rex will attempt to make his way back across the Atlantic toward North America. Even on a different Earth, he will still consider North America his territory. By placing him on a different continent from our main attack, we shall not only increase the number of lives that are being lost to multiple continents, but we will also force those who oppose us to spread their resources thin as they try to deal with threats on both sides of the Atlantic. Our power shall grow as we absorb the life force energy from this planet as Atomic Rex extinguishes it on his great journey. I shall direct the monster toward every city across Northern Africa as he makes his way to the Atlantic, ensuring the deaths of millions. The first move in our war on this Earth has been made. Our most powerful piece is on the board. Now we must surround him with pawns until we are ready to move into a position to crush those would resist us."

Tiamat turned his snake-like head around and the other two followed his gaze. In the darkness behind them, massive, terrible forms shifted in the darkness. The dragon hissed, "Go, and destroy the world that the gods stole from us. Do not stop your rampage until every last form of life on the planet has been extinguished."

The creatures slithering in the darkness walked past their masters and entered the portal that was swirling before them as the imagery within it continued to change, sending the horrors to destinations across North America. When the last monster entered the portal, Cronus peered into it and said, "Once Atomic Rex and the monsters at our command have the attention of the humans and their hybrid, and we have amassed a sufficient amount of life energy, we three shall play our parts. Surtr, you shall use your sword of flames to destroy part of the world with fire. Tiamat, you shall use your flaming breath to destroy part of the world with water. While you two are engaged in these tasks, I shall continue to guide Atomic Rex and coordinate the flow of life energy the kaiju sends to us."

Surtr stared into Cronus eyes. "I shall warn you once more. I sense great power in that monster. Be careful that your new pet does not decide to turn on his master."

At the second suggestion that Atomic Rex could be too powerful for him to control, Cronus glared at the fire demon. The two held a silent stare for a long moment, then the titan's face shifted as his glare changed into a smile. "I can control the beast for as long as we need him." He looked at the portal. "Go and prepare yourselves, while the humans and their monster are engaged with our pawns." He looked back at Surtr and Tiamat. "Within two weeks' time, we shall have all of the energy this world has to give. Then we shall seek out the gods that banished us from this planet and destroy them as well."

CHAPTER 1

Virginia

The sun was shining brightly as Luke Davis turned the ignition on in his SUV. He drove off the military base and into the forests of Virginia. His wife Melissa was sitting in the passenger seat and she smiled at him. "So what are you working on today with the big guy?"

From the back seat his daughters, eight-year-old Sally and four-year-old Suzie laughed. Sally joked with her dad. "Yeah, Dad, what's Chimera going to do today? Balance a building on his nose?"

Suzie chimed in. "Yeah, Dad, is Chimera going to throw it in the air and catch it?" The two girls continued to laugh hysterically at their jokes while their parents smiled.

Luke finally replied, "Today, Chimera is going to work on navigating through a fake town without crushing anything. He is getting better at keeping down collateral damage when moving through populated areas, but he is so big that sometimes by simply taking a step, his footfalls create shockwaves that wreck entire houses." As Luke finished what he was saying, the aforementioned fake town came into view. In a clearing in the middle of the forest was a street length's worth of quickly erected houses. Luke drove around the back of the houses to show his family that the structures were not full houses but only hollow one-sided constructs.

As she was looking at the mock street, Melissa commented, "They're just prop houses like from an old-fashioned movie. Just boards and scaffolds on the back with the front painted to look like a house."

Sally's voice rose with excitement as her mother's words sunk into her mind. "Daddy, are they going to make a movie about Chimera?"

Luke chuckled. "No, honey. I don't know if Chimera is ready for the pressures of the movie star lifestyle yet. Today, we just need to see if he can walk through this pretend street without destroying all of the houses." Luke shook his head as he contemplated the events of his life that had brought him to this point. Two years ago, he was a master teacher of students with autism who used Applied Behavior Analysis (ABA) concepts to teach his students. That all changed when representatives from the government approached Luke and told him that they needed him to be a part of an operation of vital national security. Luke had no idea what they needed an ABA teacher for, but when they offered him four times his current salary, he accepted the job. Of all the scenarios that ran through Luke's mind about what the government could have needed him for, the thought of having him train a giant monster to fight gods and mythological beasts was not one of them.

Luke was taken to a secret military installation in Virginia and introduce to General Sam Parsons. Parsons informed him that the ancient gods of Olympus, Mesopotamia, and Asgard had returned to Earth with the monsters of their mythologies to wipe out the human race. Parsons explained that conventional weapons were useless against these gods. The only option that humanity had was a giant monster that the government had created. The problem was that they needed someone to train the monster to follow directions on what to attack and what to spare. Given Luke's proven success with aggressive students, Parsons felt that he was the person best suited for the job. At first, Luke didn't believe any of the story until he found himself staring at a two hundred and fifty-foot-tall hybrid gorilla, lion, sperm whale monster named Chimera. Luke was no hero, but with the fate of the world on the line, Luke agreed to work with the monster. Chimera responded well to Luke's training and within a few short weeks, the giant monster or "kaiju," as the monster's creator Victor Toombs called him, was ready for combat.

Luke and Chimera would battle all manners of legendary gods and creatures including the hellhound Cerberus, the shark god Asag, the dragon Fafnir, and even the likes of Thor and Zeus themselves. During the course of the war, the gods used the nymphs Aiden and Allison to seduce young men and women for the purpose of using them to breed a new species of demi-gods who replace the humans after the gods had wiped them out.

Luke's wife was kidnapped by Aiden and taken to Asgard itself. This move forced Luke and Chimera to travel to the realm of the gods where the cruel but wise Odin determined that a battle between he and Chimera would lay waste to Asgard, and as such, he released Melissa and promised that the gods would end their attack on the human race. The king of the Norse gods did leave a warning that they were only seeking to slay the humans because they were destroying the planet. Odin cautioned that there were beings known as the Dark Ones in the multiverse that would seek to destroy all life on the planet. He further warned that without the gods in place to dissuade them, the Dark Ones would eventually attack the Earth as well. This warning was one of the core reasons that Luke continued to train Chimera in preparation for this second war should it ever come. The other potential threat came from the nymphs. The men who mated with the goddess were killed immediately after impregnating them, but the woman had to be kept alive until their babies were born. The beautiful and devious Allison kidnapped these women prior to them giving birth to their babies. She also managed to seduce Victor Toombs into joining her. This meant that in addition to the threat of the Dark Ones returning to Earth, there was also a power-hungry nymph with a potential army of demi-gods and a man who could create a kaiju under her sway.

Luke's thoughts returned to the present as he drove into the middle of the town and stopped his SUV. He climbed out of it, walked around to the back, and then he took out one of the huge cubes of beef, bamboo, and squid that served as an edible reinforcer for the hybrid monster.

Luke tossed the cube into the middle of the street and then he reached back into his SUV and removed a megaphone from it. Luke then gestured for his family to step out of the SUV. Over the course of the war with the gods and their monsters, Luke and his family had grown close to Chimera. Not only Luke, but Melissa and the girls all viewed Chimera as an extension of their family. They all viewed the colossal monster as if he was a well-loved family pet. Chimera loved the Davis family as well. Through his training with Luke, Chimera had grown to love Luke as Luke paired with him through the consistent process of giving Chimera a command and then reinforcing him for successfully completing the command.

After Luke had developed a personal relationship with Chimera, he slowly began having his family interact with the kaiju. While most people would have thought that exposing his wife and children to a giant monster was a bad idea, Luke knew that having Chimera build a relationship with his family was the best way that he could keep them safe. Luke's foresight in having his family form a relationship with Chimera was justified when he had to travel to Asgard to free Melissa from Odin's clutches. The moment that the monster entered the extra-dimensional realm, he was able to smell Melissa's scent and determine that she was in danger. Luke could see the anger on Chimera's face at this realization and he had no doubt that the monster's rage would have led him to a victory over the powerful Odin had the two of them clashed.

Given their relationship with Chimera, Luke had no fear of having his family stand next to the area where he was drawing the kaiju to. The monster's footfalls may shake the ground around them, but Chimera had proven on numerous occasions that he would operate with the utmost care when around Luke and his family. By having his family near Chimera's food source and by having them be part of the process of rewarding him for following directions, it would continue to build the relationship between Chimera as his family. Luke also knew that strengthening the relationship between the monster and his family would continue to increase the likelihood that Chimera would defend them in his absence.

With the threats of the Dark Ones and Allison still looming, Luke made sure that Chimera maintained a strong relationship with his family so that when these beings came and attacked, Chimera would feel the same urge to protect Melissa, Sally, and Suzie that he did.

After reminding himself of why he had brought his family with him on this training exercise, he put the megaphone to his mouth and yelled, "Chimera, come to me!"

Luke's command was answered by a roar that shook the ground and echoed like thunder across the sky. His family watched in awe as a living mountain rose out of the forest around them. Even though Chimera was nearly a mile from where they were standing, the Davis family could see the colossal monster towering over the forest. Chimera shook his head, causing large branches to dislodge from the shaggy lion mane that wreathed his head.

Melissa smiled. "It seems as if you have woken our boy up from a nap."

Luke smiled back at his wife. "He has been getting too used to sleeping in late. I think getting him up early once in a while is a good thing."

Chimera's huge sperm whale head turned in the direction of the Davis family and the mock town they were standing in. The kaiju opened his mouth and showed the long canine teeth that had torn asunder so many of the gods and their monsters. The beast then reached out with his long simian arms and placed them down on the ground. Chimera then started to walk forward with the same stride as a mountain gorilla but with his sperm whale head moving from side to side in front of him while his long, thick, fluke-like tail swayed in the opposite direction behind him. It only took Chimera a few strides to reach the faux street that the Davis family was standing on.

When Chimera was two steps from entering the mock town, Luke looked at Melissa and said, "Now it's time to see if Chimera has mastered the newest command that we have been working on." Luke held up his megaphone, pointed to the cut-out buildings, and yelled, "Chimera, be careful!"

The intelligent beast stopped walking. He then followed his trainer's finger to the fake buildings he was pointing toward. The monster lifted his hands and arms off the ground and stood on two legs. Then he slowly walked into the fake town, taking care not to step on any of the buildings while also making a conscious effort to step lightly. Chimera continued to move in a slow and steady fashion until he reached the center of the town and was standing in front of the Davis family.

Luke yelled into the megaphone, "Good work, Chimera!" as Melissa and the children cheered and clapped. Luke then pushed the huge block of food forward which Chimera carefully picked up and devoured. He then he leaned toward his adopted family and exhaled.

The force of the monster exhaling his breath blew across the Davis family, pushing the girls' hair into their faces. Suzie wrinkled her nose and said, "Eww! Chimera's breath smells like old fish!"

Melissa laughed and then looked at her husband. "It's amazing what you have accomplished with him!"

Luke shrugged. "Thanks, but I am just the facilitator. It's the ABA process and Chimera's own intelligence that really make the difference. Remember that with the best parts of a gorilla's and a whale's mind in his head, Chimera has roughly the intelligence of a three-year-old human and I think that he is actually becoming more intelligent as he grows older."

Melissa kissed her husband on the cheek. "Well, I am proud of you anyway."

Luke turned to kiss his wife back when his cellphone rang. He looked down to see General Sam Parsons' name on the screen.

Luke lifted the phone to his ear. "Yes, General."

Parsons' commanding voice didn't waste time with pleasantries. "Luke, you and Chimera need to return to base immediately. We have reports of multiple kaiju attacks taking place across the United States." There was a brief pause as Parsons chose his next words carefully. "Meet us outside of Hangar Eighteen and bring Chimera to the outskirts of the base with you. When you get here, don't let Chimera too close to the hangar. I don't want him to know what's inside."

Luke replied, "Copy that, General. I will lead Chimera to the back of the base near the hangar. Have a guard at the rear entrance to let me in."

Parsons replied with a, "Copy that." Then he hung up the phone.

Luke turned to Melissa. "There are multiple kaiju attacks occurring across the country. We need to get back to base right away." He looked at his monster. "Parsons wants us to bring the big guy back to base and then he wants me to meet him outside of Hangar Eighteen. He wants Chimera close by but he doesn't want him to know what's in the hangar."

Melissa shook her head. "Parsons doesn't have another monster in there, does he?"

Luke shrugged. "I don't know what he has in there but whatever it is, he clearly thinks Chimera might want to attack it. I need you to take the car and drop me off about a half mile from the base. I will jog the rest of the way with Chimera. Then I want you and the kids safe at home. I will send a military protection unit over to the house just in case. We don't want any more nymphs trying to kidnap you again."

Melissa nodded and then she started ushering the kids back into the SUV. Luke grabbed his megaphone and yelled into it, "Chimera, follow me!" He then jumped into the passenger side of the SUV. Melissa turned the ignition and started heading back to base with Chimera lumbering behind them.

CHAPTER 2

El Dabaa, Egypt

The moment that Atomic Rex found himself on this new Earth, he immediately began searching for both food and nuclear energy. The nuclear theropod's keen senses were able to detect a source of nuclear energy north of his current location. Atomic Rex began wandering through Egypt toward the El Dabaa nuclear power plant. The monster still had some energy left within his cells, but he was in need of recharging his body with the nuclear energy that gave him his amazing powers.

With each step that the monster took, radiation seeped out of his body and into the desert. Beneath the sand, dozens of rodents, insects, arachnids, and reptiles were infected by the radiation that Atomic Rex's body gave off. Most of the creatures that were infected with the radiation from the monster would die as a result of their exposure to the deadly energy, but some of them would survive and mutate into giant monsters themselves. Atomic Rex and the other radioactive monsters like him had spread radiation across his Earth, causing many of the animals there to turn into giant mutants. As Atomic Rex walked across this Earth, his body had the same effect on this ecosystem that it had on his own world. The threat posed by Atomic Rex went far beyond the large-scale death and destruction that he could cause directly. Much like the person designated as patient zero in a zombie film, Atomic Rex's true danger came from the countless other monsters that he would generate as a byproduct of his mere existence.

The monster's presence was first noticed by nomadic goat herders who were roaming the desert with their flocks. When he came across these flocks, both the animals and the people tending to them ran in terror from the prehistoric horror. Despite their best efforts to flee, Atomic Rex made a quick meal of both the goats and their keepers. As he continued to move farther north, the monster walked through numerous small towns and villages, crushing them beneath his colossal feet.

Local police and town militias attempted to halt Atomic Rex's advance with small hand guns and hunting rifles, but when they opened fire on the monster, he did not even notice their attacks. The few people who had access to homemade explosives attempted to hurl them at Atomic Rex's feet, and while the monster felt the explosions, they were not powerful enough to deter him from continually making his way toward the nuclear power plant and the radiation that his body craved.

The monster had left a path of destruction nearly fifty miles long in his wake when he reached the outskirts of El Dabaa and its newly constructed nuclear power plant. With the power plant recently completed, the Egyptian military had a strong presence in the city. Atomic Rex had not yet entered the city when he was met with a battalion of tanks and a squadron of attack helicopters. On his Earth, Atomic Rex had not encountered vehicles such as tanks and helicopters. Aside from other monsters, the only other resistance he had come across was in the form of giant robots. When the tanks and helicopters moved toward Atomic Rex, he looked at them with a sense of confusion rather than anger.

Atomic Rex's tail whipped from side to side behind him as he stared at the vehicles until they opened fire on him. The kaiju's body was engulfed in a maelstrom of shells, bullets, and missiles. For the first time since he had found himself on this Earth, Atomic Rex felt pain. The nuclear theropod roared at the small robots which had dared to attack him. The monster charged forward and ran over the tank battalion. Atomic Rex stomped on the tanks with the fury that had made him the king of two continents on his planet. Within seconds of attacking the tanks, Atomic Rex had crushed them as if they were made of paper. With the robots that were attacking from the ground destroyed, Atomic Rex lifted his head into the sky and glared at the helicopters that were firing on him and roared a challenge at them.

Seeing their ground forces destroyed in mere seconds, the helicopters quickly increased their altitude. The helicopters began circling Atomic Rex and firing on him. The kaiju snapped his jaws and waved his long and powerful claws at the machines, but the annoying helicopters remained out of his reach. Two of the helicopters flew straight at Atomic Rex's face and fired twin missiles into the nuclear theropod's mouth. The projectiles exploded in the monster's mouth, tearing it apart.

Atomic Rex roared in anger and pain at the tiny vehicles that had managed to hurt him. The kaiju shook his head from side to side as his frustration continued to build. As he was shaking his head, a bright blue light began to emanate from beneath the monster's scales. The helicopters continued to fire an unending barrage of missiles and bullets at Atomic Rex as the light from within the monster continued to increase in brightness. Atomic Rex was reaching into the very cells of his body to draw out the nuclear power stored within them. When Atomic Rex could feel the full fury of his nuclear power gathered beneath his scales, the monster lifted his right leg into the air. The monster stomped his foot into the ground and when he did so, a dome of pure radiation burst forth from his body in the form of his Atomic Wave. The dome of radiation engulfed everything in a three-hundred-and-sixty-degree radius around Atomic Rex for nearly one thousand feet. The helicopters that had been attacking Atomic Rex were reduced to slag in mid-air from the heat of the blast. Atomic Rex roared in victory as the flaming and melted helicopters dropped from the sky around him. The homes and small buildings that were within the blast radius of the Atomic Wave were turned to rubble and ash.

The nuclear theropod swung his head from side to side then he turned around to see if there was anything else that sought to challenge him. Just beyond the crater of destruction that the Atomic Wave had caused, the kaiju could see tiny humans running into the streets. The people were covered in burns and their skin was peeling off their bodies from the massive dose of radiation they had absorbed. Compared to the people who were dying and would die over the next few days from radiation poisoning, the pilots who were instantly incinerated in their helicopters had a merciful death.

Atomic Rex roared and then he began walking toward the newly completed nuclear power plant which held the radiation that his body now badly required. He took several steps into El Dabaa to find the streets before him filled with people trying to flee away from the horror that had come to their city. The kaiju roared, sending the people into an even greater panic. Hundreds of people were pushed to the ground and trampled by those behind them who were fleeing in terror from Atomic Rex. Seeing the river of meat in front of him, Atomic Rex dropped his head to the ground and dragged his mouth along the street until it was filled with screaming people. The kaiju took two quick bites, skewering roughly a third of the people in his mouth on his teeth and ending their lives. The people who were not chewed to death screamed in horror as Atomic Rex titled his head back and swallowed them whole while they were still alive. The monster filled his mouth with humans three more times and swallowed them before he reached the nuclear power plant.

When he reached the power plant, the monster walked directly up to the silo where the nuclear energy was generated. He roared, spun around, and then with one powerful swipe of his tail, Atomic Rex knocked the top half of the silo off. Radiation poured out of the now exposed core of the silo and into the air. Atomic Rex took a step forward and then leaned his torso over the core with his arms wide open. A blue energy began to waft from the core of the silo and into Atomic Rex. As the nuclear energy was absorbed by Atomic Rex, it not only refueled the power that had been depleted from his cells, but it also jump started the monster's amazing recuperative abilities. The wounds that had been inflicted on the monster's mouth began to heal and close. Within a few minutes from when Atomic Rex had started absorbing the radiation from the power plant, the wounds that he had suffered during his battle with the helicopters were completely healed.

The nuclear theropod stood above the core for nearly a half an hour until he drained all of the energy from the reactor. With his power fully restored, Atomic Rex lifted his head into the air and roared with a renewed vigor, announcing his presence to this new world. The roar also served as both a warning and a challenge to any other threats within the sound of his voice.

Confident that he had effectively communicated his dominance to any creatures in the area, the monster turned and began heading west toward a different but still familiar Atlantic Ocean. As he made his way through the city, Atomic Rex found the streets were filled with throngs of people trying to escape the horror that had come to their city. As he had done before, Atomic Rex bent down and filled his powerful jaws with the citizens of El Dabaa. The monster gorged himself on the people of the city until his need for meat had been satiated. Thousands of people would be devoured by Atomic Rex and tens of thousands of more people would be crushed by the monster's feet or by the falling debris that he created as he walked through the buildings within the city.

While the monster made his way through El Dabaa, radiation continued to emanate from his body. Even the people in the city who had avoided that kaiju's teeth and claws would die as a result of the radiation that had inadvertently escaped from the monster's body. Atomic Rex had come to a city that was full of people. People who had jobs, families, homes, and dreams. When Atomic Rex had exited the city, less than fifty percent of the population remained alive and many of those who were alive were condemned to a slow and painful death. In less than an hour, Atomic Rex had turned El Dabaa into a city of the dead.

In a dark dimension, the titan Cronus watched through a mystical portal as a surge of life force energy came out of the vortex and enveloped him. Just as Atomic Rex had replenished his energy by draining the power from the silo's nuclear core, so was Cronus draining the life energy on Earth. Cronus smiled as he realized that the link he created with Atomic Rex was working at optimal efficiency. He was also coming to the realization that Atomic Rex was even more deadly and destructive than he had dared dream. Cronus began to muse that with

Atomic Rex under his command, not just the life force of this Earth but countless Earths and infinite planes of existence would soon be his to consume.

Cronus gazed through the portal at the kaiju he had transported to this Earth and he said, "Yes, beast, make your way across the Atlantic Ocean to North America. Reclaim the territory that you held on your Earth. Draw out Chimera and crush him. Then the entire world will fall before your power and I shall reap the benefits of the death and decay that you leave in your wake."

CHAPTER 3

Dallas, Texas

Carlos Ramirez was driving to work along the Lyndon B. Johnson Memorial Highway. He could see the Dallas skyline looming in the distance ahead of him, foreshadowing another day at work. He was listening to Travis Tritt's *Help Me Hold On* and the song seemed to fit his mood as he made his way on a Friday morning toward the bank that he had worked at for nearly sixteen years. As he sang along with the song, he kept thinking to himself that all he had to do was to hang on for one more day and then he and his family would be spending the weekend in Dinosaur Valley State Park.

Carlos had taken his family there last year and his three sons had the time of their lives running around the park, looking at all of the dinosaur tracks that the park was famous for. His youngest son was always thrilled by the tracks. He marveled at the size of the footprints and wondered at how large the dinosaurs were. This year would be the state park again, but next year, Carlos really hoped to show his family something amazing. Next year, he would show them something that dwarfed even the biggest sauropod. With the money he had saved up on the side, Carlos was going to take his family to see Chimera! The two-hundred-foot-plus-tall kaiju that had defeated gods and monsters to save the human race from extinction.

Every three months, the government would run tours which gave people access to seeing Chimera either in his forest home or in the area of open ocean off the coast of Virginia that was set aside for the beast. The tours helped the government to cover the tremendous cost involved in sustaining something the size of Chimera. Carlos could imagine his children's faces when they saw the massive creature in person. He laughed as he thought about the look that would be on his wife's face and likely his face as well as they stared at something so large.

This thought had no sooner crossed Carlos' mind when he saw a colossal dark form suddenly appear behind the Dallas skyline. The banker quickly scanned his car for his umbrella to help keep him dry from what looked like a huge storm heading for the city. He didn't see his umbrella in the car and he cursed. "Damn weather man said that we would have nothing but sunny skies today." Carlos shook his head.

"Looks like I am getting wet on my way from the parking lot to the bank today."

Carlos continued to watch the storm and he suddenly became aware of the strange shape that the storm clouds had. Most of the time when a storm rolled in over the city, the clouds stretched straight across the horizon. These clouds were completely the opposite as they seemed to go in a straight column that started from the ground and reached high into the sky.

Carlos was still staring at the odd clouds when he heard a loud crashing sound followed by the ground shaking so violently that his car was lifted off the road. The car landed back on its tires but the impact was so great that it caused Carlos' face to smash into his steering wheel. Carlos' car swerved from side to side, as did the rest of the cars on the highway both in front of and in back of him. As soon as he was able to regain control of his car, Carlos pulled to the side of the road. Most of the other cars around him also pulled to the side of the road. Carlos opened his door and stepped out of the car as another loud crash and shockwave rocked the highway, causing him to lose his footing and fall to the ground.

He stood as the woman whose car was parked behind his walked up to him and said, "What the heck kind of storm is that?"

Carlos simply shook his head in confusion in response to the woman's question as he continued to stare at the odd cloud. It was then that Carlos' eyes beheld something that his mind could not comprehend. He rubbed his eyes, thinking that the storm, or the mini earthquakes, or whatever it was that was shaking the ground had sent him into a state of panic that was causing him to see things that couldn't exist.

His fears were confirmed by the woman who was standing next to him when she screamed, "My God, that's not a storm cloud! It's some kind of a giant!"

As soon as the woman voiced what the innermost corners of Carlos' mind already knew, his brain started to allow itself to bring into focus what he was looking at. He could see a head the size of a baseball stadium. A torso as long and as broad as an aircraft carrier. Arms and legs that were longer than any building in the state of Texas. Carlos had known fear in his life. Like any human, he experienced things that terrified him to his very core. The feeling that he was now experiencing was different from simple fear. What he felt now was the sensation of being so small as to be insignificant and that feeling was both frightening and humbling at the same time.

The giant took another step and this time, the shockwaves that it gave off were so powerful they caused the tops of several of the buildings in Dallas to break off and fall onto the streets below. Carlos gasped when he realized that, even at this early hour, there had to be several hundred people in each of those buildings. The security guards, custodians, IT people, cafeteria staff, and anyone else who was unlucky enough to arrive at work prior to rush hour had just died right before Carlos' eyes.

The buildings that were still standing had nearly every one of their windows shattered. Even at a distance of several miles outside of the city, all of the cars that were parked along the highway bounced into the air and came back down while the people standing on the side of the road were all thrown to the ground.

Carlos looked into the sky to see that the immense giant had almost reached the city itself. The giant had the appearance of a well-built man with a shaggy beard and wild hair. Carlos had been a wrestling fan since he was a young boy and all that he could think of was that the giant resembled the legendary wrestler Bruiser Brody. Carlos' mind was quickly directed off his childhood hobby and back to the horror at hand when he noticed that as the giant was standing before the city, the tallest buildings in Dallas barely reached his knees. Whatever this giant was, he would have dwarfed Chimera to the same extent that Chimera dwarfed the dinosaurs.

Carlos was crawling back into his car as he heard a voice boom across the sky that was so loud it caused his ears to bleed.

The booming voice was that of the giant as he proclaimed, "Tremble in fear, humans, as your tallest structures are crushed beneath the very feet of Atlas!" Carlos had managed to sit up in his car as he saw Atlas kick through an entire block of buildings as a child would crush sandcastles on the beach.

Carlos' car bounced again as he was trying to turn it around and drive on the shoulder in the opposite direction of the traffic that had been making its way into the city. Carlos was crying as he said to himself, "There is nothing that they can do. Even Chimera would be nothing compared to that giant." The ground shook once more, and Carlos looked in his rearview mirror to see the lower half of the gargantuan Atlas laying waste to the city. A cloud of dust that had been downtown Dallas had enveloped that titan's legs and knees, but everything above his waist was still high above the debris that was floating through the air.

Carlos looked away from the city to see the cars that he was passing turning around and driving on the shoulder or jumping the median to access the highway in the direction away from Dallas. He started talking to himself again, "That thing will have leveled Dallas within half an hour." He started driving faster as he thought about his family. "Who knows where he will go next? He could head out to the suburbs."

He switched on the radio to hear the Emergency Broadcast System. "This is the Emergency Broadcast System. This is not a drill. The greater Dallas area is under attack by an unidentified kaiju. The kaiju is larger than any other monster reported thus far. People living in or near Dallas are advised to evacuate the area. The military is working as quickly as possible to prepare a response to this attack."

Carlos shook his head. "They said a response, not a defense. My God, they are considering nuking that thing!" Carlos began driving as fast as he could away from what had once been the city of Dallas, Texas. He began to sob for all of the people that had died at the hands of the monster because as he looked back at the dust that now swarmed around the giant's feet, he could see that in mere minutes, the giant had destroyed the entire city.

Carlos was wiping his eyes clear when his car was thrown into the air and bounced down on the highway. The impact from the bounce shattered the rims of his wheels and left his car immobile. Carlos climbed out of his car to see that all of the other cars on the highway had also been severely damaged by the last impact.

The banker turned to see the giant coming toward him and everyone else who was stranded on the highway. Carlos shook his head in disbelief as the creature's neck and head literally disappeared into some low-hanging clouds. The shockwave of another of the giant's footfalls caused Carlos to lose his balance and fall to the ground. He looked up to see the sun blocked out above him as the giant's foot loomed over him. He stood up to run but when he looked at the size of the shadow around him, he quickly realized that the giant's foot was so large that even if he were driving his car at top speed, he would not be able to escape his fate.

Carlos fell to his knees and he began to pray that his family would be spared from the attack of this monster. As Carlos was praying, he heard a voice so loud that the sound of it shattered what was left of his eardrums. The voice proclaimed, "You cannot hope to flee humans! The titans have returned to end your existence!"

As blood gushed out of his ears, Carlos' mind shifted to wife and children and all of the joy they had brought him in his life. His last thoughts were of his boys and taking them to see the huge footprints that they so loved. An instant later, Carlos and countless others along with him became part of a footprint that was now the largest footprint on the face of the earth.

CHAPTER 4

Baltimore

Latoya Wilkerson was strolling the inner harbor and enjoying the fresh air, diverse shops, and multiple eating establishments that ranged from small vendors to large-scale restaurants. Latoya was working her way through med school at the world-renowned but extremely demanding doctoral program at Johns Hopkins University. She was doing well in her classes and working hard on studying and fulfilling her other obligations six days a week, but Friday was her day off. She had heard from several practicing doctors that her mental health was just as important to her being a successful surgeon as were her credentials. Dr. Price had specifically said to her, "A doctor's job is to save lives and improve the quality of life for people. That includes your own life. While it is important to have a serious commitment to your profession, you also need to remember that your quality of life needs to be something that you keep in mind as well. A happy and well-rested doctor is an effective and successful doctor."

Latoya took Dr. Price's suggestions to heart and she committed Friday to being the day that she took a break from work and made sure that her life was worth living and enjoyable. Latoya walked onto one of the many docks that extended out into the harbor. The sun was shining and there was a cool breeze blowing the salty air from the water onto the docks. Latoya walked past several people who were spending their day fishing off the pier. The fishermen included several old men sitting together, several sets of fathers and sons, and even one group that was clearly three generations of grandfather, father, and son, as all three had a strong family resemblance.

She saw a trio of men in their seventies who she had become acquainted with during her Friday visits to the inner harbor. She had learned that their first names were John, Kyle, and Randy. She walked up to the men who she playfully referred to as the "Stooges" and started up her usual line of questions. "Hey, guys, how is the fishing going today?"

The fishermen kept looking out over the bay as John pointed to a bucket full of fish at their feet. "It's been good. Really good. It's almost like something is driving the fish toward the shore."

Kyle pointed toward the horizon. "We think we might finally have realized what it is. Look out over the water. Can you see it? Sort of looks like a fuzzy distortion over the water."

Latoya put her hand over her eyes to shield them from the sun and she stared out at the horizon. In the distance, she could see something that looked like it was spinning above the waterline. She turned toward John. "Is that one of those, what do they call them, the tornadoes that form over water?"

John shook his head. "A waterspout. Sailors call them waterspouts. I have seen a few in my time, but I can't recollect ever seeing one on a sunny day like this."

Randy cleared his throat and chimed into the conversation. "I have seen many a waterspout as well, and one thing I can tell you is that they don't stay in place like that one seems to be doing. They kind of whip all around the place."

As in response to Randy's claim, the distortion started moving toward the shore. The water around the dock that Latoya and the fishermen were standing on began to ripple. They looked down to see countless fish, crabs, and other forms of sea life trying to force their way to the surface of the water. On the beach that surrounded the dock, people started to scream as thousands of fish threw themselves out of the water and onto land.

Latoya looked back to shore to see the fish flopping around helplessly as they were suffocating to death. She looked at Randy. "What on earth would make fish beach themselves like that?"

Randy shook his head. "Nothing. Nothing would make them do that. Whatever is going on out there, the fish are more scared of it than they are of dying."

Latoya shifted her gaze back to the waterspout to see that it was now moving to shore at a faster pace. Many of the people on the dock started to turn and run, but with the current training that she was engaged in, her mind was conditioned to stay calm and observe situations she found herself in.

John grabbed Latoya by the arm and started pulling her back. The med student pulled free from the fisherman and had the presence of mind to not only keep her eyes focused on the phenomenon but also to take out her cell phone, open her Facebook app, and start a Facebook Live session on what she was looking at. Within an instant, all of her followers on Facebook were seeing what Latoya was seeing. She was all too aware of the war that had raged only a few years ago between the gods and humanity. Latoya was fairly sure that what she was looking at was another attack from a parallel dimension. She also knew that the army and the people who controlled Chimera would need as much information on whatever was coming to shore as possible in order to counteract it. She kept herself from a near state of panic by focusing on her deeply ingrained desire to save lives. She laughed a little at the irony that on the day she was supposed to be focusing on the importance of her life, she could very well die trying to save the lives of countless others.

John grabbed Latoya again and managed to pull her off the dock and onto the writhing mass of fish that was littering the shoreline. When she first stepped on the dying fish, she slipped and was only held up by John's grip. Latoya took a quick look down to find a fish-free spot of sand and secure her footing. She then refocused her phone on the aberration coming toward her and she started shouting, "What looks like a waterspout has started out over the Atlantic Ocean has made its way into Chesapeake Bay! This phenomenon is occurring despite the fact that today, there isn't a cloud in the sky! Thousands of fish have swum to shore and beached themselves ahead of this disturbance, seemingly in an attempt to get away from it!"

She stopped talking for a moment and swallowed the saliva that was building up in her mouth from the tension she was experiencing. In that brief second, the disturbance had moved closer to shore and she could see that it was no waterspout. The fishermen who had been trying to pull Latoya to safety turned and ran away from her when they saw what the disturbance truly was.

Even though every impulse in Latoya's head told her to run, she forced herself to stay in place and continue to document what was happening. She aimed her phone directly at the disturbance above her and shouted, "Even in light of what has occurred over the past few years, I can't believe what I am seeing! What looked like a spinning action from a distance is not actually spinning at all but rather what has to be dozens if not hundreds of heads and arms connected to a single torso all moving at the same time! The creature has to be related to the gods and monsters that attacked our planet several years ago!"

She tried to move along the shoreline and out of the creature's direct path as she continued her Facebook Live video. "The monster appears to be in the range of three hundred feet tall!" She continued her recording as the bizarre creature came ashore and attacked the first building it came across. "The monster is tearing through a ten-story building by using its hands live a living buzzsaw!"

Her voice began to shake as she reported what she saw next. "My God! The monster is grabbing the people who are trying to flee from the carnage and devouring them! With all of its arms and heads, it's grabbing everyone in sight!"

She dropped her phone and screamed, "Randy!" when she saw her friend grabbed by the monster and devoured. The horror of what was occurring kept Latoya's focus fixed on the monster, and as a result, she did not see the mob of people running toward her. The panicked mob ran into Latoya and knocked the med student to the ground. Her body was racked with pain as people trampled her. She could hear the screams of the terrified people as they stomped over her, trying to avoid the blur of death that was attacking the harbor. A foot kicked her in the eye, causing it to swell up and obscure her vision. Latoya was starting to lose consciousness when she felt the people who were trampling her being lifted off her body. She looked up through her bruised and bloody eyes to see the monster standing above her, snatching people up and throwing them into its countless mouths.

Latoya felt a hand grab her and as she was being lifted up into the air, she saw her phone still uploading to Facebook. She tried to focus on the phone and she yelled, "I did it, Mom! I saved lives! I love you!" Latoya then closed her eyes for the final time as the monster tossed her into its mouth and crushed her to death with its rancid teeth.

CHAPTER 5

Atlantic Ocean off the coast of Boston

Mike McGrath was doing his best to maintain his footing on the fishing boat as it rocked back and forth. He was trying to tie down everything that he could on the deck of the ship with winds gusts at twenty miles per hour and a pelting rain assaulting him. Mike saw a huge wave swell up in front of the boat and he was tossed to the floor as the captain tried to steer into the wave to keep the boat from capsizing.

Mike's head slammed into the deck of the boat and he looked up toward the bridge of the ship to see the captain frantically trying to right his vessel. Mike felt a hand grab him and he looked up to see his friend Peter Jensen helping him up. Peter pulled Mike to his feet as a lightning bolt streaked over the ship and crackled when it hit the water.

Peter shook his head and pointed toward the lights in the distance as he shouted, "We are only a couple of miles from Boston! We should reach land within the hour!"

Mike nodded. "I know that we pulled in a ton of fish, but the captain should have headed to shore earlier if he knew that a storm this big was coming toward us!"

Peter shook his head. "That's the weird thing. I was watching the satellite feed myself! An hour ago, there was no indication of a storm this big coming toward us! A few clouds in the sky but nothing that looked like this!"

Mike nodded. "Well, in that case, maybe the captain needs to upgrade the weather-tracking computers on the ship because we should have seen something this dangerous coming for us!"

Peter nodded. "That's something that we can worry about when we reach shore!" A crate of life jackets ominously tumbled in front of them and spilled its orange contents across the deck.

Mike shrugged. "Let's just clean this up and secure them. God forbid we should need them and they are drifting out to sea as we fight to stay afloat!"

Mike was bending over to pick up one of the life jackets when Peter dove on top of him and forced him to the deck. Before Mike could ask what was going on, a massive swell of water ran over the deck, carrying both the extra life jackets and other pieces of unsecured cargo into the Atlantic Ocean.

Mike watched in dismay as the life jackets floated away from the boat. He turned to voice his concerns to Peter only to see his friend staring up at the bridge of the ship. Mike could see concern on his friend's face and he yelled, "Peter, what's wrong?"

Peter shook his head. "I can see the captain. He has let go of the steerage. He is just looking out the window and screaming!"

Mike looked past his friend's shoulder out toward the ocean to see more large swells of water coming toward them. The swells were so large that they blocked out the dim lights of Boston. The waves were intimidating but they were nothing that should have terrified a harden seafarer like the captain. Mike was still looking over the waves when a streak of lightning illuminated the night sky. As the lightning ducked behind the wave, Mike caught a brief glimpse of what the captain was screaming at. Mike only got a quick look before another large swell obscured the horror that was ahead of the fishing vessel.

Mike pulled Peter closer to the deck and then he grabbed onto a nearby stairway railing as the approaching swell washed across the ship. The swell was much larger and more powerful than any of the other swells that had struck them. The cold waters of the Atlantic Ocean ran across the deck, completely submerging both Mike and Peter. Mike could feel his arms nearly being pulled out of their sockets as he held onto the railing with one hand and onto Peter with the other. The swell had nearly passed over them when Mike's grip on the railing was finally pried loose. Both Mike and Peter were pushed along with the swell toward the side of the ship and the open Atlantic. As they were approaching the side of the boat, both men reached out and grabbed a hold of the railing along the side of the boat. The tail end of the swell ran over them and rejoined the ocean.

The two men were breathing hard as wind and rain continued to pelt their faces. Mike had managed to climb back onto the ship as Peter started yelling behind him. Mike turned around to see a giant yellow crab claw with tentacles writhing around it and poking out of the water.

As the claw came crashing down back into the water, it sent another swell of water rushing toward the ship. Mike took one look at Peter still hanging onto the side of the boat and quickly resigned himself to the fact that his friend was going to die and there was nothing he could do about it. Mike quickly wrapped his arms around the side railing of the ship and held onto it as tight as he could. A second later, the swell rolled over the deck. The force of the wave caused the ship to tilt onto its side and through the saltwater, Mike could see Peter being pried off the side of the ship and into the water. In his head, Mike prayed that the ship would right itself just long enough for him to reach the bridge. Mike knew that he was going to die. Between the storm and what was beneath the water, he knew that there was no way he was going to reach the shore alive.

Mike could feel his arms straining to hold onto the side of the ship as the vessel slowly listed back to its proper state. With the ship temporarily back in the proper position, Mike climbed over the railing and started moving across the deck of the boat as smaller waves rocked the vessel from side to side. Mike gritted his teeth and did his best to maintain his balance as he moved toward the bridge of the ship.

Just before Mike reached the door to the bridge, he saw the gargantuan tentacled claw rise out of the water closer to the ship. Mike grabbed the door to the bridge and pulled it open as the claw went crashing back into the water. Mike then ran into the bridge of the ship to see the captain balled up in the corner and screaming. The captain was clearly in shock and given what was happening to them, Mike couldn't blame the man. The captain knew what was attacking them and his mind couldn't handle it. Mike couldn't afford to let his fear overwhelm him. He had a wife and son back on shore in Boston. He needed to give the city as much warning as he could to evacuate before the monster that was toying with his ship reached the city.

The swell from the giant claw slapping down into the water hit the ship and caused it to shift the left. The entire room spun around Mike as he, the still-screaming captain, and everything else inside the bridge of the ship went flying through the air and slammed into the wall. Mike shook his head to clear it and then he looked out the window of the bridge to see the deck of the ship tilted vertically in the air. The ocean was pressing against the window and Mike knew that it was only a matter of seconds before the water shattered the window, rushed into the bridge, and sank the ship. Mike quickly dashed toward the radio and switched it to the Coast Guard Channel. He screamed into the radio, "Coast Guard, come in! This is the fishing troller *Manda*! We are outside of Boston and under attack by the Kraken! Call the armed forces to intercept and evacuate Boston!" He repeated the request again as the ocean water shattered the glass window to the bridge and poured into the ship. The captain didn't even bother to stand. He simply remained in his crouched position and continued screaming until the water covered him. Mike knew the fate that awaited him but he was not going to just sit there and die. Mike made his way through cold water and when he reached the broken window, he climbed out of it onto the highest part of the ship that was still out of the water.

Another swell of water lifted the boat up and in the distance, Mike was able to see the lights of Boston one last time. A tear formed in his eye as he thought of his wife and son and he said, "Dear God in Heaven, please watch over them." Mike had no sooner finished his prayer then an acrid smell struck his nose. He looked down toward the water to see long tentacles probing the sides of the sinking ship. He followed the tentacles to the water, and deep below the waterline, he could see the giant claw coming up toward the top of the ship. Mike continued to look at the water as the huge claw closed around the ship and lifted it out of the water. Mike slid off the side of the ship and fell into the Atlantic. When Mike hit the water, he immediately began swimming toward the surface. He had almost reached the surface when he felt something big and hard slam into him from below. The force of the impact disoriented Mike and when he was able to open his eyes, he found himself standing on top of something hard and yellow that was also covered in writhing tentacles. In the air above him, Mike could see his ship still being held in the grip of the giant claw. Mike shook his head in disbelief as he realized that, much like the Vikings who mistook the creature's shell for an island, he was standing on top of the Kraken.

The majority of people today thought of the Kraken as a humanoid monster with four arms or maybe as a giant squid or octopus, but sailors like Mike knew better. The original tales that the Vikings told about the Kraken described a monster that was more like a giant crab covered in tentacles than anything like a squid or an octopus. The Kraken was also said to bring about terrible storms whenever he surfaced, which explained the storm that seemed to come from nowhere.

Sailors were well aware of the original tale of the monster from the depths. During the war with the gods, Mike and many other sailors and fishermen had worried that the mythical creature might reappear in the Atlantic. The one thing that the movies got right was that the Kraken was such a powerful and dreadful beast that even the gods themselves feared it. If the Kraken did exist and was under the thrall of the gods, then most sailors felt that Odin would be wise to keep the creature trapped in whatever wretched pit he had it in.

These thoughts were running through Mike's mind until he felt the tentacles that were writhing at his feet wrap around his legs. He suddenly felt himself being lifted higher into the air as the monster that he was trapped on top of stood up. With Kraken standing at its full height, Mike had a clear view of the city of Boston. As he felt the tentacle that was wrapped around his body crushing him to death, Mike focused on the lights of the city and his last thoughts were of his family before the Kraken crushed him to death.

The Kraken brought the tiny ship that was trapped within its claw closer to its mouth and then it swallowed the vessel and all of the fish contained within it in a single bite. It had been centuries since the gods had driven the Kraken from the Earth and it had the pleasure of tasting meat. With its appetite whet, the Kraken turned in the direction of Boston and began walking toward the millions of people who lived there.

CHAPTER 6

Chimera Base, Virginia

Melissa pulled to a stop a half mile short of the outskirts of the base as Luke had asked her to do. As the car rolled to a stop, the well-trained Chimera stopped behind it. The behemoth waited patiently as he looked down through the trees that surrounded his ankles and waited for his instructor to give him his next command.

They were in a part of the forest that reached the back of the base. Luke figured that he could lead Chimera to the fence line from there. That would leave the monster roughly a quarter mile from the back of Hangar Eighteen and whatever Parsons had in there along with his usual entourage of highly trained soldiers and scientific advisors.

Luke first looked at his daughters. "I love you, girls. Keep an eye on your mom for me and make sure that she stays out of trouble."

Sally laughed, "Dad, it's Mommy's job to keep us out of trouble!"

The younger Suzie stuck out her chin and said, "Don't worry, Daddy, I will keep Mommy out of trouble."

Luke smiled and gave the four-year-old a fist pump. "Thanks, honey. I knew that I could count on you to watch Mommy for me."

Luke turned toward his wife and he looked into her loving brown eyes. She forced a smile and said, "Be safe out there when you're saving the world. I love you and I will be at home waiting for you when this is all over."

Luke smiled and kissed his wife which drew a collective "Ewww" from their daughters in the back seat. The parents laughed, and Luke once more looked his wife in the eyes. "I love you too. I will let you know what's going on as soon as possible."

Luke then jumped out of the SUV with his megaphone in hand. He tapped the side of the SUV, signaling his wife to drive away. After his family had driven away, Luke lifted his megaphone to his mouth and once again yelled, "Chimera, follow me!"

Luke then began running at a quick jog toward the back of the base with Chimera lumbering behind him. Since the loss of his horse Jason in the battle with Thor, Luke had resorted to using either trucks or helicopters to lead Chimera to where he needed to be. With the thought of Zeus and the other thunder gods still out there somewhere with the ability to shut down all electronics with an electromagnetic pulse, Luke couldn't rely solely on machines to led Chimera. Luke was training other horses to replace Jason, but it took a long time for a horse to be comfortable enough around a kaiju to not freak out when it was walking behind him and not run in fear from the monster.

As an alternative to the horse, Luke had taken up distance running to lead Chimera if he needed to and did not have the option of using an electronic vehicle. Luke was not as young as he used to be and the process of training his body to endure that type of running was taxing for him. Luke knew that he did not have too many other options. He could not simply walk in front of Chimera. Each step that the monster took was the length of a city block. Even when Luke was jogging, Chimera had to take a step and then wait a minute before taking another step to avoid getting ahead of Luke or accidentally stepping on him.

Luke ran for about five minutes before he reached the exterior gate of the base. He stopped running at the fence and then turned to tell Chimera to stop. To Luke's surprise, the kaiju was standing still and sniffing the air. Chimera looked briefly toward Luke then he looked at the base and roared.

Luke shook his head. "He smells something that he doesn't like." Luke held up his megaphone and yelled, "Chimera, stop!" He then held up his hand and said, "Chimera, stay!"

The monster looked at Luke and then he crouched down onto all fours. Luke smiled at the creature and gave him a verbal reward. "Good job, Chimera!"

Luke then jogged to the back entrance to the gate that Parsons had installed for instances exactly like this when Luke was training with Chimera and needed to return to base quickly. Luke ran up to the guard at the back of the base and he immediately began searching himself for his ID card. He cursed when he realized that he had left his ID in the SUV with Melissa and the girls. Luke didn't recognize the guard, so he doubted that the man would let him in without his ID.

He looked at the guard and said, "I forgot my ID, but I am Luke Davis. You can call General Parsons and have him come vouch for me."

The guard was staring up at the two hundred and fifty-foot-tall monster standing behind Luke and he just shook his head. "That's OK, sir, I may be new here, but from what they told me at orientation, there is only one person who Chimera listens to. Plus, I figure if you are not Luke Davis and you have control of Chimera, there really isn't much I could to do to stop you from coming onto base even if I wanted to." The guard shrugged. "Besides, General Parsons already warned me that you were coming and to let you in and direct you right to Hangar Eighteen."

Luke nodded at the guard as he opened the gate. He then sprinted toward Hangar Eighteen. When he reached the hangar, he took a deep breath and tried to slow down his heartbeat so that he could focus on whatever Parsons and likely Diana Cain needed him for.

In addition to being a key consultant for General Parsons, Diana Cain was also Luke's best friend. Parsons was the man who was in command in the war against the gods, but Diana was the expert on the gods and their monsters. She was a professor of mythology and for her graduate thesis, she had written a paper on how the ancient gods could have been trans-dimensional beings who once actually lived on Earth. Once the Greek Gods returned to Mount Olympus and started doing things like using the Charybdis to unleash a vortex that would kill all of the humans on the planet, she was one of the first people that Parsons sought out. She knew who all the gods were, how they operated, and what the monsters and other horrors that they unleashed were capable of. She was also a self-proclaimed science fiction and fantasy geek, and in addition to that, she had a knack for injecting humor into tense situations. It was this trait more than anything that had caused Luke to be drawn to her. She was quick-witted and when Luke doubted himself or was scared of what he was going to face, Diana was always there to provide a quick one-liner to make Luke laugh and help keep him from getting so nervous that he became a detriment to himself and to the mission.

Diana was a tall, athletic-looking woman in her late thirties. Most of the men on the base had their eyes on her, but they all kept away thinking that she and Luke were having an affair. In reality, Luke and Diana were not romantically involved; they were simply good friends.

Despite the fact that Luke and Melissa had been together for over twenty years, he was still madly in love with his wife. Still, Diana didn't mind the soldiers thinking that she and Luke were involved. She was the type of woman who was into nerds with a sense of humor and if that kept the muscle-heads away from her, she was fine with that. She and Luke both thought it was funny that the perception that they were a couple kept the soldiers from approaching Diana or even asking Luke about their relationship out of fear of angering him.

While any soldier on the base was more than capable of kicking Luke's ass, none of them would raise a finger against him with his connection to Chimera. Angering a former teacher by asking him if he was having an affair was one thing. Pissing off the guy who trained the monster that wrecked three different pantheons of gods was something else altogether. Luckily for Luke, Melissa was aware of the rumors and she laughed them off as well. Diana was as much her friend as she was

Luke's friend. Diana ate dinner over their house at least once a week where the three of them joked about what the men on the base must be thinking when they saw Diana go to Luke's house only to see Melissa open the door and hug her.

Thinking of his friend and his wife caused Luke to laugh. Without even seeing her yet, Diana had managed to do what she did best: cause Luke to smile and help him to calm down. Luke sighed when he was done laughing and then he opened the door to Hangar Eighteen.

Luke stopped in his tracks when he saw both Parsons and Diana standing in the middle of the hangar with two thirty-foot-tall giants in front of them. One giant had bright red hair and he was wrapped in a long white toga. As Luke looked at the giant, he could see bright blue streaks of electricity dancing across his dark brown eyes. Luke had not seen Zeus since the day that Chimera scaled Mount Olympus and reduced the god's throne room to rubble.

The second figure was much more robust than Zeus. He had wild white hair and a shaggy white beard. The giant wore a horned helmet on top of his head and his clothing was made up of something that resembled a bear's skin. Most noticeably, the giant had a huge black eye patch draped over one of his eyes.

Luke immediately recognized the being that had captured his wife and threatened to kill her, if Luke did not convince Chimera to stand down while Thor disrupted the planet's electromagnetic field. Thor's actions would have let magnetic waves from the sun cascade down onto Earth, effectively shutting down all of the technology that humans had come to rely on. With a shutdown of power on a worldwide scale, billions of people would have died in only a few short years.

Luke was seething with anger as he looked at Odin and Zeus. He was reacting on emotion rather than intellect as he lifted his megaphone to call Chimera.

Diana saw what Luke was doing and she shouted, "Luke, no!"

As much as Luke respected General Sam Parsons, had he told Luke to stop, he would still have called Chimera. Luke wasn't a soldier. He was teacher and before that, he was a husband and a father. His first thought was to protect his family. It was only the voice of his best friend that was able to stop him.

Luke was still glaring at both of the gods as he addressed Diana, "Chimera is right outside of this facility, and he smelled something he didn't like. Tell me as quickly as possible why I should not call him in here to tear these things apart before they start attacking us."

Odin voice boomed throughout the hangar. "Mortal, had we wished to attack this pathetic facility, you would all have been dead before you even had the opportunity to call upon your behemoth!"

Showing no fear of the beings that possessed the ability to destroy entire cities on a whim, Diana chastised the god king. "You came to us for help! Let me talk to Luke and try to call him down." She looked over toward Luke. "Besides even if you were to do anything, Luke already said that Chimera knows you are here. If Luke was to be hurt or killed, do you really think Chimera would need to be told who to go after for revenge?" Diana shifted her gaze back toward Odin and she smiled. "You know, for someone the Santa Claus myth is based on, you are not very jolly." With her quick verbal jab complete, she went over to her friend.

Odin didn't reply. He simply turned away from Diana as she walked over toward Luke. She took her friend by the hand and said, "I know that you feel the need to protect Melissa and the kids. I don't think they are in danger from Odin or Zeus this time, but something worse is going on. Something that could threaten every living thing on the planet and we are going to need the gods' help to stop it."

Luke shook his head as he misplaced his anger by screaming at Diana, "Their help? They are the ones that tried to kill us all in the first place! Why should they care if the human race is in danger again? I would have thought our extinction was something they would have jumped for joy over! It was only two years ago that they tried to wipe us out! They also kidnapped and impregnated all of those women only to let their damn nymphs run off with them!"

Diana placed her hand on Luke's shoulder. "The extinction of the human race would be something they want, but the death of the entire planet is another thing." She leaned in closer to her friend. "Remember what Odin told us? Remember what we have been training for? The coming of something older and darker than the gods. It's happening right now. A wave of kaiju have attacked the planet. We can absolutely confirm that. We were just starting to plan our counter-offensive when Odin and Zeus suddenly showed up inside the hangar. They are claiming that we will have to work with them if we hope to prevent Armageddon." Diana softened her voice even more. "For the sake of Melissa and the girls, try to listen to what they have to say."

Luke nodded as deep down he realized that the best chance he had of protecting his family was to work with the same beings who had once endangered them. He hugged Diana and whispered into her ear, "If they try anything... If I even think they are planning to attack us or to hurt us in any way..."

Diana whispered back to him, "Then unleash Chimera on them and don't call him off until he has torn those supposed gods to shreds."

Luke let go of Diana and they looked into each other's eyes. They both nodded and Luke whispered, "Thank you." She smiled and then two of them turned around and started walking back to where Parsons and the two gods were standing. As Luke walked through the middle of the hangar, he could see armed guards all along the walls with rifles and larger weapons. He guessed that the larger weapons were rocket launchers, aimed at the two gods. He shook his head and said to Diana, "Good old Parsons. He is willing to listen to what they are saying, but he is not taking any chances, is he?"

Diana smiled. "You don't make it as far in the military as Parsons has by leaving anything to chance. I like to think of him as our own personal Nick Fury. I think right now he is looking at the gods with the old enemy of my enemy is my friend idea."

Diana walked past Parsons and the god kings toward the main computer screen in the center of the hangar. When she reached the main screen's computer console, she turned and looked at Zeus and the electricity that was dancing around his body. "It would be extremely helpful if you could keep the electricity that you are giving off to a minimum so as not to accidentally send out an EMP that shuts down everything."

Zeus first glared at Diana and then he turned his gaze toward Luke. "The monster he controls destroyed the pillars which helped me to regulate and recharge my electrical powers. I am forced to now slowly pull ambient static electricity from the environment. Absorbing energy in this way is not the most efficient manner nor is it conducive to me controlling my powers."

Diana smirked. "Maybe you could just put yourself in a giant laundry dryer for a few hours; that would help you to build up a static charge pretty quickly."

Zeus' eyes flared up with power as General Parsons stepped toward Diana. "Ms. Cain, perhaps our time would be better focused on the monsters attacking the planet instead of on flippant remarks."

Diana shrugged. "You're the boss." She then pulled up a monitor showing multiple cities with different monsters rampaging through them. She began explaining what was happening. "According to Zeus and Odin, we are now facing an attack from the beings that they warred with millennia ago for control of the Earth. While these beings have had many different names including the Titans, we can refer to them as the Dark Ones, which is the name that Zeus and Odin use to identify them. As you can see, multiple cities around the US and Africa are being attacked by mythological monsters or kaiju." She looked Odin and Zeus. "When you attacked Earth, you primarily used your monsters to protect whatever it was you were using to try and wipe out humanity. Zeus, you used the Charybdis to try and kill humans by creating an energy vortex specifically focused on humans with the Scylla protecting it. Marduke sent the Colossus of Death to spread a plague and he sent Anzu to protect it. Conversely, these new monsters are being used as a primary method of attack by the beings who are controlling them."

Luke jumped into the conversation. "Hey, that reminds me. If you guys are here, where are Marduke and his other gods?"

Odin shook his head. "The wrath of your monster was too great for the Mesopotamians. While Zeus escaped Chimera with his life and we formed a peace treaty, Marduke, Anzu, Asag, and numerous other gods from that pantheon were slain by Chimera. It is due to the loss of the Mesopotamians and the loss of our own monsters in the war with Chimera that we now turn to you for help. We currently lack the strength to defeat the Dark Ones ourselves. We need to work with you and your monster if there is any hope of the planet surviving this incursion."

Luke nodded in reply as Diana briefly looked at the giant gods standing behind her. "If I am wrong in identifying any of these kaiju, please let me know." She zoomed in on one section of the computer screen to show a huge crab-like creature with multiple tentacles writhing around its body laying waste to Boston. "The Kraken has risen from the Atlantic Ocean and he is attacking Boston. The monster has immense physical strength and its thick shell makes it extremely resilient to physical injury. The monster is roughly two hundred feet tall and three hundred feet wide. So far, military helicopters have been bombarding the creature with no indication that they are injuring it or even slowing it down."

She then moved the focus of the screen to lower right section and she zoomed in on some kind of maelstrom of arms, legs, hands, and heads that was attacking a city and seemed to be scooping people up as it came across them. "Baltimore is under attack by the Hecatonchires. A creature with fifty heads and a hundred arms. The monster stands at roughly two hundred and seventy feet tall. Aside from its size and strength, the creature has the ability to create tsunamis by thrashing its arms when it's in the water and tornadoes by thrashing its arms when it is on land. The Hecatonchires also appears to be eating people as it comes across them."

Luke asked, "Does anyone else's head hurt when you look at thing?"

Zeus replied, "The human mind and eye is not equipped to behold the movements of a creature with so many limbs. To stare at such as the Hecatonchires is disorienting to some humans and in others it can cause madness."

Diana shrugged. "Kind of like what Lovecraft wrote about looking at Cthulhu and his writhing tentacles. I wonder if the Hecatonchires is what inspired that part of his mythos." Diana saw Parsons staring at her and she quickly refocused on what she was doing. She zoomed into the upper-left quadrant of the screen to show an immense giant that was towering over the buildings he was crushing with his bare feet.

As he was processing the scale of the giant he was looking at, Luke gasped. "My God, that thing has got to be at least three times bigger than Chimera!"

Diana shook her head. "Try more like over four times larger than Chimera. This is Atlas, the titan that was once cursed to hold up the sky. He stands at slightly over one thousand feet tall. He obviously has tremendous physical strength. With his size and power, he was able to destroy the entire the entire city of Dallas in less than half an hour. These images are from a half hour ago so that we have something to scale him with. The monster is currently making his way across the desert. I have no idea how at that height he has not been crushed under his own body weight or passed out from the thin air that he must be breathing."

Odin said, "The ways of gods and titans are beyond your mortal understanding."

Diana looked back at the screen and zoomed in on the images on the top right-hand corner of the display. She sighed. "This kaiju that appeared in Africa is the one that I can't figure out. The kaiju does not fit the description of any mythological creature that I can find. It stands at just under two hundred feet tall at the shoulder. The monster looks like some kind of a giant theropod dinosaur with notable differences from a theropod aside from its size. The kaiju has long powerful arms and claws that look much stronger and more functional than a typical theropod's more or less useless arms. The creature also appears to have a protective caprice on its back, again a trait not associated with theropods." She shook her head in disbelief as she explained the final aspect of the strange creature. "The most amazing aspect of this creature is that the kaiju has been reported to unleash some sort of dome of energy from its body that is highly radioactive. With a single pulse from this attack, the monster destroyed an entire Egyptian defense battalion." She looked toward Zeus and Odin. "Is this monster one of your monsters, that humans never recorded in mythology?"

Odin waved his hand in front of him, creating what looked like a shimmering distortion in the air. In the center of the distortion was the image of a devastated landscape. Odin looked at the humans. "This Earth is but one of many Earths. We gods can exist in the planes between these many Earths. In our plane of existence, we are able to draw the life energy that we need to sustain ourselves from these Earths. We are able to do this by the absorbing ambient energy that life gives off as it grows and reproduces. The Dark Ones that you know as titans access life energy in a different manner than we do. They require the consumption of life in order to draw energy from it. Both the Dark Ones and our kind evolved on the same Earth. It was an Earth that was much older than yours. We were sustaining ourselves off the ambient life energy of the planet while the Dark Ones were consuming it."

Odin stopped talking for a brief moment as he could see that the humans he was talking to were having difficulty understanding the concept he was explaining to them. "Perhaps if you correlate the Dark Ones and us to the plants and animals that are on your Earth. The plants take energy directly from the sun to sustain themselves while the animals such as yourselves must consume life that has already processed this energy in order to utilize it." Parsons, Luke, and Diana all nodded, signifying that they understood the analogy Odin had made.

Satisfied that the humans were following him, Odin continued on with his explanation. "We fought to drive the Dark Ones from our Earth in order to preserve it and sadly at first, we were defeated. We were forced to travel the multiverse, gathering the life energy from other Earths. We used this energy to increase our own power. In our travels, we encountered Earths where the creatures that you refer to as monsters or kaiju had developed. Much as you were able to train the beast you call Chimera, so too were we able to train these monsters to do our bidding. With these monsters under our command, we were able to attack and defeat the Dark Ones. The Dark Ones went into hiding and we placed the monsters that we had trained on different Earths at early points in each planet's development. While you humans would see these monsters as threats to local populations of your kind, in truth, they were placed here to dissuade the Dark Ones from attacking each planet. Had the Dark Ones attacked an Earth that our creatures were on, they would have risen up, not in defense of you humans, but rather the planet itself."

Odin switched the view in the distortion he had created to show some of the creatures that Chimera had slain such as the Scylla and Cerberus. "As the human population on a given Earth evolved and increased the power and technology of their weapons to the point where we felt that they could at least fight back against the Dark Ones long enough that we became aware of the attack, we would move our monsters to a less-developed Earth that was in need of protection. This removal of our guardian beasts is what led to them being regarded as legend and myth as the generations passed.

"In that time that has passed, the Dark Ones' power has slowly grown as Earths have died a natural death, or they have been killed by the human populations that had grown there. In that time, the Dark Ones also followed our example by traveling to different Earths, capturing monsters, and training them."

The distortion began to show more versions of Earth that were devoid of life. "We knew that with each dying Earth, the Dark Ones' power grew. When we suspected that their power was starting to rival our own, we decided to act and to prevent more Earth's from dying and increasing their power. Across many Earths, you humans have caused the death of your planet through its misuse. As such, we destroyed your race on several Earths before coming here where our efforts were rebuffed by Chimera, a monster far more powerful than any beast we have encountered thus far."

General Parsons gestured toward the screen. "Thank you for that backstory, but lives are being lost from these attacks as we sit here and talk about it. I assume that the loss of human lives also makes the Dark Ones more powerful? Can you explain to us what that dinosaur monster is?"

Odin shifted the distortion, showing a variety of giant monsters battling. Parsons, Luke, and Diana saw huge cybernetic birds fighting what looked like a giant Sasquatch. They saw a colossal lizard man, a Chinese dragon, and a massive polar bear with horns and a long spiked tail battling a gigantic black robot, and finally, they saw the saurian monster that was in Africa fighting a giant turtle. As the distortion settled on the saurian beast and the turtle, Odin said, "The appearance of giant monsters on multiple Earths has been increasing exponentially lately. Sometimes these creatures are created by you humans to battle each other, sometimes they are created to protect your species from interplanetary threats, and sometimes they occur by mistake. The creature you now behold is the result of the latter method of creation. On his Earth, the beast is known as Atomic Rex. Atomic Rex was the bringer of death to his planet. Humans on his Earth conducted nuclear experiments on an island that still held what you would call dinosaurs. Many of these dinosaurs would change into kaiju when they were exposed to this power. The monsters would leave their island and lay waste to their planet not only through physical attack but by spreading the deadly power that emanated from their bodies to the planet itself.

This power would either change or kill all that it came into contact with."

Odin waved his hand over the distortion to show a huge robot that resembled an ancient samurai. "As the humans on this Earth faced extinction, their guardian used his mech to lure the monsters to one another. One by one, the monsters slew each other across North America. Many of these monsters would be killed by Atomic Rex who as you reported is able to release the power stored within his body as a deadly blast." Odin shook his head. "Atomic Rex has slain countless other monsters on his Earth and because of his power and ferocity, the Dark Ones have snatched him from there and brought him to your Earth. He will destroy everything in his path until nothing remains. Furthermore, I suspect that after laying waste to Africa, he will attempt to return to what he considers his home in the Americas."

Odin shifted his one eye toward Luke as the distortion faded away. "I doubt even your Chimera will be able to stand against Atomic Rex."

Luke shook his head. "You didn't think that Chimera could defeat your son either, but he whooped Thor's ass pretty good." Odin glared at Luke in anger and clenched his fists.

It was Parsons who focused the conversation back on the task at hand. "These attacks are just a first strike. The Dark Ones are planning something else, aren't they?"

Zeus nodded. "You are indeed wise in the ways of war, General. We suspect that the leaders of the Dark Ones, Cronus, Tiamat, and Surtr, are using these attacks to destroy as much life as possible. They will then collect that life force to increase their power and use it to enact whatever tactic they have in mind to end all life on the planet."

Parsons sighed. "What can you two offer us if we work with you to fight back this attack from the Dark Ones?"

Zeus lowered his head. "As I said, I have not yet recovered my full strength since Chimera destroyed the pillars that provide me with power. I can, however, offer you the final two creatures in my stable." This time, it was Zeus who created a portal to show two winged creatures. One of the monsters was a giant bird with bright blue flames cascaded across its wings. The second monster was a huge creature with the body of a lion and the wings and head of an eagle. "The Phoenix and Griffin shall assist you in fighting the monsters that are attacking. I can also assist in transporting these beasts and Chimera to various locations as needed to battle the Dark Ones' creatures."

The geek girl inside of Diana came out as she giggled. "Since it's going up against the Dark Ones, the Phoenix isn't going to get corrupted and go all Dark Phoenix on us, is it?"

The two gods and Parsons simply looked at Diana in confusion. Luke, who had been keeping up with what Diana had referred to as essential comic reading, got her reference and smiled.

Zeus shook his head. "The Phoenix is under my complete control."

Luke quickly turned his head toward Zeus. "Wait. If you are able to teleport monsters, why can't you just send the Dark Ones' creatures and this Atomic Rex back where they came from?"

Zeus shook his head. 'The Dark Ones' power far exceeds my own at this point. They will have shielded their creatures against the use of such a tactic."

Luke shrugged. "Can you at least keep your EMPs to a minimum when you teleport us? It would be helpful to have working communications when we are entering into a battle."

Zeus nodded. "You shall have all of your technology at your disposal when entering a battle. I shall calibrate my powers to prevent them from destroying your machines."

Parsons shifted his gaze to Odin. "What can you do?"

Odin was silent for a moment as if what he was about to say was of grave importance. "If you still possess the belt of strength that you removed from my son Thor after his battle with Chimera, give it to me. I shall place it on myself and engage in battle directly."

Diana was about say something and she turned toward Parsons. She made eye contact with Parsons who winked at her. The wink indicated to Diana that Parsons knew she wanted to say something, but he wanted her to wait until later. She smiled and looked away from the general.

Parsons nodded. "I will see that you get the belt; however, be aware that we've been developing a portal to Asgard from the remains of the Rainbow Bridge you left in Norway. If I even suspect you of trying to attack us again, I will not hesitate to use the portal to send Chimera to Asgard itself with the command to destroy it."

Odin glared at Parsons. "Agreed."

Parsons held Odin's gaze for a minute and then he started shouting out orders. "This is what we are going to do! Luke, I want Zeus to send you and Chimera to Boston to battle the Kraken. If Chimera is up to it after that, I want you to travel to Baltimore to take on the Hecatonchires. In the meantime, the military will have to try and slow that monster down. The *Argos* is stationed in Annapolis. It's our nuclear-powered flagship and the vessel we use to transport Chimera over long distances. The *Argos* is currently under the command of Captain Brand. I will have him sail to Baltimore and provide backup for the ground forces there. If all else fails, the *Argos* should have more than enough firepower to at least keep the beast occupied until we can come up with an alternate plan."

Parsons looked at Zeus. "I want the Phoenix to travel to Texas and to take on Atlas."

Zeus replied, "As powerful as the Phoenix is, she is but a monster. Atlas is the largest and strongest of the titans. The Phoenix will not be able to defeat him as he is many times larger than she is."

Parsons nodded. "I don't expect her to defeat him. I just need her to hold him off. I will go to Texas as well and lead whatever military forces we have there to support her."

He turned to Diana. "Call the closest stone quarry to Atlas. Give them the size and dimensions of Atlas. I want them working on Project G in response to counteract this threat. I want you to oversee the project yourself. Tell them speed is more important than appearance."

Diana nodded. "Yes, sir." She then pulled out her phone and started dialing.

Parsons looked back at Zeus. "Send the Griffin to Africa. I want to stop Atomic Rex before he makes his way here." He then looked at Odin. "I will have your belt ready and I will give it to you when the time is right to put you into battle."

Odin's voice boomed with anger. "You presume to give me orders!"

Parsons shrugged. "You are on my base and I am in possession of the item that you desire. I hold the cards here and you will abide by my orders if you want to get your belt back and help win this war." Odin didn't reply; he simply turned away from Parsons.

With the question of command settled, Parsons finished his orders. "Luke, you and Zeus head outside. As soon as he sends the Griffin to Africa, and us and the Phoenix to Texas, I want you and Chimera in Boston."

Luke nodded and ran out the door, knowing that he needed to make sure that Chimera remained calm when he saw Zeus.

Zeus turned away from Parsons and closed his eyes. Parsons assumed that he was teleporting his monsters to their designated locations. The general gestured for Diana to follow him. When they entered his office, he closed the door. "Something caught your interest when Odin asked for the belt."

Diana nodded. "In Norse mythology, Odin dies in the battle at the end of time known as Ragnarok. In the myth of Ragnarok, the Norse gods, as well as the nearly everyone on Earth, dies."

Parsons nodded. "Explaining that mythological monsters are creatures from other worlds that were placed here by interdimensional beings is one thing that at least can be grounded in advanced science.

Predictions about the future though…are those something we can really put stock in?"

Diana shrugged. "I don't know, sir." Despite her best efforts, a small smile crept across her face.

Parsons looked at her. "What's going through your mind now?"

Diana's smile grew. "I am all for combining other mythologies for ways we can fight the gods and titans, but how cool were those Pacific Rim-style mechs we saw? If people on other Earths can make them, is it possible that we could? Just imagine the next time we go into battle if we had our own giant robot!"

For the first time since Diana had met him, Parsons smiled. He then stood up and started walking toward the door. "Right now, we have to focus on Project G, but we can talk about mechs later."

Diana grinned and said, "I want my mech to look like the robot the Kaiju Noir guy on YouTube has for a mascot. That thing is kick ass!"

When Parsons' door was closed, a young female soldier with blonde hair stood up from her workstation and walked toward the woman's room. The woman was strikingly beautiful and she caught the eye of several male soldiers in the hangar as she walked by. When she was gone, all of the men were talking to each other about the new recruit. Most of the conversation was focused on how attractive she was. The conversation over her seemingly perfect body led to the men pushing aside the fact that none of them knew her name or where she had come from.

The woman stepped outside and walked toward an alley between two hangars. When she was out of sight from any of the men on the base, she disappeared.

The Congo

The woman reappeared in a cave deep in the jungles of the Congo. Inside of the huge cave were more than a dozen children, each appearing to be roughly ten years old, running around and playing. One of the children picked up a boulder that weighed several tons and tossed it to another child who caught the huge rock and tossed it back. The woman smiled at the children, and when they saw her, they all came running over to her yelling, "Mama Allison, you are back!"

The nymph smiled at the children and she knelt down to hug them. Behind the children, she could see their mothers slumped against the cave wall. The women were exhausted, and she knew exactly why they were so tired.

One of the kids rushed up to Allison and said, "Today, we learned knife fighting from the warriors. I now know the best way to stab a man in order to kill him as quickly as possible!"

Allison patted the boy on the head. "That's excellent! Where is your Uncle Aiden? I have some very important news to discuss with him."

Allison's twin brother suddenly appeared behind her. The young man was as strikingly handsome as she was beautiful. Allison wrapped her arm around her brother's arm and she walked with him toward the front of the cave.

One of the kids grabbed Allison's hand. "Mama Allison, is today the day that we get to leave the cave?"

She smiled at the boy as several of his brothers walked up behind him with eager eyes for an answer to the question. "No, not yet. We want it to be a very special day when you leave the cave, and today is not that day. You kids go and play. Keep up that boulder tossing. I want you to be as strong as you possibly can because your time is coming soon."

The kids obeyed as Allison continued to walk her brother to the front of the cave. Aiden whispered in his sister's ear, "Did the gods or humans notice your presence on the base?"

Allison nodded. "I drew the usual attention of some of the human males but no one of importance noticed me. Luke Davis mentioned us but even then, the gods were too arrogant to see if I was around. We are only worth the gods' notice when they require our services."

Aiden nodded. "So was your prediction correct? Did the gods come here to battle the Dark Ones?"

Allison smiled. "The gods' ranks are severely depleted from their war with the humans and Chimera. They have come to forge an alliance with the humans to try and challenge the Dark Ones. In addition to their own monsters, The Dark Ones have also brought a fearsome monster known as Atomic Rex to this Earth to battle on their side."

Aiden nodded. "The Dark Ones will destroy life in all of its forms. The gods are right to forge alliances to challenge them. Should we have the children join with them and fight the Dark Ones?"

Allison scowled at her brother. "Did I somehow take your intelligence when we were in mother's womb?" She shook her head. "No. A war between our enemies will weaken them all. The Dark Ones, the gods, even the humans and Chimera will all come out weaker from this war. When the war nears its end, then if we need to strike, we will. In a war such as this, there will undoubtedly be opportunities for us to obtain weapons and artifacts that will strengthen our forces." She turned and looked back at the cave. "Besides, our young warriors are not yet ready to challenge their sires or Chimera, and should they leave the cave, the gods would immediately become aware of their existence. We want to keep all of our assets a secret for as long as possible. Just as Zeus hid in a cave from Cronus, so do his bastards hide from him." Allison looked back at her brother. "How was their training today?"

Aiden shrugged. "The warlords of the area employ remarkable fighters. The demi-gods are learning much from them. The warriors continue to accept the children's mothers as payment." Aiden rolled his head a little from side to side in discomfort. "I am not sure how much more the woman can endure. The treatment they receive at the hands of the warriors is mentally demeaning and physically harsh."

Allison turned around and slapped her brother. "We have had to endure far worse depravity at the hands of the gods and goddess for centuries! How long did we have to survive by servicing their needs? Those human females have only had a small taste of what we have gone through. Their suffering will end, and they will be rewarded when their sons inherit this planet. Our time will come when this war ends."

Aiden nodded. "What of Toombs? How is his work coming?"

Allison sneered. "That toad of a man's newest project is almost complete, but again, we shall hold that chess piece until the last minute. He is currently working in Russia. It took a few distasteful encounters on my part, but I was able to convince the men in power there that Toombs could create them a monster even greater than Chimera. The fools actually think Toombs' allegiance is to their money when in reality he is my puppet for a little more than a smile and a hug. Again, when our time arrives, Toombs' new monster will crush those who financed his creation and join us."

CHAPTER 5

Outskirts of Sahab, Libya

The hot sun continued to beat down on Atomic Rex as he made his way across the seemingly endless desert. The temperatures that were well in excess of one hundred degrees Fahrenheit did not physically affect the monster. When Atomic Rex unleashed his Atomic Wave blast, his skin was near the temperature of ground zero of a nuclear explosion. It was the endless sight of dry sand around him that was taking a mental toll on the monster.

Atomic Rex had always preferred to stay near the ocean whenever possible. He had found that food was more plentiful in the ocean. He also found that it was much easier to maneuver his massive body through the water than it was to walk across land. The lack of water around him made the volatile kaiju even more aggressive than usual. Even though he was on an Earth that was different from his own, Atomic Rex still had an innate sense of where he was in relation to the territory that he considered his. The kaiju knew exactly where North America was, and the monster was moving at top speed to reach his home. With his long strides and a body that was built for moving quickly over long distances, the monster had already traveled several hundred miles. Part of the reason that Atomic Rex found the walk through the desert so frustrating was that he knew he could reach North America much quicker by turning north and heading toward the Mediterranean Sea. By entering the water, the monster would be able to move at more than twice the speed that he was able to move on land. Additionally, he would likely find larger sources food in the water to help sustain the hunger that was slowly growing in his stomach.

The people and livestock that Atomic Rex had eaten since he had entered this world were not enough to satiate the kaiju's need for meat. Atomic Rex was sure that the seas and oceans would hold large whales and fish that he could feast on if he reached the water. The monster was quickly growing hungry once again and while he knew that heading toward the Mediterranean Sea was in his best interests, there was some force that was compelling him against his will to make the trek to the Atlantic Ocean by land instead of through the sea. As much as heat, hunger, and the endless desert angered Atomic Rex, the knowledge that something or someone else was causing him to go against his own will was enraging the beast.

Directly ahead of him, the monster could see the buildings of another city rising out of the desert. The nuclear theropod roared, as he realized that on this Earth, the sight of buildings meant the presence of humans. Atomic Rex knew that no matter how many of the small creatures he devoured, they would not be enough to truly ease his hunger. Still swallowing several thousand of the tiny creatures would ease his hunger until he reached the next city.

With the thought of eating driving out the realization that some outside force was influencing his decisions, Atomic Rex lowered his head and began charging toward the city of Sahab.

The kaiju was roughly two miles outside of the city when a strange cloud suddenly appeared in the sky above it. The cloud was dark and gray with lightning streaking out of it from all sides. Atomic Rex had seen many storms over the course of his long life, but he had never seen a single massive cloud that had lightning shooting out of it, not only toward the ground but also to the sky above it and toward the horizon.

Aside from the smell of ozone given off by the thunder cloud, Atomic Rex was also able to detect the odor of something large and organic within the strange weather formation. Atomic Rex continued to stare at the mysterious cloud as it drifted away from the city and toward him. The battle-hardened Atomic Rex was fully aware that if something was making its way straight toward him, it was a clear sign the thing was going to attack. The kaiju stretched out his powerful arms and swiped his claws at the air. The monster then reared back his head and drew in a deep breath. An instant later, Atomic Rex's head shot forward and he roared at the strange cloud that was challenging him.

In response to the roar, a high-pitched shriek emanated from the cloud. Atomic Rex watched as a thick brown beak poked out of the clouds. The beak was followed by a feathered head with harrowing yellow eyes and dark black irises in the center of them. Two long, yellow, fur-covered legs that ended in menacing claws emerged from the base of the clouds. The legs were connected to a fur-covered and a powerfully built torso. As the torso of the creature came out of the cloud, Atomic Rex saw two long brown wings attached to the back of the creature. The monster gracefully floated to the ground, revealing that it had the head and wings of a giant eagle with the body and tail of a kaiju-sized lion. The Griffin stood roughly one hundred and fifty feet tall at the shoulder, making him about two-thirds the size of Atomic Rex.

The Griffin reared up on its hind legs and roared at Atomic Rex. The Griffin then began flapping its wings behind it, causing wind gusts of one hundred and fifty miles per hour to send grains of sand flying into Atomic Rex. Despite being propelled at the speed of a hurricane, the torrent of sand bounced harmlessly off Atomic Rex's body, but the sand did manage to find its way into the beast's eyes, nose, and mouth.

The saurian monster closed his eyes and mouth. Atomic Rex's eyes became watery and his mouth dried up as his body tried to deal with the sand that had entered it. The monster put his claws in front of his face, blocking it from some of the swirling sands. Then he slowly pushed through the swirling sandstorm toward the monster that had not only challenged him but was also a potential meal.

Seeing that Atomic Rex was making his way through the sandstorm, the Griffin dropped to all fours, crouched down, and then leapt at the mutated dinosaur. Atomic Rex was shaking his head, trying to clear his orifices of the sand that was lodged in them when the Griffin slammed into his torso. The blow knocked the nuclear theropod back several steps. Before Atomic Rex was able to open his eyes, the Griffin charged and drove his shoulder into Atomic Rex's right thigh, knocking the kaiju to the ground. With his opponent downed, the Griffin leapt toward Atomic Rex, hoping to pin the saurian creature to the ground and tear his throat out.

The Griffin was in mid-leap when Atomic Rex swung his tail, striking the Griffin in the ribs and knocking off his trajectory. The blow caused the Griffin to crash into the sand to the left of Atomic Rex. Atomic Rex quickly stood up and used his claws to clear the sand from his eyes. The kaiju then opened his eyes just in time to see the Griffin leaping toward him again. Atomic Rex braced himself and opened his arms wide. He then caught the Griffin in his powerful arms. Atomic Rex roared, lifted the Griffin over his head, and then he slammed the mythological creature into the desert sand. The Griffin landed hard on his side and was in the middle of rolling over when Atomic Rex kicked him in the ribs. The Griffin screeched in pain as one of the long claws on the nuclear theropod's toes penetrated his skin and scraped across his ribcage. Atomic Rex was reaching down to sink his teeth into the Griffin's neck when the mythical monster swung out with his foreclaw and slashed Atomic Rex across his lower jaw. Atomic Rex pulled his head back, giving the Griffin the opportunity to regain his feet. With his ribs cracked and his side bleeding, the Griffin was badly injured, but the majestic creature had no intentions of retreating from this battle.

The Griffin lunged forward and clamped his beak down over Atomic Rex's left arm. The winged monster then pulled Atomic Rex toward him, causing the saurian monster to lose his balance. With Atomic Rex's weight pitched toward him, the Griffin reached out with his left foreclaw and scratched Atomic Rex across his hip and thigh several times.

Atomic Rex roared in pain as the Griffin's claws raked across his leg like giant blades. The nuclear theropod pulled his left arm toward his body, forcing the Griffin's head closer to him. The kaiju then used his right forearm to strike the winged monster in the neck. The blow caused the Griffin's vice-like beak to loosen enough so that Atomic Rex was able to free his arm from its grasp. Atomic Rex's head shot forward as he once more attempted to sink his teeth into the Griffin's neck. To Atomic Rex's surprise, the Griffin was able to shift his head to the side and avoid the bite. The mythical monster then threw his head sideways, smashing it into the side of Atomic Rex's face.

The blow caught Atomic Rex off guard and it afforded the Griffin enough time to leap into the air and start flapping his wings. Blood dripped from the Griffin's injured side as he hovered above the creature that his master had ordered him to slay. The Griffin screeched and then he dove at the head of Atomic Rex.

The Griffin moved like a blur, raking his claws across the side of Atomic Rex's face while also driving his thick beak into the top of the monster's head. Atomic Rex swiped his claws at the Griffin's face, but in the air, the creature was more than quick enough to avoid the worst of the kaiju's claws. The Griffin opened up several deep gashes on Atomic Rex's head that caused the kaiju's own blood to stream down his face and into his mouth.

While Atomic Rex's temperament often urged him to move forward when fighting an enemy, the monster's intelligence often won him the day. In the frenzy of the Griffin's attack, Atomic Rex saw the winged monster's tail hanging low beneath the creature as he fluttered in the air. Atomic Rex dropped the front half of his body low to the ground, causing the Griffin's claws to flail harmlessly in the air above him. Atomic Rex then lunged forward and closed his jaws on the Griffin's exposed tail. With the Griffin's tail caught in his mouth, Atomic Rex pulled down, causing the Griffin to slam back first into the ground at his feet. Atomic Rex saw the Griffin's hind legs pawing at the air in front of him. The nuclear theropod's arms shot out and he buried his claws into the Griffin's right thigh. The kaiju then clamped his jaws around the Griffin's right foot at the ankle. With a quick twist of his head, Atomic Rex snapped the Griffin's ankle in two.

The Griffin was still screeching in pain as Atomic Rex twisted his head the other way and completely tore off the Griffin's foot. Blood spurted out of the stump where the Griffin's leg had once been. The Griffin rolled over onto his stomach and began flapping his wings in an attempt to escape into the air. The Griffin's body was just starting to lift off the ground when Atomic Rex leapt onto his back. Atomic Rex's weight drove the Griffin's damaged ribs back into the ground with thousands of tons on top of them.

The Griffin continued to flap his wings in vain until Atomic Rex bit down into the base of his left wing. With one powerful pull, Atomic Rex tore the wing out of the Griffin's back. A crimson geyser shot into the air out the Griffin's back where the wing had been torn off. The Griffin let loose one final screech as Atomic Rex clamped his jaws down onto the beast's head and neck. With one last quick twist, Atomic Rex broke the Griffin's neck, ending the monster's life.

With his defeated opponent dead at his feet, Atomic Rex lifted his head into the air and roared in victory. The hungry monster then reached down and tore a huge chunk of flesh out of the Griffin's back. The kaiju swallowed the mouthful of blood and muscle. Atomic Rex then continued to feed on the fallen Griffin until all that remained of the once majestic beast was nothing but bones and blood.

After he had finished devouring the defeated Griffin, Atomic Rex turned his head to the north and the sea. The monster took a step toward the water when he felt something in his head urging him to turn around and destroy the city of Sahab. The influence in Atomic Rex's head wanted him to decimate the city and kill the millions of people who lived there. Atomic Rex roared at the influence. He had already fed and neither the people nor the city was a threat to him. The monster also had little interest in showing his dominance over the creatures in the city as the hot and barren desert were not lands that he saw as worth claiming for his own.

Atomic Rex then thought once more of the ocean and he turned his body so that he was facing a northern direction. The nuclear theropod took a step in that direction when the power that was influencing his mind suddenly changed from an annoying suggestion to a searing pain. Atomic Rex roared and shook his head as he tried to fight off the psychic attack.

In the dark dimension between worlds, Cronus was focusing all of his power on directing Atomic Rex toward the city of Sahab. The mad titan needed the kaiju to slay as many creatures as he could on his way to North America so that he could absorb the life energy of those the monster killed. The titan had found it easy to influence Atomic Rex when the monster's needs matched his own. Now that Atomic Rex had recharged the nuclear energy within his body and fed, the monster's desire was to return to the land that he thought of as his home as quickly as possible.

Cronus could feel Atomic Rex breaking free of his influence. The titan had known of the kaiju's fighting spirit and refusal to accept defeat, yet he did not consider that the monster's limited mind had a will power that could match his own. Cronus grunted as he redoubled his efforts. As it became apparent that Cronus could not fully dominate the kaiju's mind, he decided to change his approach. If Cronus was unable to force Atomic Rex to attack Sahab, he could at least influence the monster to continue to make his way to the Atlantic by going across Africa rather than swimming through the Mediterranean. The titan reasoned that simply by walking across Africa, the monster would inevitably take more lives by simple chance if nothing else. Every muscle in Cronus' body tightened, as he focused on convincing Atomic Rex to return to his original westbound course.

As the titan's influence seeped into his mind, Atomic Rex slowly turned west and away from the sea. The monster only glanced at Sahab and the military forces that had amassed outside of the city preparing to defend it against him as he continued to make his way back to North America.

Cronus fell to one knee when he felt Atomic Rex turn and head toward the Atlantic. He looked through his portal at the nuclear theropod as the monster made his way across the desert and he screamed, "Accursed beast! You could have greatly added to my power by destroying the city! Millions of lives were there, waiting to be added to my power! Now through your defiance, you have taxed my power reserves rather than adding to them! This affront is in addition to the fact that the Griffin's appearance indicates the gods are marshaling their remaining forces to oppose us!"

Cronus took a deep breath in an attempt to regain his composure. "Still, you did weaken our enemies by slaying the Griffin." The titan shook his head. "It is unfortunate that the energy I absorbed from the death of the beast was wasted on convincing you to continue to press through the continent."

It was at that moment that Cronus made a stunning realization about the nature of Atomic Rex. Atomic Rex had also replenished his strength by not only consuming the Griffin but also by absorbing the energy at the nuclear power plant. Cronus could already sense that after completing these tasks, Atomic Rex was far more powerful than he was when Cronus first brought him to this Earth. Cronus shook his head as he looked through the portal at Atomic Rex. "Could it be that the monster's power could potentially rival my own?"

Cronus pondered the thought for a moment, but then he dismissed it. The more pressing matter was the appearance of the Griffin. Cronus opened two more portals to reveal both Surtr and Tiamat. The ancient horrors were waiting on the outskirts of the human realm, preparing themselves for their attacks on the planet. Unlike Atomic Rex, Surtr and Tiamat knew when Cronus was looking at them through a portal. Both creatures looked back at Cronus. It was Tiamat who hissed, "What has happened?"

Cronus gritted his teeth in anger as he responded. "The Griffin has attacked Atomic Rex. He appeared out of a thunder cloud. The kaiju was able to slay the winged beast, but his presence and the way he appeared suggests that Zeus teleported him there. It seems that what's left of the gods have decided to oppose us."

Surtr grumbled, "Chimera decimated them. They are a shell of what they once were!"

Cronus shook his head. "Should they ally themselves with the humans, they could increase the threat posed by Chimera. In addition to whatever warriors and monsters they may have left, Zeus can also teleport Chimera anywhere on the planet instantaneously. We had thought that when Chimera was engaged with one of our monsters, the threat he posed would be neutralized by sheer distance if not by our creatures. Now that advantage may be lost to us."

Tiamat's head whipped around in anger. "You must gather the life energy that we require to carry out our tasks as soon as possible."

The fire that comprised Surtr's eyes grew intensity. "What of Atomic Rex? Have you been able to direct him toward population centers?"

Cronus was silent for a moment as he stared at Surtr. "Yes. He has just destroyed the city of Sahab." The titan decided that the best way to keep his allies from discovering his lie was to wrap it around a bit of truth. "Controlling the monster is more difficult than I had thought. Allow me a short time to rest and restore my own powers. Within a day's time, I shall be at full strength and the monster will arrive at the city of Adrar. After the beast destroys the city, we will have more than enough life energy for you to complete your tasks with. As soon as I have the life energy of the people of Adrar, I shall send it to you so that you may begin your attacks."

Surtr nodded. "Attain the life force that we need to destroy this Earth and be sure that energy is ready to be sent to us should a storm cloud carrying Chimera appear before us."

Cronus nodded. "Do not fret, brother. You shall be fully prepared to face Chimera when the time comes." He then closed the portal and looked back on Atomic Rex. "I must have you attack Adrar so that I have life energy to send to the others. If they suspect that I am unable to provide them with the energy I promised, they will likely turn on me and seek to take my life energy."

CHAPTER 6

Chimera Base

Luke dashed out of Hangar Eighteen to see Chimera staring at the building. He could hear the monster growling, and he could see the hairs on Chimera's mane standing up. Luke said to himself, "You don't need to be a trainer to see he's ready for a fight." Luke lifted his megaphone to his lips and shouted, "Chimera, sit down!"

The monster looked at his trainer for a second before complying with the command. Luke breathed a sigh of relief as the ground shook when Chimera's massive weight dropped down onto the soil. Chimera had reached the point in his training and in his relationship with Luke that he complied with Luke's commands instantly. Luke was well aware that the only reason the monster would hesitate to follow a command was when he felt that his trainer's life was in danger.

Luke was slowly approaching Chimera when the kaiju suddenly stood up, threw his arms out to his sides, and unleashed an anger-filled roar. Luke spun around to see Zeus walking through the hangar doors. Luke cursed under his breath as Chimera began walking toward the god whose throne room he had decimated. Luke screamed into his megaphone, "Chimera, stop!"

The kaiju stopped in his tracks. He then turned and looked at his master before returning his gaze to Zeus. Luke screamed at Zeus, "Now! Teleport us now! Before he decides to attack you!"

Luke watched as Zeus lifted his hand above his head. As the god did so, a dark storm cloud appeared over both Luke and Chimera. Lightning began to streak down from the cloud near the kaiju and his beloved trainer. Chimera roared as he remembered the battle with Zeus at the top of Mount Olympus. The beast recalled how painful the god's lightning strikes were and he refused to let them do any harm to Luke. Despite Luke's command to stop, Chimera started charging Zeus. The kaiju had only taken two steps before he was blinded by a bright flash of lightning.

Luke didn't even have time to shield his eyes as the lightning came down around him. He felt like he was suddenly dropped out of a plane with no parachute as his hair stood on end from the electrical current all around him. Luke collapsed to the ground as he felt an abrupt stop to the falling sensation. He heard screaming all around him as he blinked his eyes to try and steady his vision. He started walking forward then he tripped and fell to the ground face first into something hard and jagged.

Luke felt blood pouring down his cheek and as he crawled forward, he felt a pelting rain being driven sideways into his face by a strong wind. He blinked his eyes several more times to see that he had stumbled through what was once the brick wall of a partially destroyed building. Luke looked through the pelting rain to see the huge form of Chimera rubbing his eyes, no doubt trying to restore his vision as well.

The screaming that Luke heard suddenly became louder and with his vision finally starting to clear up, Luke stood up and took a look around him. He saw nothing but devastation around him in what he guessed was Boston. He looked back at the ground as he tried to navigate his way through the debris of the remains of the destroyed building when his nostrils were overwhelmed by the smell of rotting fish.

Luke then noticed that the rain had stopped striking him in the face and he looked up expecting to see Chimera but instead he saw something much more horrifying than his pupil and friend.

Luke saw a gigantic crab-like creature standing over him with its claws out in front of it. The countless tentacles that protruded from various points around the monster's body were all undulating back and forth. Luke quickly pulled his megaphone to his mouth, and he was about to yell for Chimera to attack when the Kraken darted past him and charged Chimera. Luke stepped through the crumbled wall of the destroyed building to see the Kraken strike the still disoriented Chimera across the jaw with his right claw. The still partially blind Chimera tumbled backward and fell onto his back. Chimera was trying to stand up when the Kraken crawled onto his chest and pinned the kaiju to the ground. Chimera had just started to roar when the Kraken's claw reached down and closed around his throat.

Luke blinked several more times and then he stared at the Kraken in awe. While not as tall as Chimera, the Kraken's overall bulk was nearly twice that of Chimera. Luke doubted that even if Chimera had not been stunned by the blinding light of teleportation, the kaiju was strong enough to push the Kraken off of him.

Chimera could feel his airway being closed off as the Kraken's claw dug deeper into his throat. The hybrid monster reached up and grabbed the Kraken's claw in both of his hands. Chimera pushed back against the Kraken's claws and for a moment, the kaiju could feel the claws sliding away from his neck. As Chimera slowly forced the Kraken's claw off his neck, the monster could feel the Kraken's sharp pincers slicing into his throat. Chimera blinked his eyes several more times and slowly the Kraken came into view. Chimera could see the two large black eyes of the sea beast staring down at him. Chimera snarled and then he unleashed a tightly focused sonar blast at the crustacean.

The Kraken's tentacles all flailed wildly and the monster fell onto his side as his central nervous system was disrupted by Chimera's blast. Chimera stood up and shook his head a few more times as he continued to recover from the effects of being teleported. Chimera looked down at the temporarily disabled Kraken. He was about to attack the mythical beast when he sniffed the air and turned his head to the side. Chimera roared in the opposite direction of the Kraken and then he began running away from the downed beast.

Luke couldn't believe what he was seeing. He had never seen Chimera run from a fight, let alone a downed opponent. Luke could only guess that there was a second monster nearby that he hadn't noticed previously. Luke darted to his left so that he could see around the fallen Kraken. Once Luke had run far enough to see past the Kraken, he could see Chimera chasing after a thirty-foot-tall giant in a toga. Luke shook his head in surprise as he mouthed the word, "Zeus?" It then struck Luke like one of the thunder god's lightning bolts. Zeus was supposed to teleport he and Chimera to Baltimore if Chimera was successful in defeating the Kraken. In his weakened state, Zeus must have needed to be close to them in order to pull off such a feat.

Zeus was still running when Chimera's massive fist struck him across the side and sent the former king of Olympus flying through the air. Zeus crashed into the upper floors of a still-standing building several blocks away. Luke watched as the Olympian's body slowly slid out of the crevice it had created forty stories up and then fell to the street below.

Chimera turned to pursue Zeus, and Luke watched as the Kraken regained his sense of balance and stood up. Chimera was still making his way after Zeus when the Kraken began chasing the kaiju. Luke grabbed his megaphone and he started running after the two monsters. The rain and wind were pushing against his body as he tried to get close enough to Chimera to call out to him. Luke not only needed Chimera to re-engage the Kraken for his own sake and for the sake of the people still alive in Boston, but he also needed Chimera to leave Zeus alive so that if they defeated the Kraken, he could transport them to Baltimore while there was still time to try and save at least some of the people there from the Hecatonchires.

Luke guessed that if there was ever a time that all of the jogging he was doing was going to pay off, it was now. Luke had never tried to run in the middle of a storm before, let alone through the debris field that was downtown Boston. He tried not to think about the obstacles he was facing and instead tried to focus on running. Luke looked at the Kraken and he could immediately see that the monster's thin crab like legs were not suited to moving through a city. Luke realized that Chimera was going to reach Zeus before the Kraken reached Chimera. Luke lifted up his head and ran as fast as he could. While he was in decent shape, he was still pushing forty years old and his body could only give him so much. Luke could feel his hamstrings tightening and he knew that at any second he could pull one of them which would stop him dead in his tracks.

Luke looked toward Chimera to see the monster standing next to the building that Zeus had crashed into. Chimera was looking down at the street and Luke could see the rage in the monster's eyes. The former teacher knew that he was out of time. He brought his megaphone up to his mouth and screamed into it, "Chimera, stop!"

The kaiju turned his head away from the fallen, and Luke hoped, still alive Zeus. Chimera saw the Kraken approaching him and the kaiju looked toward Luke for directions on what to do with the approaching monster.

Luke pointed at the Kraken and he screamed into his megaphone, "Chimera, attack!"

Chimera turned toward the Kraken and charged. The hybrid drove his spermaceti reinforced head directly into the Kraken's mouth. The impact rocked the Kraken and forced the beast to take several steps backward. Chimera stepped forward and delivered a straight fist between the Kraken's eyes, staggering the shelled monster. Chimera moved in closer to the Kraken, dropping his arms low to ground as he approached the beast. When his arms were underneath the Kraken, Chimera brought up both of his fists, hitting the Kraken with a double uppercut. The blow was so powerful that it lifted the mythical beast's front two legs off the ground.

As the front half of the monster's body was falling back to the ground, the Kraken lifted his right claw into the air. The monster then brought his claw crashing down onto Chimera's head. The blow struck Chimera with such force that it drove the hybrid face first into the street. Chimera's lower jaw slammed into the street, causing a large portion of it to collapse into the subway tunnel beneath it.

Chimera was attempting to pick himself up when the Kraken's tentacles wrapped around his body. Chimera struggled to break free of the Kraken's grip but the tentacles that had dragged thousands of ships to the bottom of the ocean held fast. The Kraken turned and started dragging Chimera back toward the ocean, hoping to drown his opponent.

Luke watch helplessly as the Kraken continued to drag Chimera toward the Atlantic Ocean. Realizing that the most productive things he could do was to try to get Zeus back on his feet, Luke started running toward the building that the thunder god had crashed into. For Luke, it was a fifteen-block jog in the rain and around debris created by the warring monsters. When he finally reached the street where Zeus had crashed into, Luke slowed down to a walk. He was breathing heavy and his clothes were soaked. Luke was in the best shape he had been in years, but he was pushing his body to its limits and it was starting to take its toll on him.

He looked down from the spot where Zeus had crashed into and at first he could not see the Olympian. Luke walked forward and put his hands over his eyes to try and shield them from the non-stop rain. As Luke continued walking forward, he saw a subway tunnel entrance and at the top of the stairs, he could see a giant sandaled foot. Luke walked up to the fallen god as quickly as he could. He found Zeus laying across the stairs to the subway completely unconscious. Luke walked over to the god and leaned down next to his mouth.

Luke threw his hands up into the air and shouted, "Great, now you're not breathing! An hour ago, nothing would have made me happier than to see you dead. Of course, when I need you, you crap out on me."

Luke climbed on top of Zeus' chest and he started jumping up and down on the god's sternum. Luke groaned when he realized that even bringing down his entire weight onto Zeus' chest was not enough to get the god breathing again. He screamed in Zeus' face, "What in the hell am I supposed to do to get you to wake up?"

The former teacher clenched his fist and gritted his teeth. "Okay, yelling at you isn't going to help the situation. What do I have around that I can use?" Luke looked around the subway entrance. When he did not see anything that could help him revive Zeus, he ran down into the subway. The first thing that he saw was a group of people huddled together in a corner. Luke guessed that the people had made their way underground in an attempt to find some kind of shelter from the Kraken's attack.

Realizing that there wasn't much that he could do for the people at that second, Luke continued to look for anything that he could use to revive Zeus. Luke scanned the subway and his eyes came to rest on a sign above the third rail on the tracks that read *Danger High Voltage.* Luke shrugged. "Well, he is a thunder god, and if nothing else, it may shock his heart back into beating. Now all I need is something to carry the current from the rail to Zeus." Luke ran back over the still-form Zeus and into the storm.

He closed his eyes as he tried to think about all of the stores he had passed on his run to the subway station. In his mind, he was slowly going back through the streets he had run past. Luke was nodding with each store that he came across when he suddenly stopped moving his head. "A Home Depot. I passed a Home Depot three blocks back. They have to have something that I can use as a conductor!"

Luke took a deep breath and then he began slowly jogging back through the wind and rain.

Chimera unsheathed his lion claws and dug them into the street. His thick claws punctured the street into the sewer system, sending a geyser of filth shooting into the air. Despite the extra resistance, the Kraken continued to drag Chimera toward the ocean as if he was weightless. The Kraken climbed into the harbor, pulling Chimera after him. When Chimera initially entered the ocean, the water reached the kaiju's chest but as the Kraken pulled him farther into the ocean, the water was quickly approaching Chimera's face. The hybrid took a deep breath as the ocean water rolled over his head.

Once he was in the water, Chimera stopped resisting the Kraken's pull. When he was being dragged on his back through the city, Chimera had been unable to fight back against the Kraken's grip. Now that he was in the water, Chimera knew that once he was deep enough, he would be able to use the ocean to his advantage.

The Kraken continued to drag Chimera deeper into the ocean in an attempt to drown his terrestrial foe, but unbeknownst to the Kraken, Chimera was as equally adept in water as he was on land. When they were deep enough in the water, Chimera began flapping his fluke and pulling back against the Kraken's pull. Remembering a tactic he had used in his battle with the Scylla years earlier, Chimera waited until he stretched the Kraken's tentacles to their limit. The kaiju then switched the direction that he was flapping his fluke and in doing so, he used both his strength and the Kraken's own might to send his body hurtling toward the ancient nightmare. Chimera's thick head slammed into the top of the Kraken's shell, driving the beast into the ocean floor. Before the Kraken was able to stand up, Chimera latched his jaws and hands onto the base of the Kraken's left claw. The kaiju began to chew and pull on the claw, causing the Kraken to instinctively pull away. Once more, Chimera had caused the Kraken to use his own strength against himself.

Under the strength of the two giant monsters pulling on the appendage, the Kraken's claw tore free from its body.

Chimera held the severed appendage in his mouth as the Kraken scurried away from him. Ichor poured out of the Kraken's shell from the joint where the claw had been torn free and it shrouded the water in a thick black cloud. The Kraken spun around to face Chimera only to find himself blinded by his own bodily fluids. Chimera sent out a wide sonar blast and when it bounced off the Kraken and returned to him, he knew exactly where the monster was in the pitch-black water.

Luke was panting when he reached the Home Depot. He breathed a sigh of relief when he saw that the doors were unlocked. He had been in enough Home Depots to know where he needed to go. Luke ran along the front of the store until he found multiple rolls of chains rolled up on large wheels. He found the lightest chain that he could carry and said to himself, "I guess I need about fifty feet." He then pulled out the chain to a little past that length and used the bolt cutters hanging on the wall to cut it.

Luke then grabbed a shopping cart and began loading the chain into it.

He heard a voice yelling out from the dark isles of the store, "Looting is illegal! I am calling the police!"

Luke threw his hands in frustration. "The hell with the police, call the Army! Ask for General Sam Parsons and tell him that Luke Davis commandeered this chain to save Zeus' life." He then placed both hands on his shopping cart and jogged back out into the rain.

The Kraken was spinning around on the ocean floor, trying to clear his vision from the cloud of black ichor that was pouring out of his body when Chimera slammed into the side of his shell head first. The blow pushed the Kraken along the ocean floor, but the monster was able to lash out with his tentacles and wrap them around Chimera. The Kraken pulled Chimera in close to him and then closed his remaining claw on Chimera's throat.

Chimera unsheathed his own claws then drove them into the Kraken's mouth. Once his claws were embedded in the monster's mouth, Chimera pulled down as hard as he could, ripping off the bottom portion of the Kraken's maw. The Kraken tightened his grip as he writhed in pain and more black ichor poured out of his body. Chimera drove his right hand back into the hole where the Kraken's maw had once been and used his claws to tear the Kraken apart from the inside.

The Kraken's grip on Chimera slowly loosened and then went completely limp when he finally inflicted enough damage on the crustacean to end its life. Chimera felt the Kraken's dead body drift away from him and then he headed back toward the surface.

By the time Luke had made his way back to the fallen body of Zeus, he was exhausted and could barely breathe. Several of the people who had been hiding in the subway were now gathered around the unconscious Zeus. Luke was too tired to explain what was going on so he just shouted, "US military! Get away from that thing; he is under quarantine!" The crowd quickly backed away as Luke pushed his shopping cart up to the giant. He grabbed one end of the chain he had stolen and he wrapped it around Zeus' wrist. He then grabbed the other end of the chain and immediately dropped it to the ground as he realized he was too fatigued to carry it. He looked around at three twenty-something men with Boston College jackets on and he shouted at them, "You guys! Help me carry this chain into the subway."

The college students looked at each other for a second and then one of them said, "But you just said that thing was under quarantine?"

Luke pointed at them. "I know what I said! I also said I was US military! Now if you don't want to go to federal prison for obstructing a federal mission, come help me!"

The college kids gave Luke a strange look as if they knew there was no way that not helping him would put them in jail. Luke thought that his bluff had failed until the three young men started walking toward him. They all grabbed the chain and then Luke led them to the subway rails. He stopped short of the third line and looked at the college kids. "On three, throw this chain onto the third rail and then get down and cover your head."

Luke could see the fear in their eyes. In his head, Luke silently prayed that he was not about to get these kids and himself electrocuted to death. Luke counted, "One, two, three!" Then he and the students he drafted into helping him tossed the chain onto the third rail. None of them hand the chance to duck before sparks lit up the subway and electricity caused the chain to flail. Luke heard a crashing sound at the top of the subway stairs. He turned to see Zeus sitting bolt upright at the subway entrance with a huge hole in the ceiling above his head from where his skull had crashed through it.

Luke motioned for the college kids to back away from the chain then he walked up to Zeus. The god looked beaten and broken but alive. There was a roar from the harbor and both Luke and Zeus looked toward the water to see Chimera standing at the shoreline. Luke panted out, "Good boy, Chimera. I knew you would crush that giant crab."

Zeus looked at Luke. "Mortal, thank you for reviving me."

Luke held his megaphone against his chest as he continued to try and catch his breath. "Shut up. Just get us to Baltimore."

CHAPTER 7

Fort Hood, Texas

The soldiers of Fort Hood were dashing around the base in preparation for two major events. The first was Atlas. Atlas was a giant far larger than any of the kaiju they had seen in the war with the gods. Atlas was making his way across the state and wrecking everything in his path. The titan had laid waste to the entire city of Dallas in less than half an hour. The soldiers of Fort Hood were put on immediate alert that they were going to intercept Atlas before he made his way to the city of Waco. The thought of battling a giant that was over one thousand feet tall was nearly incomprehensible to the men and women of Fort Hood. Despite their trepidation, the men and women of Fort Hood were soldiers and they were more than ready to carry out their duty to protect not only their country but their planet.

The second thing that the soldiers were preparing for in addition to the battle with Atlas was the coming of the legendary General Sam Parsons. Parsons was the man who led the armed forces in the war with the gods and they hoped that when he came he was bringing Chimera with him. Some of the soldiers at Fort Hood had actually seen Chimera in person and they stated that as massive as Chimera was, pitting him against the approaching Atlas would be akin to sending out a Chihuahua to fight a Great Dane.

Parsons had ordered jet fighters and attack helicopters to be ready to take to the air and attack Atlas. The last of the helicopters were fueling up when a huge storm cloud suddenly appeared in the middle of the base no more than a few feet off the ground. Lightning shot out from the cloud and somehow managed to streak off into the sky without hitting any people or buildings. The soldiers of Fort Hood watched as a giant bird with blue flames dancing around its body burst forth from the storm cloud, took to the sky, and began circling the base.

At the sight of the fire bird, alarms went off around the base as the soldiers thought that they were under attack. Anti-aircraft missiles were aimed and the kaiju and ready to fire when people started yelling that a man was also walking out of the storm cloud.

General Parsons was partially blind and disoriented, but he was well aware of what the appearance of the Phoenix would set off on the base.

He had asked his secretary to contact the base and warn them of his unorthodox method of travel and of the monster that he was bringing with. From what he was able to see going on around him, it appeared that he and the Phoenix had arrived prior to the message.

Parsons stumbled out of the dissipating storm cloud. Once the cloud had completely vanished, he started yelling out orders, "Do not attack the monster. The creature is the Phoenix and for now, it is helping us out! Where is the commanding officer for this base? I need to see him immediately!"

A short man came running out from the crowd. He stopped short of Parsons and saluted before introducing himself. "General Dan Cabollo, reporting for duty, sir. The jets and helicopters are ready to attack."

Parsons returned the salute. "Very good, General. My apologies for my unorthodox method of travel and the disruption it caused on your base." Parsons pointed to the Phoenix flying overhead. "Our jets are going to fly with the Phoenix in the first wave of the attack. You and I will follow in the helicopters as the second attack wave. Our objective is to keep Atlas in the desert and away from any populated area!" He pulled out a piece of paper from his pocket and handed it to Cabollo. "I will need one transport helicopter to fly to this location and rendezvous with Diana Cain. She will tell the pilot what he needs to do when he gets there."

Cabollo took a quick look at the Phoenix. "Sir, permission to speak freely?"

Parsons nodded. "Granted."

"Sir, we were expecting Chimera to be here to help us. Can we trust the Phoenix in this mission?"

Parsons shrugged. "I honestly don't know. Chimera is engaged with other monsters as we speak. So, for now, the Phoenix is going to have to be enough to help us hold the line until the third wave arrives."

"Sir, if I may be so bold, what is the third wave we are expecting?"

Parsons smiled. "Son, even I don't know exactly what to expect. If there is one thing I have learned over the past two years, it's to trust Diana Cain when it comes to myths and legends."

The Hoskins Clay and Limestone Quarry was roughly thirty miles outside of Waco, Texas. The place was alive with action as the manager of the quarry, Ian Reece, had recently received a phone call from a Ms. Diana Cain at the Department of Defense. Ms. Cain had put a massive request for rock and clay to be gathered into a specific position as quickly as possible. Reece explained to Ms. Cain that with a giant walking across Texas, most of his men were either home with their families or trying to evacuate and that very few of them had come into work. When Ms. Cain offered to pay three times what the materials she was requesting were worth and to pay each man quadruple his hourly rate, Reece started making calls. Within an hour, the entire quarry was filled with workers operating cranes, bulldozers, and even shovels to try and fill the strange request made by Ms. Cain.

Reece was standing on an observation platform, overseeing the progress on the odd but high-paying request when a massive storm cloud suddenly appeared on the far side of the quarry. The cloud was hovering just above ground level and bolts of lightning were coming out of it. Reece was staring at the storm cloud when he saw what looked like an attractive middle-aged woman walking out of it. She had her hands placed over her eyes and she appeared slightly disoriented as she moved away from the quickly dissipating cloud.

The woman took a few steps forward and started calling for Reece. When he heard the strange woman calling for him, Reece ran down from the observation platform to meet her. By the time Reece had reached the woman, several of the workers from the quarry were escorting her to him. The woman thanked the workers for their help and said that she was now able to see and could walk on her own. Reece ran up to the woman. "I am Reece. Are you okay? Where did that thing come from? How did it bring you here?"

Diana waved her hand in the air, brushing off the questions. "My name is Diana Cain. I am the woman from the DoD that contacted you. Let's just say that the storm cloud is a classified method of transportation for the military." She looked over at the colossal mounds of clay and stone that the workers had gathered in the middle of the quarry. "Looks like it's coming together well. How much longer until it's finished?"

Reece shrugged. "My best guess is about a half an hour. The design is simple enough and constructing it here in the quarry is saving us a lot of time, but the sheer size of it is what is going to take some time." He looked at Diana. "Are you sure you need it to be eleven hundred feet long, two hundred feet across, and one hundred and fifty feet deep? I mean, that's a hell of a lot of stone and clay."

Diana nodded. "Let's just say that I hope it's enough." A military helicopter soared over the quarry and they both looked at it. Diana smiled. "That helicopter is for me. I need to go and talk to the pilot. Let me know as soon as the project is finished to my specifications."

Reece nodded. "Will do, ma'am." Diana thanked him and then she ran off to the spot where the helicopter was landing.

Parsons climbed into one of the attack helicopters as it took to the air. The hardened general has seen all manner of enemy and horror during his time in the military which stretched from the first Gulf War to now. During the war with the gods, Parsons had seen many strange and gigantic creatures. He had even seen footage of Atlas from his attack on Dallas, but nothing could have prepared him for the experience of seeing Atlas in person.

The helicopter had no sooner risen off the ground than the outline of Atlas could be seen on the horizon of the desert. Parsons shook his head and he whispered, "My God."

Cabollo turned to Parsons. "What was that, sir?"

Parsons did his best to recover his composure. "Nothing. Are the jets in the air yet?"

"Any second now, sir. They are just waiting for the helicopters to clear their take-off path and then they will be in the air."

Parsons nodded then he switched the channel on his radio. "Diana, come in. What's the status of Project G?"

Diana's voice came back over the radio. "The quarry workers will be done with their task in another fifteen minutes. My part should only take a minute or two. Given the distance between us, and assuming that everything goes as it should, Project G should be to your position within half an hour."

Parsons looked through his window to see the Phoenix taking position in front of his helicopter. The flaming bird flapped its wings twice and then streaked toward the incomprehensible form of Atlas. As the Phoenix approached Atlas, six fighter jets took a V-formation behind the monster. Parsons took a deep breath and then he radioed back to Diana. "The Phoenix seems to be carrying out the commands I suggested to Zeus. It appears to not only be going after Atlas, but it is also falling into formation with our jets." Parsons dropped his voice slightly so that Cabollo wouldn't hear him. "Diana, I am looking at Atlas. I can tell you right now that the Phoenix, the jets, and the helicopters won't be enough. We need Project G up and running as soon as possible."

The Phoenix flew straight toward the humongous Atlas. When the titan saw the flaming bird approaching him, he stopped walking and snarled at the creature. As large as she was, the Phoenix was barely a quarter of the size of the mountainous Atlas. The titan reached out his long arms towards the Phoenix, but the bird stopped short of Atlas' reach. She hovered in the air and then she began flapping her wings in rapid succession. The Phoenix's wings soon became a blur of motion and as their speed increased, the blue fire that was circling them began to expand. The flames grew until they completely covered the monster's wings. Then in a bright burst of fire, the flames shot out from the Phoenix's wings and enveloped the entire top part of Atlas' body.

The flames that were enveloping Atlas were so bright that Parsons had to look away from them. He heard Cabollo say, "It's like looking at the Sun!"

Parsons ignored Cabollo, switched his radio to the channel the jets and helicopters were using, and shouted, "All jets, fire at will on Atlas!"

The already blinding light of the Phoenix's attack was made even brighter as missiles and machine gun fire struck Atlas as well. Cabollo shook his head as he continued to stare at the unmoving form of Atlas' feet and legs. He tapped Parsons on the shoulder and said, "How is he still standing? Between the monster and our jets, that was enough firepower to destroy the top of a mountain!"

Parsons shook his head. "Atlas is beyond our understanding. According to the legend, he was once tasked with holding up the very sky itself. His strength, stamina, and durability may be without limit." The two generals watched through the windshield of their helicopter as the Phoenix slowed down the flapping of her wings and stopped the barrage of flames on the titan. Two jets were flying toward the cloud of smoke that covered the top half of Atlas' body when the titan's hand reached out from the cloud and swatted the jets, causing them to explode.

The titan stepped out of the pillar of smoke that was clinging to him. He then fixed his huge eyes on the Phoenix and the remaining jet fighters. The titan opened his mouth and Parsons thought that Atlas was going to roar or scream at his attackers. Instead, Parsons heard a much more terrifying sound. He heard the sound of Atlas laughing.

Cabollo's voice was shrill and high pitched as he placed his hand on Parsons' shoulder. "He is laughing at us! That didn't even scratch him! What are we going to do?"

Parsons ignored the lower-ranking general and kept his eyes on Atlas. He watched as the Phoenix flew a circle around the titan's head and then dove straight for his eyes. The Phoenix flew in a frenzy in front of Atlas' face, pecking and scratching at his eyes and mouth with a relentless fury. This time, Parsons heard Atlas scream in a mix of pain and anger as he reached up for the Phoenix only to have the bird avoid his grip and continue her attack.

Parsons yelled into his radio, "All remaining jets, target Atlas' knees and feet while the Phoenix is engaged with him!"

The remaining jets flew toward Atlas and fired at the giant's knees and legs. The bullets and missiles exploded against the giant's lower half, but they yielded the same ineffectual result as the attack on his torso. The jets flew past Atlas and then they circled around to attack again.

As the jets flew past the titan, he reached out and grabbed the tenacious Phoenix in both hands. Atlas crushed the bird's fiery wings then he slammed the disabled Phoenix to the ground. The fire bird looked up at Atlas and screeched defiantly at the titan. The Phoenix then propped herself up on her broken wings, opened her beak, and spit out a fireball that exploded against the titan's hip.

Atlas glared down at the Phoenix then lifted his huge foot in the air and brought it down on the monster, crushing her into the sand. Parsons and Cabollo watched as a plume of flames from beneath Atlas' foot signaled the end of the Phoenix. Atlas lifted his foot off the dead Phoenix to reveal nothing but a pile of ash where the corpse of the mighty fire bird should have been.

Atlas had just lifted his foot off the dead Phoenix when the fighter jets renewed their attack on him. The pilots were still following Parsons' last order and trying to attack the giant's legs. The jets were flying at Atlas and spending the last of their ammunition when Atlas kicked out with his long leg and destroyed all of the remaining jets with a single blow.

Inside of his helicopter, Cabollo shook his head and looked over at Parsons. "Sir, the jets and monster are down without so much as injuring Atlas. All that we have left are our helicopters. What do we do now?"

Parsons kept his gazed fixed on Atlas. "We use our helicopters to draw Atlas as far away from populated areas as we can. We try to buy Diana more time and we hope for a miracle." The moment that Parsons had finished speaking, a plume of fire arose from the ashes of the fallen Phoenix. The bird that mere moments ago had been slain was now reborn from her own ashes. The Phoenix took to the sky and flew in front of Atlas. Once more, the fire bird began rapidly flapping her wings until a continuous wave of blue fire shot out from them and struck Atlas. Parsons grabbed his receiver. "All helicopter pilots, follow the formation of my helicopter! We are going to fire on the giant and attempt to draw him farther out into the desert!" Parsons watched as the Phoenix cut off her flame blast and again flew at Atlas. This time, the bird's beak struck Atlas directly in the right eye. A river of blood flew out of the titan's damaged eye while the Phoenix flew away from him. Atlas placed his hand over his injured eye as blood continued to flow between his fingers. Parsons looked over at Cabollo. "Can't ask for more of a miracle than that. Now, all we need is Diana to come through."

Diana was sitting and repeating phrases in Hebrew from scans of ancient manuscripts when Reece called out to her that the project she had ordered was finally complete. She nodded and said to Reece, "Your men have five minutes to clear the area. Tell them to get as far away from this project as possible. Just leave your machines where they are. If any of your machinery is damaged as a result of what happens, the US army will reimburse you twice what they were worth."

Reece shrugged and then gave the order for all his workers to clear the area.

As soon as Reece gave Diana the thumbs up that the area was clear, she ran over to the helicopter pilot who was assigned to her. She climbed into the helicopter and yelled to the pilot, "Take me to the smaller mound at the northernmost part of the land mass!" As the pilot was in the air, Diana removed a piece of paper from her pocket and she quickly wrote the name *Atlas* on it.

The pilot brought the helicopter down on top of the mound and then he turned around to look at Diana. He held out a cylinder to her that was roughly the size of a cigar. "Ma'am, here is the charge with the remote detonator that you asked me to prepare for you."

Diana slowly reached out and took the charge. "So this thing won't explode until you push the button on the detonator, right?"

The pilot nodded. "Yes, ma'am. That's correct."

She nodded. "Okay. I am going to perform the ceremony. If it works, we need to be off this thing ASAP. So, keep the motor running and be ready to go."

The pilot nodded in reply and then Diana jumped out of the helicopter and onto the mound of clay covered stone. Diana was extremely knowledgeable in all forms of mythology. In addition to the myths of the Norse and Greek gods, she was also well versed in the Christian, Jewish, and Muslim legends as well. The Greek and Norse gods had proven to be real. Today, Diana hoped that one of the legends of the world's major religions was as real as Odin, Zeus, or in this case, Atlas. She began walking around the huge mound and saying letters from the Jewish alphabet. She had practiced each word every day since she had come up with this idea over a year ago.

Diana thought of her favorite movie, *Army of Darkness,* and how Ash had raised an army of the dead but not taking the time to learn a series of words correctly. Diana was confident that she had said all of the words correctly but now came the hard part. It had taken Diana several months to convince an extremely knowledgeable rabbi to tell her the secret name of God. Normally, no rabbi would have given this name to anyone let alone someone who was not of the Jewish faith. In this instance though, the rabbi understood that if the gods who had attacked mankind ever came back, the most powerful creature in his religion could be a valuable weapon for the human race.

Diana closed her eyes and she focused on making sure that she pronounced every syllable of the name correctly. She then took a rubber band out of her pocket and used it to attach the piece of paper with Atlas' name on it to the charge in her hand. She then knelt down, scooped out a wad of clay in the shape of a mouth, placed the charge with the name on it in the mouth, and then brushed the clay back in the hole she had dug.

The moment that the last bit of clay was back in place, the ground beneath her feet began to rumble. Diana stood up, bolted back to the helicopter, and jumped into it. She shouted, "Go! Go! Get us clear of this thing!"

The pilot pulled the helicopter off the mound it was resting on and then flew it clear of the quarry. Diana then asked the pilot to turn the helicopter around and to hold his position. Once the pilot did as she ordered, Diana climbed into the seat next to him and she watched through the windshield as the mound that she was standing on and the larger mounds connected to it continued to shake.

The small mound that Diana was on only a moment ago pulled itself off the ground and lifted into the air. This was followed by other parts of the construct which revealed themselves to be arms pulling off the ground and reaching into the air as well. With a few more movements, that entire construct had pulled itself off the ground to reveal a humanoid being of immense proportions. The creature stood up and it looked in the direction of Atlas. The stone giant then began walking toward the titan that had been identified as its prey. Diana pumped her fist and said to the pilot, "We did it! We have successfully made a golem! I wasn't it sure it would work at all, let only for something as big as we needed to fight Atlas, but it worked!"

The pilot nodded. "Yes, but is that big boy going to be enough to defeat Atlas?"

Diana shrugged. "There's only one way to find out." She grabbed her radio and called to Parsons. "General Parsons, this is Diana Cain. Project G was a success! The golem, codenamed Grimm, is up and heading toward Atlas. His dimensions place him at one hundred feet taller than Atlas! ETA to you is ten minutes, but you should see him coming over the horizon before that!"

Diana turned to look at the pilot. "Follow Grimm. We need to be able to deactivate him as soon as his mission is complete."

The pilot smiled. "A giant man made of stone and clay codenamed Grimm? Fantastic Four fan, are we?"

Diana smiled back. "Oh yes! If Grimm defeats Atlas and saves the world, I am going to demand two things from Parsons. First, that he calls Marvel Comics and tells them to start making FF comics again, and second, call Fox and tell them to make a good freaking FF movie! I mean, Disney basically made a great Fantastic Four movie with the Incredibles! Can't Fox just follow that format and get it right?"

The pilot laughed. "Let's hope that Grimm there does his job so you can get Parsons to make those calls. I am a big FF fan too." The pilot kept his eyes on Grimm and said, "By the way, the name is Todd Pressley. If they do ever make a good FF movie, would you mind going with me to see it?"

Diana gave the pilot a quizzical look. "Are you asking me on a date in the middle of a battle?"

Pressley nodded. "We could die today if things go bad. I figured this might be my only chance to ask."

Diana smiled. "If Grimm wins this fight, I will pick a movie that we can go see. It could be awhile before Fox gets their act together."

Pressley smiled and pulled the helicopter a little closer to Grimm. "All right, big boy, go out there and win me a date!"

Parsons watched as the helicopters and the Phoenix unleashed high-caliber bullets, missiles, and mystical flames at Atlas. The titan seemed unfazed by the attacks as he moved forward with his hand still holding the bloody socket where his eye had once been. As the giant lumbered forward, he continued to reach for the Phoenix. Parsons guessed that the giant wanted revenge on the monster for pecking his eye out.

The helicopter that Parsons was in suddenly stopped firing on Atlas. Parsons yelled at the pilot, "Why did we stop firing?"

The pilot turned his head. "Sorry, sir, but we have used up all of our ammunition."

One by one, the remaining helicopters all stopped firing on Atlas as they ran out of ammunition. Parsons looked out his window and saw that only the Phoenix was still attacking Atlas. The kaiju was flying around the titan and continually hitting him with bursts of flames from her wings and mouth.

Cabollo shook his head. "That's it, General. We have tried everything. Even the fire bird is useless against that thing! Sir, we need to call the president and advise him to use the nuclear option on Atlas."

Parsons scowled at Cabollo. "Under no circumstances would I advise the president to use a nuclear weapon over US soil! As

Commander and Chief, if he decides to use that option, I will respect his decision, but I will not recommend that course of action."

Cabollo shrugged. "With all due respect, sir, I don't think we have any other option."

Parsons pointed his finger in Cabollo's face and he was about to verbally assault the man, when the pilot called out, "Sir, I have something coming in on the radar!" The pilot shook his head in disbelief. "It appears to be huge! If this reading is correct, whatever is headed toward us may be even bigger than Atlas!"

Parsons kept his finger pointed at Cabollo. "There is always another way. You just have to be creative enough to find it." Parsons then yelled up to the pilot, "Turn us around! I want to see what's coming!"

The pilot responded with a quick, "Yes, sir!" Then he turned the helicopter around and flew toward the setting sun. When the helicopter had turned one hundred and eighty degrees, Parsons yelled into his radio, "All pilots, converge on my helicopter and follow it!" The other pilots flew into formation behind Parsons. They had only flown for a few seconds toward the sunset when a gargantuan shadow stood up in front of it and blocked out the entire sun.

Parsons smiled when he saw the unfathomably large rock giant walking toward them. He said to himself, "Good job, Diana. I can only imagine what kind of ridiculous request you are going to make of me for pulling this off."

Cabollo gasped. "What in the hell is that? A living mountain?"

Parsons shook his head. "No, that's Project G. It's a Golem, codenamed Grimm. It's an ancient Jewish legend brought to life, and it's our best bet at stopping Atlas."

Diana's voice suddenly came through on the radio. "Do you see our boy Grimm, General? He is going to kick Atlas' titan-sized ass!"

Parsons smiled. "Excellent work, Diana. Now, all pilots, follow us in a south-by-southwest direction. We don't want to be in between these two mountains when they clash!" When they were roughly a mile away from the path of Grimm and Atlas, Parsons called over the radio for the pilots to turn around and hold their position so that he could witness the titanic battle that was about to ensue.

Grimm continued to walk across the desert in a straight line. The golem had no expression on his bland face nor did his body convey any type of emotion or sentience. Grimm existed for one reason and that reason was to destroy Atlas.

Atlas was continuing to swipe at the Phoenix when the flaming bird suddenly turned away from Atlas and flew toward the sunset. Atlas had been looking down at the ground as he held his badly damaged eye. As the Phoenix flew off, Atlas lifted his head to see where the bird was going and it was then that he saw Grimm walking toward him.

At the sight of the colossal Grimm, Atlas dropped his hand from his injured eye. Blood poured down the face of the titan, as for the first time in his thousands of years of existence, he finally beheld something larger than himself. Atlas continued to stare at the golem when the stone giant came to a stop in front of him. Atlas had the unique experience of looking up into the face of a being that stood an entire one hundred feet taller than him.

Grimm shifted his gaze down toward Atlas then he pulled his right hand back and drove it into the titan's face. There was loud crack when Grimm's stone hand shattered Atlas' nose. The titan fell backward and he crashed into the earth with enough force to register as a 2.3 on the Richter scale. Between the blood seeping out of his eye and gushing from his nose, Atlas' face and beard were covered in red. The titan looked up to see a stone foot the size of a warehouse coming down toward him. Grimm stomped on Atlas' ribs and drove the air out of his lungs. The golem then took a step forward and kicked Atlas in the face, snapping the titan's head to the side.

With his opponent stunned on the ground beneath him, Grimm lifted his stone foot to stomp on Atlas' head and end the titan's life. Reacting on instinct, Atlas rolled to the side and avoided the blow, letting Grimm's heavy foot crash down into the sand next to his head. Atlas sat up and punched Grimm in the midsection. While the blow managed to knock the golem back a step, it didn't cause any damage to the rock monster. Atlas growled as he stood up. He then punched Grimm twice in the chest with enough force to shatter a building but against the stone giant, the blow only managed to shake off some loose sand and clay.

Grimm responded by bringing down a hammer fist down on top of Atlas' head. The blow dropped Atlas to his knees. The groggy titan shook his blood-soaked head and face as his hands reached out and grabbed onto Grimm's legs. Atlas slowly started to pull himself back to his feet, using the golem as a crutch.

Cabollo looked over at Parsons. "Why does Atlas keep trying to trade blows with that mountain? He could have tried to take out the golem's leg and get him to the ground, but instead, he keeps trying to outmuscle it."

Parsons shook his head. "Isn't it obvious? Since the dawn of time, Atlas has been the biggest, baddest thing in existence. In every fight he has ever been in, he was able to use his size and strength to crush his opponents. He doesn't know any other way to fight but to overpower someone. Atlas has one method of fighting and we got something that is better at it than he is. This fight was over before it even began."

Atlas had managed to pull himself back to his feet and he looked up into Grimm's face. The golem looked down at Atlas and then he landed a right hook to Atlas' torso that cracked his ribs. The titan bent over in pain and grabbed his bruised sides. Grimm stepped forward and then hit Atlas in the face. The force of the blow sent teeth the size of row homes flying out of the titan's mouth and caused him to stumble backward for several steps before falling onto his back. The bruised and battered titan looked up through blood and tears to see Grimm standing above him with his foot raised. Atlas knew that he could roll to the side and avoid the blow again, but he also knew that doing so would only delay the inevitable. He knew that if he kept fighting, he would only increase and prolong his suffering. Atlas closed his one remaining eye as Grimm brought his foot down and crushed the titan's head.

With his opponent defeated, Grimm turned and looked at the helicopter carrying Diana. The stone colossus then began walking toward the person who had created him.

Pressley looked at Diana. "I think you had better blow that charge now."

Diana nodded. "Ya, I think that's a good idea." She pushed the button on her detonator and the charge blew up, destroying the paper with Atlas' name on it. With the name of his target gone, Grimm crumbled into a huge pile of stone and clay.

Pressley smiled. "What was he going to do after he killed Atlas? Was he coming here for you?"

Diana shrugged. "I don't know, and I don't ever want to find out."

Parsons' voice came over the radio. "Great job everyone. We need to head to back to Fort Hood and see what happened with Chimera and the Griffin in their missions."

Pressley was turning around his helicopter when Diana smiled at him and picked up the radio. "Parsons, do you have any connections with Fox studios?"

Parsons was laughing at what he could only guess Diana would ask of him when the Phoenix flew past the helicopters and over to the bloody corpse of Atlas. The giant bird landed atop of the gargantuan carcass and proceeded to devour it.

Cabollo pointed at the carrion-eating monster. "Sir, what are we going to do about the Phoenix?"

Parsons shrugged. "She did her job, let her eat. My guess is we will be sending her back into battle before too long."

CHAPTER 8

Baltimore

The *Argos* pulled into the harbor of what had once been Baltimore. The ship that was large enough to carry a kaiju across the ocean cast a majestic and awe-inspiring scene against the turmoil that was occurring in Baltimore. At the sight of the ship, a few survivors who had managed to make their way to waterfront started to cheer. During the war with the gods, the media had covered the *Argos* taking Chimera to places like Greece and the Middle East. The public had come to associate the *Argos* as a sign that Chimera had arrived to battle whatever malevolent creature was on the prowl. This time, however, the *Argos* was not bringing Chimera, nor was it bringing hope or salvation to the few people who remained in Baltimore. Today, the *Argos* was bringing enough firepower to destroy a large metropolitan city and hopefully an ancient monster.

Baltimore was in ruins as the Hecatonchires continued to the ravage the city in a blur of chaotic motion. The *Argos* was captained by Charles Brand. Brand had over thirty years of naval experience, and yet today, he found himself faced with an order that he never thought he would be asked to carry out. Today, he was ordered to fire on an American city.

As the ship came to a stop in the inner harbor, Captain Brand turned on the ship's communication system to address his crew. He took a deep breath and began speaking, "Men, the situation is as follows. The monster known as the Hecatonchires has destroyed more than fifty percent of the city of Baltimore. In the process of destroying the city, he has killed hundreds of thousands of people. Many of those people have died as a result of the Hecatonchires devouring them. The Army and Air Force have attempted to drive off the creature with a tactical assault, but their efforts have been in vain. We have been given orders to stop the monster here and now by using every weapon at our disposal, short of our nuclear arsenal. This order comes despite the fact that there are undoubtedly still US civilians alive in the target area."

Captain Brand let the crew consider his words for a moment before continuing. "Now I know that carrying out this order will be a difficult task for you men. As we perform the difficult task before us, I want you to remember two things. First, that we are following orders. This decision does not fall on you. This falls on me and the people above me. Second, I know that if I were trapped in the target area, I would want that monster to be stopped here and now before it destroyed another city. I would also prefer to die in a bright painless flash instead of being eaten alive by a monster from ancient history."

The captain looked at the stunned faces of his crew and he hoped that his words would help to ease their consciences. He doubted that they did because despite directing the speech as much at himself as he was at his crew, he still was having difficulty giving an order that would kill the citizens he was sworn to protect.

Brand made the sign of the cross over his chest and then he turned to his XO. "Target all weapons on the Hecatonchires and open fire."

The outer hall of the *Argos* lit up as dozens of missiles shot into the sky. The missiles with the most powerful payloads rose high into the air, arching over the city before taking a downward turn and heading for the Hecatonchires. The smaller shells and lower-grade missiles rocketed over the ruins of the inner harbor. Several of the smaller shells crashed through the still-standing buildings. When Captain Brand saw the buildings falling, he reminded himself of his own words. He said to himself, "You're just following orders too." He then said a silent prayer that the buildings had long ago been evacuated.

All fifty of the Hecatonchires' heads turned toward the oncoming barrage. The monster's body was shook as the first barrage of shells struck it. Captain Brand watched as the monster convulsed under the first wave of the attack. Brand allowed himself a brief smile when he saw several of the kaiju's heads look straight up at the larger payload of missiles falling toward him. At the realization that the larger attack was coming from above it, the Hecatonchires crouched down and put all one hundred hands and arms over its head and body.

When the larger payload of missiles struck the monster, the explosion tore through the remains of the city. Buildings that were still standing were reduced to ash in the blink of an eye. The Hecatonchires himself was completely engulfed in flames. Captain Brand kept his binoculars fixed on the inferno that was raging over the Hecatonchires. The shock wave from the blast raced across the decimated remains of Baltimore and into the harbor itself. Even a ship as large as the *Argos* felt the concussive force of the blast it had unleashed as the shock wave rocked the vessel from side to side.

After the shock wave passed, the sailors aboard the *Argos* began to cheer and congratulate each other. Brand held up his hand and screamed, "Quiet!" The hardened captain had served on the *Argos* in the first war with the gods and he was fully aware that the monsters they were fighting were incredibly durable.

For several minutes, the flames continued to burn on the spot where the Hecatonchires had been standing. The flames slowly began to die out and turn into a pitch-black smoke. Brand was straining to see the Hecatonchires or hopefully its remains at the epicenter of the blast. Brand continued to stare at the wall of smoke when he saw movement behind it. The captain cursed when she saw no less than thirty hands reach through the vale of smoke. As the arms of the Hecatonchires continued to emerge from the pillar of smoke, Brand could see numerous burns and chunks of skin missing from several of the arms.

A second later, the monster's heads began to emerge from the smoke and all of them were screaming in an odd mixture of agony and anger. The screaming heads all looked out over the harbor at the *Argos*. Dozens of heads roared in unison as the Hecatonchires started running toward the harbor.

Brand gritted his teeth at the sight of the oncoming kaiju. He had already attacked the monster with the most powerful weapons aboard the *Argos* and all he had managed to do was to anger the beast. Brand grabbed the ship's radio and yelled into it, "I want all remaining weapons to fire on the monster. I want every sailor that is not controlling weapons, steerage, or communications up on deck and armed with a rifle firing on the beast! We are not retreating. We did not sacrifice a large section of Baltimore and the people within it to turn tail and run! We either stop this beast here or we keep it focused on us as long as we can until help arrives or we give our lives in service of the human race!"

A communal "Aye, Aye!" rang out over the ship as every remaining cannon on the *Argos* began to fire on the Hecatonchires. With each passing second, more and more sailors ran up on deck armed with rifles and rocket launchers.

The writhing form of the hundred-armed monster waded through the barrage and walked to the water's edge. When the Hecatonchires entered the Chesapeake Bay, the beast began slamming its arms into the water and churning them both in the water and in the air above his heads. The motion of the kaiju's hundred arms caused the water of the bay to shift back and forth, causing huge waves to slam into the *Argos*. In addition to water, the waves also bombarded the *Argos* with the remains of dozens of ships and docks that had been reduced to floating debris in the bay.

The rough waves rocked the *Argos* from side to side and forced the sailors on deck to stop firing their weapons for fear of pitching off balance and hitting their shipmates. The remaining cannons were still firing at the Hecatonchires with far less accuracy than they were able to on a calm sea, but even their limited effectiveness was soon countered by the second part of the Hecatonchires' attack.

As the monsters continued to swirl countless arms through the air, a vortex began to form around them. The vortex quickly grew into a tornado that jumped off the monster's arms and landed on top of the water. When the tornado hit the bay, it quickly filled with water and began moving toward the *Argos*. As the *Argos* rocked from side to side, the crew managed to fire several more shells toward the Hecatonchires, but they never reached their target as they were sucked into the waterspout. The first waterspout was halfway to the *Argos*, when the Hecatonchires placed a second a tornado on top of the bay. Behind the protection of two waterspouts and torrent of rogue waves, the Hecatonchires started making its way toward the *Argos*.

The captain was holding onto his swivel chair as he tried to maintain his footing. Brand had decided that if he was going to die fighting a monster, he would do so on his feet rather than on his knees. Brand continued to struggle to maintain his balance when he saw a massive storm cloud with lightning streaking out of it suddenly appear on shore near the now destroyed national aquarium.

Brand thought that the storm cloud was some other phenomenon generated by the Hecatonchires that would end the lives of him and his men. The captain started to pray that the good Lord would accept him into his kingdom when his prayers were answered in a very different way. Brand's eyes went wide when he saw the distinctive sperm whale head and lion's mane of Chimera burst out of the cloud. The captain called out over the communication system. "All hands, work to stabilize the ship and keep it afloat! Chimera has just arrived! We need to hold out until he can take care of this monster!" Brand heard a cheer echo throughout the ship at the mention of Chimera's name and the captain allowed a miniscule sliver of hope enter his mind that his ship and his crew might survive this attack.

Chimera roared the moment that he saw the Hecatonchires heading for the *Argos*. The hybrid often slept and was fed aboard the *Argos*. To Chimera, the *Argos* was a second home. The kaiju did not wait for Luke's command. He simply charged into the water toward the misshapen horror.

Luke emerged from the cloud to see Chimera wading into the Chesapeake Bay. Once he saw the *Argos*, he immediately understood why Chimera had not waited for him. Luke was fully aware of the relationship that Chimera had formed with the ship. He screamed, "That's it, Chimera! Go and protect your territory!"

Chimera looked toward the *Argos* as it listed dangerously from side to side with waterspouts spinning around it and the Hecatonchires quickly closing in on it. The kaiju realized that he was not going to be able to reach the many-armed giant before he destroyed the ship. Chimera fell into a crouching stance and unleashed a tightly focused sonic blast at the mythical monster. Chimera watched in surprise as several of the Hecatonchires' arms and heads spasmed but for the most part, the monster seemed unaffected by the blast. Chimera leapt forward, deeper into the water, and he fired a second sonic blast with the same result.

Luke was watching from the shoreline and doing his best to avoid flying debris. He whispered to himself, "All of the arms and heads. The Hecatonchires has fifty brains and a nervous system that is incalculably long. If Chimera's sonic blast is spread across a nervous system that large, its effectiveness must be severely diminished."

Luke lifted his megaphone to his mouth and yelled into it, "Chimera, swim! You are going to have to swim out and attack him!" Luke stared at Chimera after he had given the command. Up until this point, Luke had only given the kaiju one-word commands such as attack or stop. Luke had no idea if the monster would be able to understand a complete sentence.

Chimera briefly looked at Luke and then he turned back around and strode out into the water. Luke didn't know if Chimera understood his order or if the kaiju simply realized that his sonic attack was not working on his own and decided to use a new approach. Whatever the reason for Chimera's change in tactics, Luke was glad that the monster was going after the Hecatonchires because the ancient creature had reached the *Argos*.

The storm and the rough seas were tossing the *Argos* from side to side. With each wave the rolled over its bow, the *Argos* tipped closer to capsizing. Captain Brand was doing his best to keep his composure as he screamed out the orders for his men to continue to try and balance the ship and pump out any water that had managed to find its way into the *Argos*. Brand knew that his crew was only buying time and that their only hope was Chimera. He was doing his best to hold onto his chair and keep his eye on the approaching Hecatonchires. The ancient beast had just about reached the *Argos* and between his limited weapons and the rough storms and waves, Brand was helpless to do anything to stop the creature.

Luke watched from the shoreline as the Hecatonchires approached the *Argos*. When the ancient horror reached the ship, Luke was slightly relieved to see that the monster was roughly a quarter the size of the

Argos. Luke thought to himself that the *Argos* was designed to carry Chimera, so it made sense that the Hecatonchires would not be as large as the huge ship. Luke shifted his gaze to Chimera and he could see the monster stretched out and swimming along the surface of the water like a living torpedo. Luke breathed a brief sigh of relief. "There is no way the monster can do enough to seriously damage the *Argos* before Chimera reaches him." As if in response to Luke's claim, the Hecatonchires walked up next to the hull of the ship and the monster's hundred arms began moving in a blur. Luke shook his head. "My God, it moves like some kind of a giant tree shredder."

The blur that was the Hecatonchires' arms connected with the hull of the *Argos*, tearing through thick steel as if it were paper. Luke watched in horror as water rushed into the hull of the ship. He then watched as the Hecatonchires reached into a chasm he had created to grab several sailors and toss them into his mouth. Luke saw Chimera rear up behind the Hecatonchires and he cheered at the thought of the horror of the attack being over, but his hopes were quickly dashed.

Chimera stood up behind the Hecatonchires in what was hip-deep water to the two monsters. The hybrid reached out to grab the Greek horror, but as soon as Chimera's arms touched the spinning blur, Chimera was thrown backward into the ocean. Chimera fell beneath the churning waves and then he immediately stood back up. When he resurfaced above the water, the Hecatonchires was staring at Chimera. The monster had taken his focus off the now sinking *Argos* and was completely focused on Chimera. The Hecatonchires' arms were still moving in a blur around his body with his fifty heads just above them, all snarling at Chimera.

The hybrid kaiju roared and then threw a punch at the Hecatonchires only to have his hand sliced open and deflected by the movements of the mythical creature's arms. Chimera pitched forward off balance and before he could regain his footing, several of the Hecatonchires' countless arms reached out and grabbed the hybrid's arms. With the man-made kaiju caught in his grasp, the Hecatonchires turned his buzz saw attack on Chimera. The Hecatonchires struck Chimera dozens of times per second, both rocking the kaiju and cutting into him with each blow. Chimera could feel the skin being flayed off his face. The kaiju instinctively tried to fire a tightly focused sonic blast at the ancient beast but as before, the attack was ineffectual against the complex central nervous system of the Hecatonchires.

Chimera's own blood was spraying over his body and dripping from his face. Trying desperately to find a way to escape the Hecatonchires' death grip, Chimera dropped to his knees and submerged his head and body below the waterline. Above the waterline, the Hecatonchires still had a grip on Chimera's hands and arms. With Chimera's face and torso below the water, the Hecatonchires turned his swirling attack on Chimera's arms. Beneath the waves, Chimera roared in pain as the sheer speed of the Hecatonchires' attack began to tear the skin off his arms. Chimera opened his eyes to see that in contrast to the Hecatonchires hundred arms and fifty heads, the strange creature only had two legs. Realizing his opponent's weakness, Chimera's head shot forward and he closed his jaws on the Hecatonchires' left leg. Chimera tasted the satisfying sensation of the Hecatonchires' blood filling his mouth and he continued to tear into the beast's leg. Chimera felt the Hecatonchires' release the hold on his arms and the buzz saw-like attack stop as all one hundred of the monster's hands tried to reach down and grab him.

Chimera felt several of the hands reaching for his mane. The intelligent hybrid knew that if the Hecatonchires was able to pull him back to the surface, he would die. To prevent this from happening, Chimera used the same tactic that the Kraken had tried to utilize on him. Chimera flapped his powerful fluke tail and began swimming farther out into the Atlantic with the Hecatonchires' leg still trapped in his mouth. The moment that Chimera took off, the Hecatonchires fell back into the water.

Luke was watching the Hecatonchires' arms and heads all writhing on the surface of the bay as Chimera dragged the creature out to deeper waters. Diana had recently insisted that he watch the film *Jaws* with her and as the writhing heads and arms of the Hecatonchires were pulled out to sea, Luke was reminded of the young Chrissy screaming for her life as the shark had its way with her. While Luke felt pity for the character in the movie, he hoped that the Hecatonchires was experiencing the same fear of dying as all of the people he devoured felt as he was eating them. As Chimera pulled the Hecatonchires farther out to sea, the storms, waves, and waterspouts the monster had created began to dissipate. Luke watched as the *Argos* began to slowly stabilize. He could see the sailors who had managed to survive the beast's attack manning lifeboats. Luke had been on the *Argos* long enough to know that the men and women on board were more than capable of making it to shore from their current position. He figured that the *Argos* was most likely lost, but he thought that most of the crew would escape with their lives. Luke ran to the most stable remaining dock where he guessed that the sailors would head to in order to assist them in any way possible. As he was standing on the dock, he took one more look at the horizon to see Chimera and the Hecatonchires dive beneath the water.

When the Hecatonchires felt himself being pulled beneath the waves, all of its heads that were above water inhaled. With lungs connected to fifty different heads, the beast could hold its breath for hours at a time, so it was in no danger of drowning. The danger of losing his leg, however, was very real as Chimera continued to maul the appendage.

Chimera dove and pulled the Hecatonchires underwater where he bit down hard into the misshapen creature's leg. When Chimera felt his teeth strike bone, the monster twisted his head, causing the Hecatonchires' left leg to break.

A stream of bubbles escaped the Hecatonchires' heads as they screamed in pain and unleashed the oxygen that had been stored in their lungs. When the air left the monster's body, Chimera could feel the beast's buoyancy dramatically decrease. With the Hecatonchires left leg still trapped in his jaws, Chimera unsheathed his thick claws. He then reached behind the Hecatonchires and raked his claw across the back of the creature's right leg, slicing its hamstring to pieces. Chimera put his feet out in front of him as he landed on the ocean floor. He then jerked his head down and slammed the Hecatonchires onto the rocky ocean bottom. A cloud of blood and sand formed around the Hecatonchires as the monster struggled to stand up and make its way to the surface to fill its lungs with air.

The Hecatonchires had managed to get its legs under itself, but the badly damaged appendages immediately gave way under the beast's disproportionately weighted body. Chimera swam circles around the Hecatonchires as it struggled to find a way to swim back to the surface. Chimera watched as the Hecatonchires began to move its arms in unison below it to propel itself up. With the monster's hundred arms now in motion behind it, its fifty heads were exposed.

When Chimera saw that the Hecatonchires was defenseless, he darted toward it. Chimera slammed his thick skull into nearly a dozen of the Hecatonchires' heads that were positioned at the top of his body. Most of the heads were completely crushed, while those that survived were badly stunned. Additionally, the blow also knocked the Hecatonchires back to the ocean floor. The Hecatonchires' lungs were close to bursting from lack of oxygen and its legs were bleeding badly as the monster tried to pick itself up off the bottom of the ocean yet again. The Hecatonchires looked above him to see Chimera swimming down toward him. At the sight of the approaching hybrid, the Hecatonchires panicked. The Hecatonchires' arms and heads began moving wildly in uncontrolled motions. The beast's remaining heads looked up one last time to see Chimera's skull collided with them. Several more heads were crushed by the impact of Chimera's spermaceti reinforced head. With nearly half of its heads destroyed, and its remaining brains suffering from lack of oxygen, the Hecatonchires' arms fell limp to its sides. With the monster standing helpless before him, Chimera unsheathed his claws and he began to tear apart the misshapen monster one arm at a time until all that remained of the Hecatonchires was a bloody pillar of crushed heads.

Chimera pushed the lifeless body of the Hecatonchires away from him and then he swam back to the surface. When Chimera surfaced, he looked toward the shore to see the remains of the *Argos* sticking out of the water. Chimera dove forward and swam back to the remains of the ship that housed and fed him from most of his life.

When Luke saw Chimera approaching the *Argos*, he grabbed his megaphone and yelled, "Chimera, stop!" The monster complied with the request and Luke yelled, "Good job, Chimera!" Luke wanted to at least give the kaiju a verbal reinforcer for following his command. There were still roughly twenty lifeboats trying to make their way to shore and Luke was afraid that the act of Chimera simply swimming to shore could endanger them. Luke looked at Chimera standing next to the demolished *Argos*. Aside from the blood dripping out of the wounds on Chimera's arms and face, Luke could see that the kaiju was hurt by the loss of the ship that he thought of as a part of his home. Luke heard a crack of lightning behind him and turned around to see Zeus standing behind him. The sailors that were coming ashore were reaching for any weapon they could find to attack the god. Luke saw what was happening and he yelled, "Wait! I am Luke Davis. Many of you know me and for those who don't, I am Chimera's trainer. I can speak for General Parsons that for now, Zeus is on our side!"

Some of the sailors shook their heads in compliance with Luke's declaration while others kept their gaze fixed on Zeus. The King of Olympus pointed out over the water at Chimera. "The beast has not only defeated me, but he slew the Kraken and the Hecatonchires in consecutive battles. Truly, he is a force to be reckoned with." Zeus looked down at Luke. "The general known as Parsons has asked me to return you and the monster to Chimera Base. He wishes to review the battles that have occurred and plan our next missions in this war."

Luke nodded in reply. "That sounds good. I am exhausted, and Chimera will need time to recover as well before he fights again." Zeus nodded and as he lifted his hand, storm clouds formed around both Luke and over Chimera who was still in the water. There was a bright flash and then they were gone.

Luke found himself back at Chimera Base standing in front of Hangar Eighteen. Luke looked up into the bloody face of Chimera. Luke smiled at his friend and shouted through his megaphone, "Good work, Chimera! You can eat!" He then pointed to the hangar that held the thousands of pounds of beef, squid, and bamboo that Chimera ate on a daily basis. The weary monster walked over to the hangar and as he was approaching it, the men who worked there pulled back the retractable roof so that the kaiju had access to his food. As Chimera was eating, a storm cloud appeared near Luke. General Parsons, Diana, and Zeus all walked out of the cloud. As if he sensed their arrival, Odin also walked out of the hanger to join the others.

Parsons looked at the bloodied Chimera and then he turned to Luke. "I take it that you two were successful?"

Luke nodded. "Chimera is a little beat up, but the Kraken and the Hecatonchires have both been slain." Luke frowned and shrugged his shoulders. "Sadly, we lost the *Argos* in the process. What about you guys?"

Diana smiled. "Project G was a success! Grimm kicked Atlas' ass!"

Parsons nodded. "We lost some jets and pilots, but we stopped Atlas from reaching another city and the Phoenix is still alive." He turned to Zeus. "How did the Griffin fair with Atomic Rex?"

Zeus shook his head. "The reptile's power is greater than I had thought. Atomic Rex slew the Griffin and he is still making his way across Africa."

Parsons looked at Chimera and then at the rest of his team. "It's clear that Chimera, as well as the rest of us, need some rest. I will suggest that the cities directly in front of Atomic Rex be evacuated as quickly as possible. It's clear that having the military attacking him will only cost us more lives. We are going to take tomorrow to rest and we will not go back into battle until two days from now. Throwing Chimera into another battle while he is hurt may cause us to lose him. It's better to have him rest up to fight another day than to rush him into a fight he isn't ready for."

Luke nodded. "When he is done eating, I will tell him to go into the forest and sleep. He heals pretty quickly. I think in twenty-four hours he will be pretty much one hundred percent."

Parsons nodded. "Good. You and Diana rest up too." A soldier came running out of Hangar Eighteen with a tablet in his hand that he gave to Parsons. Parsons read the information on the device and then he reported it to the rest of the group. "It's a report from Captain Brand. Most of the crew of the *Argos* has survived. The *Argos'* sister ship, the *Hudson*, is currently being constructed in the bay of the same name. The ship is roughly fifty percent complete. The construction of the *Hudson* is now a top priority and it should be seaworthy in a few days. I have also been in touch with General Cabollo. He will see to the disposal of Atlas' corpse down in Texas. I will catch a few hours of sleep. Then I will confer with Zeus and Odin on what the next moves our enemies will be and how we can address the threat of Atomic Rex."

CHAPTER 9

Chimera Base

Luke stumbled into his house on the base. He was exhausted and barely able to stand, but when his two daughters came running toward the door to hug him, he felt slightly invigorated. He knelt down and wrapped his arms around his children. Suzie yelled, "Dad, you're home! What happened? Is Chimera okay?"

Sally echoed her sister. "Yeah, Daddy, did Chimera get all of those bad monsters?"

Luke smiled at the girls and at the sight of his wife walking in from the back of the house to see him as well. He looked down at the girls. "Chimera is a little scratched up, but he is going to be fine. He beat up a giant crab octopus monster and a giant with like a hundred arms and heads. He ate his dinner and now he is resting."

Melissa came over and gave Luke a kiss. She then looked down at their daughters and said, "It looks and smells like Daddy could use a shower, something to eat, and some rest too. Why don't you two let Daddy shower off? Then we can eat dinner and let Daddy get some rest."

Luke hugged his wife. "Maybe you girls can eat without me. I am going to shower and then catch a nap. I'm really tired. I'll eat something when I wake up."

The kids hugged their dad again and then they ran off to play. Melissa followed Luke toward the shower. She didn't want to press her weary husband too much, but she knew that he would feel the need to talk to her about what happened.

When they entered the bathroom, Luke looked at Melissa. "Sorry, I couldn't talk to you sooner. We had to move. It's even worse than last time."

Melissa closed the door so that the girls would not hear the more horrific parts of their father's adventures. "I saw on the news about the attacks in Texas, Boston, and Baltimore."

Luke turned on the shower to further block the sound of their conversation. "Stay calm when I tell you this until I can explain the entire scenario. Zeus and Odin are on the base."

At hearing that Odin, the god who had kidnapped her and used her to ransom against Luke and Chimera, was on the base, Melissa gasped. She took several deep breaths. "Have we finally captured them?"

Luke shook his head. "No, they have come to us for help to fight creatures they call the Dark Ones. Titans and other beings older than themselves. While the gods just wanted to wipe out humans, these guys want to destroy all life on the planet. It seems they eat life force or something. Anyway, they came to see Parsons to enlist Chimera's help in fighting off this threat. The titans unleashed some of their monsters on Earth and some kind of atomic dinosaur from another Earth who destroyed his world. Chimera fought off the two monsters I told the girls about, and Diana made some kind of a rock giant that killed the titan in Texas. It seems that the atomic dinosaur killed the god's monster they sent after him."

Melissa nodded. "So is this dinosaur the only threat left?"

Luke shrugged. "Parsons and the gods think that this is just sort of a first strike. There may be more coming, and the Dark Ones are most likely planning some sort of Doomsday move to end the world." Luke finished taking off his clothes and he climbed into the shower.

As Luke climbed into the shower, Melissa locked the door to the bathroom, stripped off her clothes, and climbed into the shower with her husband. Luke looked at her with surprise. "Honey, the kids are still awake."

She placed her finger over his mouth. "They'll be fine for a while. Besides, we need to make sure that you sleep well so you can go and save the world later."

Diana was too excited to sleep when she returned to her house. She was slightly intrigued by the prospect of a date with Captain Pressley. She knew that the pilot was a few years younger than her, but Diana also knew that she was not a typical woman in her late thirties either.

What really intrigued her was the fact that the ritual for creating a golem had worked. Given all that occurred in the war with the gods, she had some hope that the ritual would work, but she was far from sure. Her main concern was the fact that Zeus, Odin, and the other beings that she had encountered were not actually gods but interdimensional beings of vast power. The legend of the golem was connected to the Hebrew God of the Old Testament. This concept had several thoughts running through Diana's mind and her vast knowledge of mythology and legend. Diana sat down at her computer and began typing out some of her thoughts.

Does the fact that the golem was created mean that what people think of as God truly exists? If the golem does confirm God's existence, does it also confirm that like Odin and Zeus he is an extra-dimensional being? Will this question bring all of the world's religion into question? Diana smiled to herself. *Am I being too philosophical about all of this? Yes.* She stood up from her computer, laughing at how deeply she was examining the entire situation when another series of thought crossed her mind. As she sat down, she added one more sentence to her hastily scrawled notes. *If the Judeo/Christian God does exist, does that mean that creatures like the seven-headed dragon and the Leviathan mentioned in the Bible exist as well? If so, will we one day have to face them also?*

Suddenly feeling much more fatigued than she had a moment ago, Diana closed out her computer and stood up. She shook her head. "Let's focus on one Apocalypse at a time."

Parsons allowed himself six hours of sleep before returning to Hangar Eighteen at three a.m. the morning after his mandatory twenty-four rest period. He walked into the hangar where one of his assistants greeted him with an egg sandwich, a black coffee, and the latest reports on the movements of Atomic Rex. Parsons read the reports as he walked to the command center of the hangar where both Zeus and Odin were waiting for him beneath the main display screen. Behind the two gods, Parsons communications team was tracking Atomic Rex and looking for the appearance of any other new kaiju.

Zeus was the first to speak. "The need you mortals have to sleep is quite time-consuming. We could have been planning the next phase of our defense hours ago if you were able to stay awake."

Parsons was not usually a man who allowed himself to be irked by petty comments, but the stress he was under combined with a minimal amount of sleep had shortened his temper. He looked at Zeus. "Sleep allows us to refresh our minds and see things with a new clarity. Perhaps if you slept, you would have won the war and we wouldn't be here right now. Of course, if that happened, you wouldn't have had us and Chimera around to defeat three monsters for you already."

The gods didn't reply; they simply stared silently at Parsons. Seeing that he had made his point, Parsons got down to the task at hand. He turned on the display screen to show a map of Africa with a dot moving across the country of Algeria. "Atomic Rex is still making his way across Africa in a westerly direction. It seems that he is headed for the city if Adrar." Parsons turned to the gods with a quizzical look on his face. "You had said that the Dark Ones absorb life force and that they would use Atomic Rex to kill as many people as possible. However, when he was approaching the city of Sahab, the kaiju simply passed by it. Any idea why the Dark Ones would've had him skip a city with several hundred thousand people in it when they supposedly want to kill as much life as possible?"

Zeus and Odin exchanged glances. "I cannot say. Atomic Rex is unknown to us and his power is far greater than any other creature that we or the Dark Ones have ever commanded. They are not as adept in controlling their monsters as we are. It is possible that their control over the kaiju is not as complete as it is over their other monsters."

Parsons nodded. "That's something to keep in mind." He turned his focus back to the monitor. "Whatever level of control the Dark Ones have over him, Atomic Rex is closing in on the city of Adrar and it doesn't look like he is going to pass it by. The city is being evacuated, but the evacuation will only be twenty percent complete by the time the monster reaches it. I want you to send the Phoenix to intercept him. Atomic Rex seems like a nasty character, but our reports indicate that he needs to absorb nuclear energy to survive. I saw in her battle with Atlas, that the Phoenix can regenerate herself when she dies. While Atomic Rex may initially slay the Phoenix, your monster can win a battle of attrition. She may die several times, but from what you've said and what we have seen of Atomic Rex, he won't back down from a battle. The idea will be for the Phoenix to battle Atomic Rex until he runs out of energy."

Zeus nodded as Odin replied, "You are indeed wise in the ways of war, General. You have a talent for noticing and utilizing the strengths of those under your command."

Parsons nodded in reply and then he took a sip of his coffee. The general had been in enough negations to know when someone was patronizing him. He was also wise enough to not let the other party know he was aware of the patronizing. He focused back on the issue of the Dark Ones. "We will have to teleport the Phoenix to Algeria in the next twenty minutes before Atomic Rex reaches Adrar. Before we do that though, you had said the attacks so far were simply first strikes designed so that the Dark Ones could amass more life energy to mount a world-ending assault. Do you have any idea what form this assault might come in, and do you think we will need the Phoenix on hand to fight off this assault should it occur soon?"

Odin shrugged. "When the Dark Ones have the power they require, they will attempt to cause some extinction-level event. This event could be in the form of directing a comet or asteroid to Earth. It could be the creation of a new ice age or any other catastrophic event that would extinguish all life on the planet. To attempt such an act, the Dark Ones themselves will need to be on the Earth. The moment that they enter this plane of existence, we shall be aware of it."

Parsons nodded. "When they enter this plane of existence, will Chimera be able to defeat them?"

Zeus laughed. "Millennia ago, it took the combined might of my gods and the cyclops when I was at full power to defeat Cronus and his titans! Your beast may be mighty, but these are cosmic beings he will be facing. Your monster will die if he challenges one of the Dark Ones alone. He will be as a lamb challenging a lion!"

Odin placed his hand on Zeus' shoulder. "Still, if you were to return Thor's belt to me, it would significantly increase my own strength and power. Together, Chimera and I could defeat the Dark Ones. Should the Phoenix be available to us as well, the three of us will crush the Dark Ones!"

Parsons nodded and shifted his gaze to Zeus. "All right then. I want you to send the Phoenix to intercept Atomic Rex before he reaches Adrar. Otherwise, we will wait and see what the Dark Ones' next move is."

Zeus nodded and then in a flash of lightning, he was gone.

Parsons looked over at the main display screen. He could see the dot that was Atomic Rex closing in on the city of Adrar. He yelled out to the people working the communications display. "I want the satellite feed as close on Atomic Rex as possible! I also want Luke and Diana here ASAP!"

One of the people at the display screen yelled, "Yes, sir!" He then focused the satellite's camera as tightly as he could to show Atomic Rex walking through the desert. The monster was moving at a steady pace until he saw a large storm cloud suddenly forming in front of him.

CHAPTER 10

The desert, 6 miles west of Adrar, Algeria

Atomic Rex could feel whatever force was influencing him attempting to direct him to the city ahead. The kaiju was not hungry, having devoured the Griffin only a day ago. The monster did, however, feel a slight desire to replenish the nuclear power stored within his cells. Atomic Rex could not sense any source of nuclear energy within the city and his keen sense of smell told him that even if he was hungry, the city was already partially empty.

The city currently held no value to the monster and he desired to walk past it and continue his journey back to the Americas, but the entity that was in his head continued to push him toward Adrar. In his mind, Atomic Rex continued to struggle against the will of Cronus, but for now, the will of the titan was winning out.

In the space between dimensions, Cronus struggled to keep his hold on Atomic Rex. The monster's fighting spirit simply refused to give in to another's will. Cronus realized that he was using nearly as much energy to control Atomic Rex as the beast gained for him by killing people. He began to reconsider his plan to have the nuclear theropod trek halfway around the world while he directed the monster's will. Had Cronus simply placed Atomic Rex in the Americas, the monster may very well have taken more than enough lives to deliver the power that Cronus and the others needed to defeat the humans. Cronus had underestimated Atomic Rex and put too much value in his own abilities. The titan considered simply teleporting the kaiju to the Americas, but such an act would prove detrimental to him in numerous ways.

First of all, teleporting the creature would take a tremendous amount of energy and there was no guarantee that the monster would immediately head for the most populated areas on the continents. If the beast did not head for population centers, then Cronus and the other Dark Ones would not receive the amount of life energy that they required to be assured of completing the tasks before them.

The second and more grievous concern was that veering away from his stated plan would show Tiamat and Surtr that he did not have total control over Atomic Rex. Cronus knew that the other two Dark Ones were already beginning to suspect that this was the case. Surtr and Tiamat reluctantly viewed Cronus as their leader since he was inherently the most powerful between the three of them. If they were given the slightest evidence that Cronus was not as all powerful as he portrayed, there was every chance that his fellow Dark Ones would turn on him.

With those factors weighing on his mind, Cronus continued to struggle against Atomic Rex's will power in order to control the beast. The titan was slowly forcing the kaiju toward Adrar when a storm cloud appeared in front of him and the flame-covered Phoenix sprang forth from it. Cronus could feel the anger swell within Atomic Rex at the sight of another kaiju. The titan knew that attempting to steer the nuclear theropod toward the city was a useless gesture at this point. Once Atomic Rex saw another kaiju, he was immediately overwhelmed by the urge to slay the creature and no force in the cosmos was capable of dissuading him from doing so.

Atomic Rex shook his head and roared at the Phoenix as it flew circles in the sky above him. The Phoenix circled the nuclear theropod three times before slowing down and hovering directly over the reptile. Atomic Rex looked up and roared at the fire bird as it floated just out of his reach. The Phoenix screech in reply to Atomic Rex's challenge and began to flap her wings in rapid succession. The rate of flapping increased until a pillar of flames shot down from her wings and engulfed Atomic Rex.

Atomic Rex was driven to the ground by the force of the Phoenix's attack. The monster was lying flat on his stomach as the heat from the Phoenix's flames scorched his body and turned the sand he was laying on into molten glass. Atomic Rex's body was racked with pain, but the searing pain only served to further enrage the monster. As the pillar of flames continued to push Atomic Rex to the ground, the kaiju placed his powerful arms beneath his body and began to push himself back into a standing position. The beast's outer layer of scales was beginning to burn off by the time he had reached his feet. The monster shook his head in anger at the thought of the Phoenix trying to kill him with flames. Atomic Rex had been born in fire and that power was his to control.

The monster lifted his leg into the air and as he did so, he reached deep into his cells to extract the nuclear energy within them. The outer layer of Atomic Rex's scales began to glow blue. As they did, the flames that were surrounding him began to be pushed back. Atomic Rex roared as he slammed his foot into the ground and unleashed his devastating Atomic Wave. A blue dome of pure radioactive energy expanded out from Atomic Rex's body. As the dome expanded, it pushed the pillar of fire away from Atomic Rex and when the apex of the dome struck the underbelly of the Phoenix, it burned the creature and threw her into the air.

The Phoenix tumbled through the air and came crashing down onto the desert floor several hundred feet from where Atomic Rex was standing. The nuclear theropod turned toward his prey and charged. The Phoenix was in the process of standing up when Atomic Rex crashed into her and wrapped his arms around her. Atomic Rex lifted the Phoenix over his head and then he slammed her down hard onto the desert floor. The Phoenix was lying flat on her back when Atomic Rex lifted his foot into the air and stomped hard on her chest, breaking several of her ribs in the process.

The Phoenix screeched in pain as she felt her bones crack. The Phoenix then threw her wings up toward Atomic Rex. When her wings reached their full extent, twin fireballs sprang forth from them. The fireballs struck Atomic Rex in the chest and face, knocking the kaiju off the Phoenix and causing him to take several steps backwards. The Phoenix regained her feet and threw another pair of fireballs at Atomic Rex before she took to the sky once again.

Once she was in the air, the Phoenix flew away from Atomic Rex and over the city Adrar. When she reached the edge of the city, she made a tight turn and began flying back toward Atomic Rex. As she approached the nuclear theropod, the Phoenix increased her speed and with the increase in speed, the flames that wreathed her body began to expand. The Phoenix had covered half of the distance between herself and Atomic Rex when her entire body became covered in flames.

Atomic Rex saw the living comet streaking toward him and he roared as he braced himself for impact. The Phoenix flew directly into Atomic Rex and when her flaming body struck the reptilian creature, it caused a massive explosion. Both Atomic Rex and the Phoenix disappeared within the blast. The flames from the explosion raced across the desert and toward the outskirts of Adrar. When it had reached its full extent, the blast had covered nearly three-square miles of the desert in flames.

When the flames reached their farthest point, they suddenly snapped back to their point of origin. The Phoenix was standing in the center of a smoke-filled crater as she drew the fire back into her body. Once she had absorbed all of the flames back into herself, The Phoenix turned around to look down at the dead body of Atomic Rex. To her surprise, the kaiju's body was nowhere to be found. The Phoenix shifted her head from side to side looking for the corpse of Atomic Rex, but her vision was obscured by the smoke that surrounded her. The fire bird began to flap her wings as she attempted to rise above the smoke when Atomic Rex's jaws closed around her neck.

The Phoenix flapped her wings wildly, clearing the smoke from the air as she tried to free herself from Atomic Rex's death grip. The saurian kaiju clenched his jaws tighter around the Phoenix's neck until he felt his teeth reach her spinal cord. With the Phoenix firmly in his grasp, Atomic Rex swiped his claws across the Phoenix's mid-section, ripping her stomach open. As a mix of blood and organs fell out of the Phoenix's body, Atomic Rex twisted his jaws and snapped the Phoenix's neck.

The nuclear theropod let the lifeless body of the fire bird drop to the ground. He then lifted his head into the sky and roared, letting this world know that he was its master. The monster had taken a few steps away from the dead Phoenix and toward the ocean when he felt the strange presence within his mind urging him to attack the city. The saurian creature was fighting against the influence when his body suddenly became very aware of something that it craved suddenly appearing behind it.

Blocking out the influence attempting to take over his mind, Atomic Rex spun around to see the Phoenix's body burning with bright blue flames. The cells in Atomic Rex's body were immediately able to identify the power that the Phoenix used to regenerate itself. It was the power that Atomic Rex had sought his entire life and had not been able to find. The Phoenix was able to regenerate herself through the power of nuclear fusion. Until now, Atomic Rex had to absorb radiation from external sources that generated radiation through fission. The absorption of radiation from nuclear fission was able to temporarily satiate Atomic Rex's need for radiation, but the absorption of a nuclear fusion power source would give him the ability to generate his own energy as he needed. Atomic Rex realized that in order to obtain that power, he would have to kill the Phoenix once again. With a desire to slay something that he had never felt before, Atomic Rex roared and charged at the reformed Phoenix.

The Phoenix took to the sky and streaked toward Atomic Rex. The fire bird fluttered above the kaiju's head, using her flaming beak and claws to ravage Atomic Rex's face. Atomic Rex attempted to use his own teeth and claws to tear into the Phoenix, but the nimble bird proved too evasive for the nuclear theropod to touch. Blood started to slide down Atomic Rex's face from the damage being inflicted upon it.

Atomic Rex changed tactics by lowering his head and spinning around so that his tail struck the Phoenix on her right side.

The blow sent the Phoenix tumbling through the air. The Phoenix had nearly crashed into the ground before regaining control of her flight pattern. Once she had steadied herself, The Phoenix increased her altitude to put some distance between herself and the charging Atomic Rex. The fire bird circled above Atomic Rex then she looked skyward and flew into the stratosphere. When she had flown as high as she could, the Phoenix turned and dove directly toward Atomic Rex. As she was diving, the flames around her body began to grow. The fire bird once more intended to unleash her full power on Atomic Rex, but this time, she would do so with the force of a meteor falling from space behind her attack.

Atomic Rex looked skyward to see the flaming form of the Phoenix plummeting toward him. Knowing what the Phoenix was attempting to do, Atomic Rex shook his head and once more he began to call forth the nuclear energy stored within his cells. Just prior to the moment that the Phoenix would have struck Atomic Rex, the saurian beast unleashed his Atomic Wave. The Atomic Wave collided with the streaking hulk of flames that was the Phoenix. The blue dome of the Atomic Wave pushed against the mushroom-cloud explosion created by the Phoenix. The result of the conflicting attacks was an explosion that shook the Earth and caused many of the buildings in the nearby city of Adrar to crumble from the shockwave.

As the flames and smoke dissipated from the dual attack, both Atomic Rex and the Phoenix were lying still above the field of glass they had created from the heat they released. It was Atomic Rex who rose to his feet first. The nuclear theropod was exhausted and nearly drained of energy, but when he saw the Phoenix still on the ground a few hundred feet away from him, he forced his body to move as quickly as it could. The glassy ground that Atomic Rex was forced to walk across was difficult to traverse, but the monster continued to push himself toward his prey.

Atomic Rex was a few steps away from the Phoenix when the mythical creature began to stir. The Phoenix had managed to lift her head off the ground and she was starting to lift herself up when Atomic Rex drove his clawed toes into the back of the fire bird and through her chest. Blood spurted out of the Phoenix's beak as she tried to shriek in pain. The fire bird looked down at the claws protruding from her chest and then her head fell limp.

Rather than walk away as he had the previous time he slayed the Phoenix, Atomic Rex kept his foot embedded in the fire bird's body and he waited. When the Phoenix's body began to glow with blue flames, Atomic Rex absorbed the power that the Phoenix was trying to use to regenerate herself. As the energy of the Phoenix filled Atomic Rex's body, he felt a power the likes of which he had never experienced before. The Phoenix's ability to generate energy through nuclear fusion was purging Atomic Rex from the need to feed off nuclear reactors. From this moment on, Atomic Rex would be capable of creating his own nuclear energy.

The power that was running Atomic Rex extended throughout his entire body. When the energy that was once the Phoenix's entered Atomic Rex's brain, it forced out the presence that had been attempting to influence him.

In the space between dimensions, Cronus screamed in pain as his physical body was tossed backward as a result of Atomic Rex's mind freeing itself from the titan's consciousness. Cronus staggered back to his feet and looked through a portal at Atomic Rex in awe. Now that the creature was infused with the power of the Phoenix, it had the potential to destroy even him. Cronus' sense of awe turned to fear when Atomic Rex looked back at him through the portal and roared. Cronus quickly shut the portal and then he shook his head in disbelief. "The creature has not only broken free of my control but by taking the power of the Phoenix, it has gained the power to sense me." A shiver of fear ran down the titan's spine. "Could he perhaps have the power to reach me now if he so wished?"

Through his attempts to control Atomic Rex's mind, Cronus was well aware that the kaiju hated him and longed to destroy him. Cronus was weak from his attempts to control the monster and he doubted his ability to defeat Atomic Rex should he appear to attack him. Cronus knew that he needed to reenergize as quickly as possible should Atomic Rex realize that the mastery of nuclear fusion would now give him the ability to travel between dimensions. The titan opened a portal to both Surtr and Tiamat. He screamed at his brother Dark Ones. "Begin your attacks now! I will send you the life force energy I have gathered from Atomic Rex momentarily!"

Surtr growled and Tiamat hissed in anger, as they knew that without the life energy Cronus had promised them, they would be unable to teleport to the exact spot where they needed to be to start the apocalypse. As the two Dark Ones pierced the thin veil separating them from Chimera's Earth and set foot upon it, their thoughts were fixed on first ending all life on this Earth, and then ending Cronus.

When Cronus saw Surtr and Tiamat both on Earth, he said to himself, "No more energy is coming to you, my brothers. You shall have to initiate Armageddon with the energies that you now possess. Hurry in this task, for I fear that Atomic Rex may come for us, and if he does, we shall need to have gathered the lives of as many organisms as possible."

CHAPTER 11

Chimera Base

Luke and Diana both ran into Hangar Eighteen just in time to see Atomic Rex absorb the power of the Phoenix. Diana frowned. "That can't be good, can it?"

Before anyone could respond to Diana's comment, alarms started to go off throughout the hangar. Zeus' face showed his sudden panic. "I can sense it. Two of the Dark Ones have set foot on Earth."

One of the soldiers sitting at a computer by the main display screen called out, "General Parsons, sir, we have reports coming in from Yellowstone National Park in Wyoming! They are reporting that a giant demon with a flaming sword is making his way through the park and setting everything on fire!"

Parsons yelled, "I want visual on this creature now!" The computers at Chimera Base had access to every camera on the planet and above it. The soldier accessed this system to bring up security cameras and feeds from peoples cellphones to bring the monster into focus. An image that was close to the popular description of Satan himself quickly filled the screen. The creature had a distorted human-like face with two black horns sticking out of the top of it. Two long bat-like wings protruded from his back. The beast's body was that of a stout but heavily muscled human. The demon had a hunched stance that made it appear more menacing. Its body had flames flickering around in the same fashion that the Phoenix's body did. In the horror's right hand was a flaming sword that was causing everything around it to catch fire.

It was Luke who voiced the thoughts of nearly every human in the room. "Is that the Devil?"

Diana shook her head. "Not quite, but close enough. I would bet that's Surtr. A fire demon from Norse Mythology."

Odin's voiced boomed out, "Indeed, you are correct, human."

Parsons could tell that Surtr's demonic appearance was deeply disturbing to his mainly Judeo/Christian subordinations. The hardened general swallowed his own fears and tried to refocus the group on the task at hand. He looked toward Odin. "I take it Surtr is one of the Dark One's you mentioned would be coming to end the world?" The ancient god nodded in reply. Parsons took a step closer to Odin. "What is he doing there that could end the world?"

The answer came not from Odin but from Diana. "During the events of Ragnarok, Surtr is said to defeat the gods and then with his flaming sword set the world on fire. If he is in Yellowstone, he could use his sword to cause the super-volcano beneath the park to erupt. If that happens, the eruption alone would devastate most of the middle of the country. The debris from the explosion will cover the world in ash and block out the sun. Within six months, nearly half of the world population will die. After that, things will get really bad."

Parsons looked at Luke. The general didn't say a word, but Luke replied, "On my way to Chimera, sir. We should be ready to be teleported out there in five minutes. I have a radio if you need to get in touch with me!" Luke ran out the door, sprinted to his truck, and then he took off into the woods after Chimera.

One of the soldiers yelled out from his computer, "Sir, Atomic Rex is turning north and away from the city Adrar! We have a helicopter following him to track his movements more closely!"

Parsons nodded. "Well, at least a bit of good news." He turned toward Zeus. "You said that two of the Dark Ones have come to Earth. Where is the second one?"

Zeus closed his eyes. "He is somewhere north. It is difficult to say where exactly. There is something blocking my perception of the creature."

Diana placed her hand on Parsons' shoulder. "That's why you should never say we've got good news. It's like Fight Club, and what did I tell you is the first rule of Fight Club?"

Odin's voice boomed throughout the Hangar, "General, your monster is not prepared to face Surtr alone. Bring me my belt so that I may join him battle! We can deal with the other Dark One and Atomic Rex after we address this immediate threat! I will need the belt to meet the demon on equal terms!"

Parsons nodded. "Head outside. We don't need you growing to kaiju size in here and destroying the hangar." He turned to Diana. "Go and get the belt as quickly as you can." Diana ran out of the room. As she was sprinting down the hallway to the locked vault where Thor's belt of strength was located, she kept thinking about Ragnarok and trying to decide if it was a myth or a prophecy.

Luke was driving as fast as he could to Chimera. He had seen and fought many strange creatures over the past two years, but nothing chilled him to the bone the way that Surtr did. Luke had been raised as a Catholic and seeing Surtr had a disturbing effect on him. He kept reminding himself that even if he looked like it, Surtr was not the literal Satan. Still, no matter how many times Luke told himself this, he couldn't shake the feeling that he was charging off to confront the Devil himself.

Luke's mind was snapped back to what he was doing when he heard Parsons' voice come over the radio, "Luke, come in! Have you reached Chimera yet?"

Luke could see the massive form of his friend sleeping in the woods ahead of him. He sped up and said, "Yes, sir, waking him up now!"

Parsons' responded, "Good. As soon as he is awake, radio us back. We are giving Odin Thor's belt. He will grow to kaiju size and then Zeus will teleport you, Chimera, and Odin to Yellowstone!"

Luke yelled into his radio, "Copy that." Luke pulled his truck to a stop in front of the living mountain of flesh that was Chimera. He grabbed his megaphone and yelled, "Chimera, wake up!"

The monster stirred and then lifted his head up into the sky. Luke was glad to see that most of the wounds Chimera had suffered in his previous battles had healed over. Luke would have preferred to have given Chimera a small reward just for waking up, but he knew that time was of the essence. He yelled into his radio, "Parsons, we are good to go!"

Parsons was standing outside of Hangar Eighteen with Zeus and Odin when he got the word from Luke that Chimera was ready for battle. He called back, "Copy, we are just waiting for Odin to put on the belt and then Zeus is going to transport you!"

A garage door opened, and a golf cart driven by Diana pulled out of it. On the back of the cart, was a belt made for the thirty-foot-tall gods. She pulled alongside Odin. The Norse god promptly grabbed the belt and wrapped it around his waist. The belt immediately caused Odin to grow to a height of three hundred feet tall.

Parsons looked at Zeus and yelled. "Teleport them now!"

Zeus lifted his hand into the air and storm clouds surrounded Odin. There was a flash of lightning and then he was gone. Deep in the woods, another storm cloud surrounded Luke and Chimera. Lightning flashed around them and a moment later, Luke was struck by a wave of intense heat. Luke found himself in the center of a raging forest fire. His eyes immediately teared up as he was coughing from the smoke and soot in the air. He looked up to see what he could only describe as a creature of pure evil coming toward him. Surtr was huge. Chimera stood at roughly two hundred and fifty feet tall and Surtr had at least thirty feet on the hybrid.

Luke looked to Chimera and was surprised to see the mighty kaiju taking a step back as he stared at Surtr. Luke shook his head and said, "If even you find that thing disturbing, I am glad that we have back up." Luke looked around for the giant form of Odin but he could not find the King of Asgard. Luke didn't know what had happened to Odin, but when he saw Surtr getting closer with his flaming sword raised above his head, Luke grabbed his megaphone, pointed at Surtr, and yelled. "Chimera, attack!" Chimera roared and then charged the demon.

Outside the city of Adrar, Atomic Rex was trying to orient himself to the new sensations he was experiencing since he had absorbed the power of the Phoenix. The monster could sense the presence that had been trying to control him being forced out his mind. He could also sense that the presence was watching him from somewhere far away. Atomic Rex could not comprehend how, but when he focused on the presence, he could see it watching him. He could also sense that two creatures similar to one that was trying to control had suddenly appeared on Earth. One of the creatures was on the land across the ocean that he considered his territory. The other was up north where ice covered everything. Neither of the creatures was the one that had tried to control him but that didn't matter to the nuclear theropod. Something had tried to control him and that thought enraged Atomic Rex. The saurian kaiju needed something to take his anger out on and the closest creature that he could find was the one in the Arctic.

Atomic Rex was heading north when another storm cloud appeared in front of him. The kaiju was surprised to see a human that was even larger than he was emerge from the cloud. The giant had one eye and a long white beard. Atomic Rex roared at the giant and then he began running toward him. The giant held up his hand and the movement stopped Atomic Rex in his tracks.

Atomic Rex was trying to move forward, but he found that he was unable to do so. He looked at the bearded giant who yelled, "Hear me, monster! The Dark Ones tried to control you and they have failed! The Phoenix belonged to the gods and she was under our control! You have since taken in her essence and you have now put yourself under our control as well! You will now follow my commands! Together, you and I shall put an end to the Dark Ones and then we shall slay Chimera! After that, I shall lead my fellow gods as we extinguish the blight of humanity from this world and restore it to its natural state! Now, monster, bend to my will and follow me!"

Atomic Rex could feel the presence of the giant in his mind. The giant's control over the kaiju's body was far greater than the influence that had possessed him before. Atomic Rex could feel his body being moved against his will in the direction of the giant. Atomic Rex's anger grew to an inferno within his mind. Atomic Rex refused to let another being control him. The mutated dinosaur reached deep into cells, and Odin watched as the scales on the body of the nuclear theropod began to give off a bright blue glow.

The Congo

Allison and Aiden were sitting inside of their cave, watching the events unfolding before them through a portal just as Cronus was doing from his dimension. Aiden shook his head in fear and disbelief. "The Dark Ones have come to Earth! They will end all life on this planet including ours!" He turned to his sister. "You must send Toombs' new monster into battle Surtr with Chimera! Together, they may stand a chance against the demon!"

Allison rolled her eyes at her brother. "Don't be so dramatic. We can easily escape with the children to another dimension and even the monster if we need too." She pointed back to the portal. "Look all three sides of this a war and the wild card that is Atomic Rex are engaging in battle. Our enemies are destroying each other for us. As these battles play out, we shall be provided with opportunities to strengthen our position. We will not attack anytime soon but will act at the conclusion of these battles in some fashion."

CHAPTER 12

Chimera Base

General Parsons clenched his fists in anger as he stared at two separate scenes on the large screen before him. The first part of the split screen was showing a satellite video of Chimera as he charged toward Surtr. The second screen showed the now giant Odin standing before Atomic Rex. The helicopter that was following Atomic Rex was sending the video feedback to Chimera Base. Parsons screamed, "I want audio from Odin! Now!"

The soldier controlling the feed brought up the audio. Parsons heard Odin declaring that he would control Atomic Rex and use him to defeat the Dark Ones as well as the humans. Parsons cursed, "Goddamn traitors." He watched the feed for a few more seconds as Atomic Rex's body took on a blue hue. There was a bright flash and Parsons saw a dome of blue light coming toward the screen and then the feed turned to static.

Parsons screamed, "What the hell happened to the feed?"

A soldier called back, "We're not sure, sir. Whatever that flash was that Atomic Rex gave off either knocked out the feed or totally destroyed the helicopter."

Parsons continued to bark orders. "There has to be a dozen more news helicopters on the way to cover this. Find one with audio and get the visual feed, back online! I want to know what's going on with Atomic Rex and Odin!"

He yelled, "I also want a satellite feed from the North Pole and recon planes flying over it. We need to know what's going on up there." Parsons took a look at Chimera squaring off with Surtr. He looked toward Diana. "What do you know about Surtr? Can Chimera defeat him?"

Diana's eyes were wide as she shook her head. "In the story of Ragnarok, Surtr is said to be able to battle Odin, Thor, and the rest of the Asgardians to a draw or to outright defeat them. Surtr could be more powerful than all of the gods Chimera has faced so far combined."

Yellowstone National Park

Chimera was only a few steps away from Surtr and he reached out his arms to grab the demon. Surtr smiled at the charging Chimera and then he leapt into the air. Surtr was leaping over Chimera when he opened his wings and started flapping them. Chimera looked up, expecting Surtr to attack him from above, but to his surprise, the demonic creature simply flew past him.

Luke was doing his best to refrain from coughing as he yelled once more into his megaphone, "Chimera, attack!" Chimera roared and then he started following the flying demon as he made his way deeper into Yellowstone Park.

As Surtr glided over the forest, the very heat that his body was giving off caused the trees that he passed over to catch fire. Chimera was running on all fours as he pursued the Dark One. Luke was doing his best to keep up with the hybrid but with the fire burning around him and smoke filling his lungs and eyes, the best that he could manage was a quick walk. Luke watched as both Surtr and Chimera pulled away from him and within a few minutes, he could no longer see them through the thick black smoke that was filling the air. Two thoughts filled his mind as he looked at the fire raging around him. The first thought once more took him back to his childhood and Sunday school when the teachers told him about Hell. Luke looked at the inferno raging around him, and he thought that this was probably the closest thing to Hell on Earth that someone could imagine. He shifted his gaze to the wide path of trees that had been crushed in front of him as he voiced his second thought, "Well, on the bright side, at least Chimera's path will be easy to follow."

Sweat was pouring off Chimera's body as the kaiju chased the Dark One through the ever-growing forest fire. Despite Chimera's considerable speed, Surtr was slowing pulling away from him. Chimera was starting to think that Surtr might escape from him when the Dark One suddenly landed on the ground. The demon laughed loudly as he lifted his sword over his head and drove it into the ground. Lava erupted from the ground on the spot that Surtr's sword had touched.

Surtr pulled his sword out of the ground which caused even more lava to erupt from beneath the earth. He screamed, "Only a few more blows and my sword shall pierce deep enough into the ground to ignite the flames that will cover this world in ash!"

The Dark One was lifting his sword over his head to once more drive it into the ground when Chimera rammed his head into Surtr's back. The blow knocked Surtr to the ground and sent his sword flying off into the woods. Chimera shook his head in pain as the very act of touching Surtr had scorched his flesh where he made contact with the demon.

Surtr stood up and he screamed, "Pathetic beast! Do you truly think that you have the strength to challenge me? I am the destroyer of worlds and you are but a mockery of life created by the puny creatures whose meaningless lives shall soon end to sustain me!"

Chimera responded by throwing his arms out at his sides and roaring at the demonic Surtr. Chimera then charged the Dark One again. This time, instead of trying to avoid Chimera, Surtr stood his ground. When Chimera reached Surtr, the kaiju wrapped his arms around the demon. Every inch of Chimera's skin that was touching Surtr burned from the heat coming off of the Dark One. Chimera blocked out the searing pain as he tried to throw Surtr to the ground. Chimera pushed Surtr hard to the side, but the Dark One did not move.

Surtr laughed at Chimera and then with a shift of his weight, he threw Chimera to the ground and sent him rolling through the burning trees that surrounded them. Chimera rolled over twice before he was able to stop his momentum and stand up. The kaiju had no sooner reached his feet than Surtr flew over to him and punched him in the face. The blow staggered Chimera, causing the monster to lose his balance. Surtr then kicked Chimera in the stomach, once more knocking the kaiju to the ground. Chimera landed hard on his back directly on top of a group of burning trees. The hybrid tried to stand up only to have Surtr kick him in the face once more. Chimera's head snapped backward as blood trickled out of his nostrils. Surtr then kicked Chimera in the ribs with such force that blood spurted out of the monster's mouth. With his opponent down, Surtr turned away from Chimera and began walking back toward his flaming sword.

Chimera looked over to see Surtr pick up his sword and walk back to the point he had previously struck with the weapon. The demon lifted the sword and drove it into the ground for a second time. Surtr drove the entire top half of the sword into the ground and it caused multiple geysers of lava to shoot into the air. One of the geysers opened up near Chimera and showered the monster in the scoring liquid.

The kaiju rolled around, and he could see Luke stumbling through the woods toward him. Luke was holding up his megaphone and yelling to Chimera, but the between the heat, smoke, and the beating he had taken, Chimera was unable to hear what his trainer was saying.

Luke could see that Chimera was stunned if not injured beyond the point of being able to carry on. The former teacher was doing his best to keep moving forward through the flaming, trees, blistering heat, and geysers of lava shooting into the air. Luke had seen Chimera like this before where the monster seemed defeated. He had also witnessed what happened when the monster received an adrenaline surge through his body. Most importantly, Luke was aware that one of the things that was sure to trigger an adrenaline surge in Chimera was when he saw his trainer in danger.

Luke watched as Surtr pulled his flaming sword out of the earth and lifted it over his head to drive it through the ground. Luke wasn't a professor of mythology like Diana, and he sure as hell wasn't a geologist, but he was pretty sure that if Surtr struck the ground one more time, he would ignite the super-volcano that would end the world. Luke pushed aside his fear of Surtr and of death. He pushed aside the thoughts that he was trying to save the world. He pushed every other thought aside and he focused on his loved ones. He thought of his best friend Diana and how much he enjoyed spending time with her. He focused on Parsons, a man that he admired and respected more than any other person he had ever met. He thought of the bloody and beaten Chimera. The monster who he had trained and who he had fought countless battles with. The monster whose love and loyalty to him was beyond question. Most of all, he focused on his family. He thought of Melissa, his wife and the love his life. He thought of his girls who were the wonder, awe, and joy of his existence.

Luke focused on these things and what a great life he had lived. He didn't know what happened to people when they died, and he didn't care. He knew that he had lived his life in a state as close to Heaven as any man had a right to. If giving up his life even provided the smallest chance of saving all those people, he thought that dying was a small price to pay.

Luke ran up to Surtr with his megaphone in hand. As he stood in front of the monster, he could feel his skin starting to blister from the heat being given off by the Dark One. Luke held his megaphone to his mouth and he screamed, "Stop! You can't do this! I won't let you!"

Surtr looked down at the mortal standing at his feet and he laughed. "You won't let me! Mortal, I shall drive my sword through you and ignite the flames of doom with your bones!"

Chimera watched as Surtr aimed his sword at Luke. When he saw that the Dark One was about to hurt Luke, rage ran through the kaiju like a river shattering a dam. The monster felt the strength return to his body as he sat up and fired a sonic blast at Surtr. Surtr's body convulsed as Chimera's blast disrupted the horror's central nervous system, causing him to drop his sword. Chimera stood and he fired a second sonic blast at Surtr that caused the Dark One to fall to the ground with his limbs and head twitching and shaking. The kaiju threw his arms out to his sides and he roared. He then dropped to all fours and charged the demon.

Luke ran to the side to clear out of Chimera's way but he took the time to yell, "Good boy, Chimera!" as the monster sprinted past him.

Chimera climbed on top of the flaming creature and he unsheathed his claws. The monster raked his claws across the demon's face and chest, causing an orange lava-like substance to seep out of the fresh wounds.

Surtr roared in pain and then he flapped his wings, creating a wall of flames that pushed Chimera off his chest. The moment that the Dark One regained his feet, Chimera drove his head into Surtr's midsection. The blow knocked the demon back several steps and as he was trying to regain his balance, Chimera stepped forward and delivered another slash across Surtr's face. The boiling yellow liquid that spurted from the new wound landed on Chimera's chin and burned the monster, causing him to grab his face.

While Chimera was grabbing his face, Surtr struck the monster in the jaw, knocking him to the ground. Rather than pressing his advantage on the kaiju, Surtr ran after his burning sword. The demon grabbed his sword and he turned around to see the seething face of Chimera standing between him and the area where he needed to drive his sword into to ignite the super-volcano. Surtr screamed, "Enough, beast! You have kept me from my goal for too long! Die like the animal you are!" Surtr swung his sword at Chimera but the monster ducked under the swing, charged forward, and wrapped his arms around Surtr. The very act of grabbing Surtr burned Chimera's flesh. The kaiju roared in both pain and anger as he lifted Surtr into the air and then slammed him into the ground.

Surtr was attempting to stand up when Chimera spun around and used his tail to strike the demon in the face. The blow knocked Surtr onto his side and caused him to drop his sword.

Seeing a possible chance to end the battle, Luke ran as close to the giant flaming sword as he could. He then grabbed his megaphone and yelled, "Chimera, watch me!" He then picked up a burning tree branch and made a stabbing motion toward Surtr. He then pointed at the sword and again made a stabbing motion toward the Dark One.

Chimera was reaching down to pick up the sword when Luke saw Surtr stand up behind him. Luke screamed into the megaphone, "Chimera, tail swipe!"

Following his master's command, Chimera bent low to the ground and swung his tail behind him. The blow struck Surtr in the ribcage and knocked him to the ground. The kaiju then wrapped his hand around the flaming sword and as he did so, he screeched in pain. Luke had never heard a sound like this one come from Chimera before. For a brief moment, Luke wondered if Chimera did indeed have a soul. He also wondered if Chimera's soul was burning at that moment from grasping the demon's sword.

With the burning tree branch still in his hand, Luke pointed at Surtr and again made a stabbing motion. Chimera turned around to see Surtr standing up behind him. The hybrid roared and then he drove Surtr's own sword into his chest. The Dark One screamed as he grabbed at the sword. Luke and Chimera watched as the area around where the sword had entered the demon's chest turned a bright white color. The white color quickly spread across the demon's body, cracking his skin as it moved.

Luke shook his head. "Is his fire sword turning him into ice?" He had no sooner finished his sentence than the dead, rigid body of Surtr fell to the ground. When the icy form of Surtr hit the ground, it shattered into a large cloud of ice particles that blanketed the immediate area. As the ice particles fell onto the raging forest fire, it doused the flames caused by Surtr. Luke looked over toward the area where Surtr was trying to ignite the super-volcano. He noticed that as the ice particles fell onto the geysers of lava, they slowly died down as well. Luke then a felt a strange cooling sensation on his face and hands. He looked at his hands to see that the ice particles were healing the burns he had suffered. Luke shifted his gaze to Chimera to see that the monster's burns seemed to be healing as well.

He shrugged at the kaiju and said, "I guess this is some kind of magic thing we are going have to ask Diana about. I am also guessing that the lack of Odin being here means something went wrong and we can't expect Zeus to teleport us. So that means we're walking out of here." Luke then grabbed his megaphone, pointed at himself, and yelled, "Chimera, pick up!" The kaiju gently reached down and placed his open hand on the ground for Luke to climb into. Luke made his way into Chimera's hand and once he was in the middle of it, Chimera lifted Luke up to his face. Luke looked down at Surtr's sword which seemed to have lost its flames. Luke shrugged. "We can't just leave the sword here either." He then directed Chimera to pick up the sword as well. Chimera was hesitant at first but when he felt that the blade was no longer giving off heat, the monster grabbed the hilt and lifted the weapon.

Luke then lifted his radio to his mouth. "Parsons, come in. Chimera has defeated Surtr. It seems as if the super-volcano has subsided as well." When only static came back over the radio Luke said "Okay, I guess that we are a bit out a range with this thing. Let's find a ranger station, get in touch with Parsons, and get you a well-deserved meal." He then pointed to the east of the forest and told Chimera to walk.

Through a portal to the Dark Dimension, Cronus watched as his brother Dark One's life force left his body. The titan could see the essence of what had once been Surtr starting to become one with the cosmos. Before Surtr's life essence could finish its transition, Cronus reached out across time and space and grasped the life essence in his hand. In his mind, Cronus could hear Surtr's life energy yearning to return to the multiverse. Cronus smiled. "No, brother, your part in this war is far from over. I told you that you will have the life energy from this world and you shall still have it, as part of me." Cronus then absorbed Surtr's life force into himself and vastly increased his already immense power.

CHAPTER 13

Adrar

Atomic Rex could feel the giant's consciousness entering his brain. This was not like the will that had tried to influence him earlier. This giant was trying to completely take over Atomic Rex's mind. The nuclear theropod could feel that his control over his own body was slipping away. The monster's consciousness was being forced into the back of his mind. While the kaiju could not fully comprehend what was occurring to him, he knew that if he did not act quickly, he would be a prisoner in his own body and a slave to the giant's will. Rage welled with Atomic Rex and he used that emotion to tap into the now unlimited supply of nuclear energy stored within his cells. The nuclear theropod lifted his leg into the air and roared in defiance at the giant. The monster slammed his leg into the ground and in doing so, he unleashed his Atomic Wave attack.

The blue dome of energy burst out of Atomic Rex's body and slammed into Odin. The heat from the blast scorched the god king's skin and the force of it sent him flying through the air. Odin was pushed several hundred feet before he crashed down into the desert. The Asgardian sat up and saw Atomic Rex roaring at him in defiance. Odin knew at that moment he would never be able to control the monster. He also realized that if left unchecked with his newly acquired power, this monster was more than capable of doing exactly what he was trying to prevent. Atomic Rex had the ability to end all life on Earth!

The god king stood and yelled, "You think you possess power, monster? Odin is power!" Odin then stretched out his hand and fired a bolt of bright yellow energy at Atomic Rex. The blast hit the kaiju in the chest and left a dark black burn mark on his scales. Odin sneered at the creature when he saw that Atomic Rex was still standing. The Asgardian took a step forward, yelled, and threw out both hands in front of himself. Twin blasts shot out of the god king's hands and this time, the blast was so large that it enveloped Atomic Rex's entire upper body. The blast knocked the kaiju backward and caused him to stumble and fall on his back.

Atomic Rex rolled over onto to his stomach to see Odin running toward him with both of his fists clenched and glowing orange with power. Atomic Rex stood up a moment before Odin was able to reach him. The saurian monster sprang forward with his jaws agape in an attempt to bite into the god's arm. Odin countered by striking the beast with an uppercut that snapped his jaws shut. Odin then landed punches to Atomic Rex's ribcage and the right side of his jaw. With each blow that Odin landed, the energy that was emanating from Odin's fists burned Atomic Rex where they struck him.

Atomic Rex shook off the blows of the god king and then sprang forward toward him. The kaiju wrapped his powerful arms around Odin and then threw the giant to the ground. Odin landed hard on his back but as he hit the ground, the ancient warrior instinctively threw his arm up in front of his face to protect it. Odin had no sooner lifted his arm up then Atomic Rex closed his jaws around the Asgardian's forearm. Odin screamed in pain as the nuclear theropod shook his arm from side to side, driving his teeth farther into the giant's forearm with each movement. Atomic Rex pulled back hard on Odin's arm then he kicked the god hard in the ribs with his clawed foot. The kaiju's toes pierced the right side of Odin's abdomen, causing a stream of blood to flow down his side.

Odin grimaced then he landed three punches to Atomic Rex's side that forced the kaiju to release his grip. Odin then brought his fists together and once more fired twin beams of energy that knocked Atomic Rex to the ground. The Asgardian stood and grabbed Atomic Rex by the legs while he was still flat on his back. Then, in a display of his awesome strength, Odin pulled hard to his right and threw Atomic Rex several hundred feet across the desert. The saurian kaiju landed face first into the sand and skidded to a stop. The kaiju was in the middle of standing when Odin grabbed him by the tail. The god then pulled back hard on Atomic Rex's tail and tossed the kaiju to the ground once again.

Atomic Rex was still on the ground when Odin wrapped his muscular arms around the nuclear theropod's throat. Odin saw several news helicopters now swarming around him. The arrogant god wanted the humans to know how helpless they were before him and he knew that killing Atomic Rex would prove that point to Parsons in particular. Odin looked at the helicopters as he screamed, "This is how you die, monster! Helpless in my grasp! Unable to even utter your death moan as I crush the life out of you! Know that of all the creatures and constructs you have battled, it was Odin who—" Odin stopped boasting when he felt the skin on the arm he was using to choke Atomic Rex burning. He looked down to see the monster's scales glowing a familiar bright blue color. The god released his grip on Atomic Rex's neck just as the Atomic Wave exploded from monster's body. Odin was directly next to Atomic

Rex when the kaiju unleashed his Atomic Wave and he caught the full fury of its power. The god king was carried the full distance that the blue dome of energy traveled before he was dropped to the ground a half mile away from Atomic Rex.

Odin found himself lying face down in the desert sand as a burning sensation wracked his entire body. He looked at his right arm to see that the skin had been completely burned off it. Odin's bicep had been completely destroyed, leaving only a gaping hole with visible bone at the bottom of it. His left arm was badly burned as well but it was still functional. The injured Asgardian was making his way back to his feet when Atomic Rex closed his jaws on what was left of Odin's right arm. Odin screeched in agony as Atomic Rex tore off a piece of the hanging muscles and tendons that were still connected to his disabled arm and swallowed them.

Odin's pain turned to rage at the thought of Atomic Rex eating him while he was still alive. Odin held up his left hand and he fired a bolt of energy into Atomic Rex's face that drove the monster back from him.

A storm cloud started to form around Odin and the god felt a wave of both relief that Zeus was saving him and shame that Atomic Rex had defeated him so soundly. Odin was in the middle of being teleported when he felt a sharp pain in his shoulder. He looked down to see Atomic Rex biting into his chest and shoulder. Odin yelled, "Do not send us to Asgard!"

Chimera Base

Parsons was watching the battle from the feed provided by the helicopters that were following Atomic Rex and Odin's battle. He saw Odin and Atomic Rex vanish when they were both teleported away from Africa. Parsons yelled. "Dammit, where did they go!"

Diana rushed over to the soldier who was managing the feed from the helicopter. She put her hand on his shoulder. "Playback the last part of that video. I thought I heard Odin shout something."

The soldier compiled. As they listened to the recording Diana shouted, "I knew I heard something! He said not Asgard!" She turned to Parsons. "Start scanning the woods of northern Norway where Chimera battled Thor. That's where the portal for the Rainbow Bridge was that connected Earth and Asgard. If Zeus was trying to send Odin back home, it's possible he was going to retrace the path of the Rainbow Bridge. If Zeus had to stop teleporting Odin and Atomic Rex halfway through the process, then they may have been dropped back in those same woods!"

Parsons nodded. "Good thinking." He yelled out to everyone in the hangar, "Start scanning northern Norway for any signs of radioactive blasts! If Atomic Rex is fighting Odin up there, that's the best way we can find them!"

Norway

Odin came crashing down into an area of a vast forest where all of the trees had been crushed flat from the battle between his son and Chimera. Thor had survived his fight with Chimera but as Atomic Rex tore out a mouthful of flesh from his right shoulder, Odin began to suspect that this might be his final stand. Atomic Rex was in the middle of swallowing another mouthful of Odin's flesh when the god kicked the reptile in the stomach. Odin then threw a left hook that slammed into Atomic Rex's jaw and knocked the monster to the ground.

Odin was standing above Atomic Rex and he was about the kick the monster when he suddenly felt dizzy and fell to one knee. The god king looked at the blood pouring out of his body and he realized that he would not live much longer. Atomic Rex stood and he was glaring at the god king, waiting for him to expose his throat.

Odin tried to scream but the most he could muster was a barely audible whisper as he reached up with his remaining hand and grabbed the patch that covered his missing eye. "I traded this eye a long time ago, monster. I traded it for knowledge. Know now that knowledge is indeed power." Odin lifted the eye patch and from beneath it a vortex of swirling black energy shot out and totally enveloped Atomic Rex.

Atomic Rex roared in anguish as what physicists know as Dark Energy tore into his body. Odin's body tilted from side to side as he tried to stay alive long enough for the Dark Energy pouring out of his eye socket to slay Atomic Rex. Odin whispered, "For Asgard, for my children, though I may die, today you fall, monster."

Atomic Rex was experiencing a level of pain that exceeded anything he had felt before. He could feel his scales being torn off his body. The vortex of Dark Energy was pushing him backward and destroying everything around him. The very ground on which Atomic Rex was standing on was disintegrating beneath his feet, causing the monster to lose his balance and fall over. Atomic Rex was completely surrounded by darkness and overwhelmed by pain. The saurian monster roared in defiance of his own demise and then he unleashed his Atomic Wave in attempt to free himself from the agony he was in.

Odin watched as a bright blue light formed within the all-consuming darkness of his attack. The god king sighed in disbelief as a blue dome of energy began to force its way out of the vortex of Dark Energy. The last thing that Odin saw was his own Dark Energy being pushed back onto him by the Atomic Wave. A wall of Dark Energy backed by nuclear power moved toward Odin. Through his one eye, the god king briefly saw the overlapping wave of nuclear and Dark Energy take on the form of a giant wolf's head with its jaws open. Odin's last thoughts were of Ragnarok and the prophecy that he would die in the jaws of Fenrir the wolf. The wave of opposing energies washed over Odin, destroying what was left of his skin and ending his supposedly immortal life.

Atomic Rex opened his eyes to find himself half buried in dirt and rock. The kaiju had bad burns and deep wounds all over his body. He pulled himself out of the pit to see the remains of Odin laying on the ground. As he was walking toward the dead god, the mutated dinosaur could already feel his advanced healing abilities beginning to repair the wounds he had suffered.

The healing process was costly on Atomic Rex's body and he knew that he would need rest and food in order for his body to completely recover. The monster walked over to what remained of Odin and began devouring the remains of the Asgardian. After he had eaten his fill, Atomic Rex laid down in the quiet woods. He could still sense the other presence like those that had tried to control him to the north. The monster pushed the thought of the other creature aside and drifted to sleep.

Chimera Base

Parsons and Diana were standing at the control center of Chimera Base, waiting for any sign as to where Odin and Atomic Rex may have been transported to. In front of them, dozens of soldiers silently searched the incoming information that would indicate the location of their targets. After several minutes of silence, one of the soldiers shouted, "Sir, I have a reading of a small radioactive blast from the woods of northern Norway!"

Parsons nodded. "Put it on the main screen." When the feed came up to reveal Atomic Rex devouring what looked like the charred corpse of Odin, Diana pumped her fist in triumph. "Yes, they are in the exact spot where Chimera battled Thor." She turned to Parsons. "At least we know that Atomic Rex is in a spot where it will take him a day or two to reach any highly populated area."

Another soldier called out, "Sir, I have Luke Davis calling in from a ranger station in Yellowstone Park. He confirmed what we saw through the satellite video. Chimera has slain Surtr and retrieved his sword. He also says that with Surtr's death, the super-volcano seems to have returned to its natural state and that many of the fires burning in the park have gone out."

Diana smiled. "There's some good news that we can build from!"

A call came from soldier manning a computer station on the far side of the hangar. "General Parsons, I have an abnormal energy reading coming from the Arctic! I am patching it through to the main screen now!"

Parsons looked over at Diana. "Isn't it you who is always telling me not to talk about Fight Club?" Diana smiled and shrugged.

An image appeared on the screen of the dragon Tiamat standing on the Arctic ice near the shoreline. The ancient dragon was moving across a glacier and blasting it with fire. The fire spewing out of the dragon's mouth suddenly split into two beams. At first, the people watching from Chimera Base couldn't understand how the split flame was occurring. It wasn't until Tiamat's neck and head began shaking that they saw why there were twin beams coming from the dragon. Tiamat's shaking head and neck suddenly split into two separate and unique heads. The flames coming from the two heads suddenly split into four beams as the heads split once more into four distinct heads. The heads continued to split until Tiamat had seven unique heads all spewing fire in a three-hundred-and-sixty-degree radius.

Everyone watching the screen could see what was happening as the ice around Tiamat turned to first to slush and then to water. Once he had melted everything within reach of his fiery breath, the dragon began moving forward and melting more ice.

Parsons voiced the concern that everyone was thinking. "We need to know how long it will take him to melt enough of the polar ice caps to cause catastrophic damage to the planet." Several soldiers and scientific advisors began running calculations and simulations on the effect Tiamat was having on the ice caps.

Diana was staring at the screen as she shook her head in disbelief. "He has seven heads. Just like the dragon in Revelations."

One of the advisors came running over to Parsons. "Sir, if Tiamat continues to melt ice at the rate he is now, the world will face dire consequences in forty-eight hours for coastal regions and worldwide flooding within seventy-two hours."

Parsons sighed. "We haven't seen Zeus since he and Odin betrayed us. Even if he did show up, we can't trust him anymore, which means that we can't just teleport Chimera up there to battle Tiamat." Parsons looked at the map to see that Hudson Bay and the nearly finished *Hudson* carrier were between Chimera and Tiamat. Parson called out to the people who were tracking Luke and Chimera's movements. "What if we could get Chimera to the *Hudson*? Would it be able to reach Tiamat before it was too late?"

Several more simulations were run and one of the advisors yelled back to Parsons, "No, sir. We would still fall short of our deadline by five hours."

Parsons shook his head. "We can assume conventional weapons won't stop Tiamat. There is the nuclear option, but would dropping a nuclear bomb up there cause even more damage than the Dark One?"

Diana ran over to Parsons. "There may be another way! A small nuclear attack that we could send toward Tiamat. Atomic Rex is already in Norway. He could reach the Arctic in a day if we were to lead him there!" Diana smiled. "It's a classic monster movie theme! If you have two monsters that are a threat, bring them together and have them fight each other! At worst, eliminating one and weakening the other or at best killing them both!"

Parsons frowned. "Tiamat is one of the Dark Ones who were trying to control Atomic Rex."

Diana shook her head. "No, we can bring back up the audio of when Odin was talking to Atomic Rex. He said the Dark Ones tried to control you and they have failed. Atomic Rex is no longer under their control. Everything that we know about Atomic Rex suggests that he is extremely aggressive. I firmly believe that if we draw Atomic Rex to Tiamat, they will fight. Atomic Rex just tore freaking Odin to pieces! If there is anything on this planet that can stop Tiamat, it's Atomic Rex!"

Parsons was staring at Diana as he considered his options. The mythology professor threw her hands up in the air. "Look, you can always nuke the North Pole if this doesn't work, but it's the safer option and could kill two birds with one stone."

Parsons nodded as a plan formed in his head. "All right, this is what we are going to do. We are going to address all of our remaining issues in a two-phase plan. Phase one, have Chimera continue to head in a northwest direction toward Tiamat. We also attack Atomic Rex and draw him to the Arctic and into what is hopefully a confrontation with the Dark One. If Tiamat kills Atomic Rex, then we use the nuclear option. If Atomic Rex wins, we continue to track his movements. The limited intel we have on the monster suggests that his ultimate goal is still to come here to North America. Should that plan hold true, we will already have Chimera on an intercept course with Atomic Rex. Also, we load our portal to Asgard on a cargo plane and have it fly on an intercept course with Chimera."

Parsons stopped and took a deep breath. "Phase two of our plan will go as follows. I want our portal to Asgard up and running as soon as possible. With Odin dead, we can assume that Thor is now in charge there. We will contact him and inform him of my intention to carry out the threat I made to his father for betraying us. We are either going to have Chimera force, Atomic Rex through the portal or if Atomic Rex dies fighting Tiamat, then we are sending Chimera through the portal. If Atomic Rex fights Chimera and defeats him then we will try to use helicopters to lure Atomic Rex through the portal to Asgard. Thor can then either deal with consequences of his father's betrayal or if it's within his power, he can send whichever monster goes through the portal directly to Cronus."

Diana nodded. "Now that is a plan right out of a monster movie."

Parsons smiled and shouted, "All right everyone, now we all know the plan. Diana, I want you with me and the squad that is prepping the portal. Have them load our portal onto a carrier jet. We are heading directly to Luke. When we reach Luke, we'll secure Surtr's sword and inform him of the plan. From there, we will follow Chimera until he engages Atomic Rex, or we hear that the dinosaur is dead. Either way, make sure the portal is ready to send a kaiju through it."

Diana nodded. "On it! I just need to grab a few things while they are loading the portal onto the plane!" She then turned and ran out of the hangar.

Parsons then yelled out to his communications team, "I want whatever aerial forces we have in Northern Europe making a bombing run at Atomic Rex to draw him to the North Pole ASAP! Have a second retrieval unit ready to go in and get Thor's belt as soon as Atomic Rex has left the area."

The general scratched his head for a moment and then he added one more command, "Also, keep an eye out for any atmospheric anomalies that could be Zeus. He has a lot to answer for and I doubt that his part in this war is over yet!"

CHAPTER 14

Norway

Captain George Travis was stationed at the joint Alconbury RAF/USAF Base when he was contacted by General Parsons and given the order to fly over Norway and to attack the kaiju designated Atomic Rex. His job was to lure the monster to the Arctic and lead him into a confrontation with the Dark One known as Tiamat who was trying to melt the polar ice caps and effectively end the human race.

Travis relayed the orders to his team. He didn't have to explicitly tell them that the fate of the world depended on their success. Travis took some small comfort in the fact that he and his squad were not trying to kill Atomic Rex but rather just to anger him and point him in the right direction. He had already seen the footage of the kaiju slaying both the Griffin and the Phoenix. The last images that they had of the monster's battle with Odin seemed to indicate that he had just about killed him as well.

Travis had seen Chimera live and he had an appreciation for how powerful the hybrid was. From what he heard, Chimera had barely managed to defeat Thor when they fought several years prior. Travis figured that Odin had to be as powerful if not more powerful than Thor. It was clear to Travis that Atomic Rex was far more powerful than Odin, which in Travis' mind, suggested that Atomic Rex was even stronger than Chimera. Any creature with that type of power was something that Travis wanted to avoid directly engaging if at all possible.

Travis had been leading his fellow pilots over the vast and beautiful forests of Norway when they saw the destruction caused by their target ahead of them. Travis decided that it would be prudent to fly past the target once before attacking him. Flying over the monster would give Travis and the rest of his fellow pilots a chance to see with their own eyes exactly what they were up against. Travis shook his head in disbelief as he flew past Atomic Rex. The monster looked absolutely terrifying and the sense of dread that the beast gave off was accentuated by the burned and eaten remains of Odin that were lying on the ground next to him.

After flying by the target, Travis began to circle back around. He called out to the pilots under his command, "Okay, boys, let's piss that thing off and get him to chase us to the freaking North Pole!" Travis then armed his bombs and began decreasing in altitude. Travis' hands were sweating as he pulled the release for his payload. The deadliest creature on earth was asleep below him and it was Travis' duty to wake up the monster and aggravate it enough to chase him to the end of the world. Travis bowed his head and said a quick prayer for the success of his mission and the safety of squadron. As his bombs were falling toward Atomic Rex, Travis wondered how much sense it made to pray for protection from a monster that had already killed a god.

Atomic Rex had been sleeping for roughly two hours when he heard a high-pitched noise coming from above him. The nuclear theropod opened his eyes and looked skyward to see roughly a half dozen jets flying overhead. He also saw smaller objects falling from the jets as they flew over him. Atomic Rex stood just as the first bomb exploded against his back. The first explosion was followed by dozens of other explosions that occurred both on and around him. None of the explosions were capable of injuring the near indestructible monster, but they did cause him pain and anger him.

Atomic Rex roared in anger at this newest attack as the jets flew past him. The monster's anger grew as he watched the jets circle around and head back toward him. As the jets were approaching for a second time, they opened fire with their machine guns. The large-scale bullets bounced off Atomic Rex's thick hide without penetrating it, but once more, the attack caused the monster pain. Atomic Rex watched as the jets circled around him and headed north. The jets were racing over the horizon when Atomic Rex roared in defiance and then sprinted after them. The second that Atomic Rex sprinted away, a blonde woman with the figure of a supermodel stepped out the trees. Allison walked over to the still-smoking corpse of Odin. The nymph knelt down next to the remains of the god and she smiled. "With you out of the way, and Chimera fighting the Dark Ones, everything I planned is falling into place. All of that time I spent on my back for you and the other gods, you never put any thought into what I was capable of." Her thin hand reached out and grabbed Thor's belt. "With this is in our possession, Zeus will come looking for me." Allison stood up and laughed. "When he finds us, he is going to fall as well. With the gods out of the way, the other players on the board will weaken themselves to the point that we shall sweep in and destroy the victor. Then the world will be mine to deal with as I see fit." Allison then disappeared with the belt, leaving only the charred remains of Odin behind.

Travis and the other men in his squadron were tracking Atomic Rex on their radars after they had flown over him. Travis called out over the radio, "Okay, boys, we may need to slow down a little. We want to make sure we are not moving so fast that Atomic Rex can't follow us."

One of the other pilots responded to Travis' direction. "I don't think that will be a problem, sir. According to my radar, the monster is actually gaining on us." Prior to coming to this world, Atomic Rex was able to run at incredible speeds for long periods of time, but since he had consumed both the Phoenix and Odin, the monster's speed and stamina were beyond belief. The monster was leaving a path of crushed trees in his wake as he sprinted after the fleeing jets moving at a speed of over five hundred miles per hour.

Atomic Rex chased the jets for roughly a half an hour, until they reached the coast of the Norwegian Sea. The monster took two steps into the water and then he stopped while the jets continued to fly in a northern direction.

Captain Travis noted that Atomic Rex had stopped moving. He called out to the rest of his squadron. "We are going to have to loop back around and engage that monster again to get him to follow us into the water."

Travis decreased his altitude to only a few hundred feet above sea level. He then flew directly at Atomic Rex and aimed two missiles at the nuclear theropod. Travis pulled back on his trigger and watched as his missiles went streaking toward Atomic Rex. His missiles were quickly followed by those fired by his fellow pilots. Travis watched as Atomic Rex's body was rocked with explosions. Travis flew his jet directly over Atomic Rex as the smoke from the attack was clearing. For a brief second that seemed like an eternity, Travis found himself looking into Atomic Rex's eye. As he was staring into the monster's eye, Travis could see the monster's rage at their continued attacks. At that point, the pilot had no doubt that Atomic Rex would follow them to the Arctic and beyond.

Travis led his squadron back out over the sea and called out, "Fly just above the water, boys. We want to make sure that Atomic Rex can see us so that he can follow us to the target."

Atomic Rex watched as the jets flew out over the water and this time, the monster dove into the sea after them. The monster was now determined to destroy the tiny machines that had attacked him. Atomic Rex dove into the water in pursuit of the jets, unaware that once again he was being drawn into a battle with another creature with the fate of the human race hanging in the balance.

Once Travis was sure that Atomic Rex had followed them into the water, he called back to base, "Atomic Rex is on his way to intercept

Tiamat. You can send the retrieval team in after the secondary target, over."

North Dakota

Luke and Chimera were following Parsons' last orders and continuing to head north. Chimera was still carrying Luke in one hand and Surtr's sword in the other. They had just about reached the Canadian border and Luke was beginning to worry if there would be an issue with Chimera entering another country carrying a giant sword. Luke was trying to decide what he would say to the Canadian border patrol when he saw a US military transport plane fly low past Chimera. The plane shot out flares that Luke was pretty sure was a signal for him and Chimera to follow. Luke looked up from the palm of the Chimera's hand at the kaiju's face. He was glad to see that Chimera was looking down at him for direction. Luke grabbed his megaphone, pointed at the plane and shouted, "Chimera, follow."

The monster grunted and then he began lumbering off in the direction of the plane. The plane was flying as slow as it was able to and it occasionally circled around so that Chimera could follow it at a leisurely pace. At full sprint, Chimera might have been able to keep pace with the plane but if he was moving that fast, he would have inadvertently crushed Luke to death.

The monster followed the plane to the Grand Forks Air Force Base. The plane landed and Chimera walked up next to it. Then at Luke's command, the kaiju placed his hand on the ground so that his trainer could climb out of it. Luke slid out of Chimera's hand as five forklifts pulled up to the back of the plane. The plane lowered its rear hatch and a horrible but familiar smell wafted out of the back of the plane. The second the odor reached Chimera, the monster began salivating.

Luke looked at Chimera to see the monster staring expectantly at him. Luke smiled as the first forklift drove onto the truck and came out with a pallet full of the massive cubes of beef, squid, and bamboo that were Chimera's food source. Luke grabbed his megaphone and shouted, "You did good, Chimera!" He then pointed at the growing pile of food being dropped off by the forklifts. "Eat! You have earned it!"

Chimera sat down and began devouring the food cubes as Diana Cain came walking out of the plane with her hands behind her back. When Luke saw Diana, he immediately ran toward her with his arms open to hug his friend. Diana saw him coming for her and she held out her right hand and yelled, "Stop! I have orders that you need hear before you come any closer to me!"

Luke stopped running and raised his eyebrow as he addressed his friend, "Orders from Parsons?"

Diana shook her head. "No, he is getting ready to have a chat with Thor. Your orders come from a higher authority!" She pulled her other hand from behind her back to reveal a pair of jeans, a T-shirt, and a flannel shirt. She said, "Your wife says that you need to take a quick shower and change while Chimera is eating before you talk to me. She said she can only imagine how bad you smell after being in Chimera's palm all day, and that there was no way she was going to let you walk around smelling like that!"

Luke laughed and he quickly sniffed his shirt which had the fish-like smell that Chimera gave off. He jogged over to Diana and took the clothes from her. "Can I assume that when we return home, you will inform Melissa that I followed her orders explicitly?"

Diana laughed. "That depends on how much you get on my nerves for the rest of this mission. So, you had better be on your best behavior if you want me to give her a good report."

Luke smiled. "I'll try." He then ran toward the base for a much-needed shower.

Luke was able to shower and change his clothes in just under fifteen minutes. Luke quickly slapped his sneakers on then he jogged back out to where Chimera had been eating. He was slightly surprised when he saw Chimera's back toward him and about three dozen armed soldiers standing in front of the kaiju also with their backs toward him. It was clear that they were all looking at something, but Luke couldn't see around Chimera to determine what had their attention. Luke could tell that Chimera was tense and the soldiers were obviously at the ready as well. When he finally reached Chimera's leg, he was able to see what the soldiers were all looking at. The portal to Asgard had been set up and it was functional. The portal consisted of two forty-foot-tall pillars which created some kind of space bridge between Earth and Asgard. In between the two pillars, Luke could see a bit of a distortion. He walked closer to the distortion and when he saw who was on the other side of it, Luke knew why Chimera was on edge. Parsons was standing on the Earth-bound side of the portal with Diana next to him with the soldiers and more importantly, Chimera behind him. On the other side of the portal was the god that Chimera had battled several years ago and the new king of Asgard.

Luke realized that he had walked into the middle of the conversation when he heard Parsons yelling, "That is what we are going to do. The previous king of Asgard broke our treaty with him and we shall follow through on the consequence we gave him for breaking that treaty. If you are able to redirect the attack toward another mutual foe of ours, then we are fine with that course of action. Be assured, however, that as soon as the threat of Tiamat has been addressed, we will be sending a kaiju to Asgard."

Thor grumbled, "You are being a fool, Parsons. Return my belt to me. Then I shall work with your monster to battle both Tiamat and Cronus. Together, we shall crush the Dark Ones and Atomic Rex!"

Parsons shook his head. "Then with your belt, you can attack us again. I am sorry, we are not at liberty to give you that opportunity. Make whatever preparations you see fit, but I would highly advise that you find a way to send the kaiju that comes through the portal to Cronus. When you had your belt of power and all your monsters, you were not able to defeat Chimera. I shudder to think what he or an uncontrolled Atomic Rex would do to Asgard now. We suspect that you have roughly twenty-four hours before a kaiju is at the gates of your city. Be thankful that we gave you the warning that you didn't offer us."

Parsons then signaled for the portal to be closed. After the portal had closed, Luke had made his way up to Parsons. "Wow, I want to be sure that I never piss you off."

Parsons only nodded in reply as another soldier came running over to him. "Sir, we have a report that the retrieval team has reached Odin's body, but they are reporting that the belt is not there."

Parsons shrugged. "Were there any signs of weather anomalies around Odin's body?"

The soldier shook his head. "No, sir. No anomalies of any kind reported. The belt is just gone."

Luke jumped into the conversation. "So, we don't think it was Zeus then who grabbed the belt?"

Diana nodded. "As far as we know, every time that Zeus has teleported us or anyone else, he has used a mystical storm cloud."

Parsons rubbed his temples. "Does this mean that Cronus has the belt now? Are we looking at fighting an enhanced version of him now as well?"

Diana sighed and frowned. "We will know soon enough if Cronus took the belt, but there is another possibility. Allison could have taken it."

Luke eyes went wide. "Allison, as in the nymph who kidnapped all of those men to breed with goddesses? Allison who turned Toombs against us? Allison who kidnapped all of those women who were pregnant with demi-gods?"

Diana nodded. "The one and the same. If it was her, she now has a man capable of making a monster as powerful as Chimera, twenty-some, two-year-old demi-gods who we don't know how fast they reach maturity, and a belt that makes anyone who wears it infinitely more powerful. Oh, and did I mention that we have no idea where she is?"

Parsons nodded. "We will worry about Allison later. Right now, we have to make sure that Atomic Rex engages Tiamat and then worry about the next step of dealing with both him and the Dark Ones after the conclusion of their battle." He turned to the soldier who had given him the information about the belt. "Get me an update on the progress of luring Atomic Rex to Tiamat." The soldier saluted and then ran back to his communications post.

The Arctic

Travis received the communication just as a massive swirling pillar of fire came into view. The flames presented an odd sight with the white Arctic ice and the grey sky it was set against. He radioed back, "Tell General Parsons that we've arrived in the Arctic, we have visual on Tiamat, and Atomic Rex is in pursuit." Travis then changed his radio over to the channel his squadron was using. "That's got to be our target, boys. We are going to circle around him and draw Atomic Rex right into him." Travis flew over the ring of fire and he looked down as the seven heads of Tiamat spun in all different directions, spewing fire everywhere and melting the ice around him at an alarming rate. The one good thing for Travis and his men was that Tiamat appeared to be so preoccupied with what he was doing that he didn't notice the jets circling above him.

Atomic Rex was doing his best to move through the now slushy terrain of the Arctic. The kaiju had chased the jets that attacked him across a forest and a sea. Now the objects of Atomic Rex's anger were circling above a wall of fire and the nuclear theropod was determined to finally destroy them. Atomic Rex roared and then charged fearlessly into the raging wall of fire. Atomic Rex passed through the flames relatively unscathed, but the moment that he came out of the wall of fire, he slammed into Tiamat and knocked the serpent to the ground.

Tiamat was both stunned and surprised that something had passed through his flames and attacked him. All seven of the serpents' multifaceted heads sprung up and hissed at whatever had dared to attack him.

Atomic Rex was shaking his head to try and clear it from the unexpected impact when he suddenly found Tiamat's heads hissing at him. The kaiju was immediately able to detect that this creature was not only challenging him, but that it was also the creature he had sensed previously. This creature was like the other one which had tried to control him.

With the knowledge that this creature was like the one that had tried to control him, Atomic Rex forgot about the jets that had pestered him. The kaiju reared back and roared at Tiamat. The saurian kaiju then leapt forward and closed his jaws on the closest of Tiamat's seven necks.

Travis radioed back to base. "We can confirm that Atomic Rex has engaged Tiamat."

By this time, Parsons was live on the other side of the radio. "Good. Move away from directly over the monsters but circle the area for as long as you can and keep us posted on the battle."

Travis acknowledged Parsons orders and then he carried them out.

CHAPTER 15

The Arctic

Atomic Rex bit down into one of Tiamat's necks that ended in a goat-like face. The goat face bleated in pain while the other six heads all turned on the saurian kaiju and unleashed their flames on him. Tiamat's mystical flames scored Atomic Rex's scales and the monster realized that he would not be able to withstand them for long. Refusing to withdraw from his attack without making it worthwhile, Atomic Rex bit down hard on the goat-head neck and used his claws to slash at it. Atomic Rex endured the barrage of Tiamat's flames for several more seconds during which he continued to ravage the goat-head's neck. When the kaiju could no longer stand the mystical flames, he pulled away from Tiamat with his jaws still latched onto the neck.

There was a wet popping sound as Atomic Rex tore the goat head from Tiamat's body at the midpoint of its neck. The six remaining heads of the monster looked up into the air and shrieked in pain at the loss of the other head. Atomic Rex pulled the dead goat head from his mouth and then charged his injured opponent. The nuclear theropod slammed into Tiamat's torso with enough force to move the ancient dragon back nearly fifty feet. Atomic Rex then bit down onto another of Tiamat's heads at the base of the neck while simultaneously using his claws to rake the dragon's chest.

Blood poured out of the base of the neck that Atomic Rex was attacking and his claws were tearing long strips of flesh from Tiamat's torso. Tiamat could sense that he was about lose another of his heads so he used the remaining five to wrap around Atomic Rex.

With Atomic Rex in the ever-tightening grasp of his heads, Tiamat lifted the kaiju off the ground. The Dark One then threw Atomic Rex to his right. The saurian monster flew for several hundred feet before he hit the icy ground and slid along it for another hundred feet.

When Atomic Rex finally stopped sliding, he looked up to the see the blood-soaked form of Tiamat coming toward him. The dragon stopped just short of Atomic Rex's reach and then all six remaining heads opened their mouths and together unleashed a wall of flames.

Atomic Rex's scales began to crack and peel away from the intense heat that was assaulting them. The monster's body was in incredible pain, but his mind was overrun with anger. Atomic Rex had been taken from a world in which he was the undisputed ruler of two continents and placed on a similar but vastly different version of his home. The monster's mind was then assaulted by a creature who sought to dominate him for his own ends. These were offenses that Atomic Rex would not abide. With Tiamat's mystical flames burning his body, Atomic Rex roared and stood up. He then took one agonizing step forward after another forcing his way through Tiamat's barrage. When he had closed half the distance between himself and Tiamat, Atomic Rex leapt forward.

Tiamat's eyes went wide with fear and disbelief when they saw Atomic Rex's jaws coming out of the maelstrom of flames. The mutated tyrannosaur crashed down into Tiamat with enough force to knock the Dark One onto his back. Atomic Rex was standing on top of Tiamat with the dragon pinned beneath him. Tiamat's heads were flailing and spewing flames in every direction in an attempt to force the monster off him.

Atomic Rex roared as he stood atop of the fallen dragon and then he lashed out with his claws and tail. Atomic Rex spun from left to right, swiping at Tiamat's heads and necks with his claws and swatting them aside with his tail. When Atomic Rex had first pinned Tiamat to the ground, he was still being sprayed by the flames emitting from the dragon's mouths. As Atomic Rex continued his attack, the flames died out and were replaced by blood flying out of the wounds Atomic Rex had torn open with his claws.

Tiamat abandoned his flame attack and once again used his remaining heads and necks to wrap around Atomic Rex. Two of Tiamat's heads wrapped around Atomic Rex's arms, restraining the monster from using his claws to cause further damage. The dragon then used two more of his heads to ensnare the nuclear theropod's tail and prevent it from striking him. With his final two heads, Tiamat reached up and latched his jaws onto Atomic Rex's neck.

Blood poured out of the kaiju's neck as Tiamat tried to rip out his jugular and cut off his oxygen supply. Atomic Rex shook his head and pulled with his arms in an attempt to free himself from Tiamat's necks, but the Dark One's grip held firm. Atomic Rex continued to struggle against Tiamat's grip until blood loss and an inability to breath caused the kaiju's head to slump down. The monster was blacking out when his eyes fell upon his clawed feet pressing down into Tiamat's stomach. Seeing his chance of breaking the dragon's hold, Atomic Rex lifted his foot into the air and then he drove his clawed toes into Tiamat's stomach. Blood gushed out of the gaping wound in Tiamat's gut as all of his heads released their hold on Atomic Rex and hissed in pain. With his arms and mouth free, Atomic Rex lashed out.

His jaws shot forward and closed on one Tiamat's heads that had the visage of a moray eel. With two quick bites, the nuclear theropod crushed the skull of the eel head and then let it slip lifelessly from his mouth. Another head with a hood like that of a cobra around it sank its fangs into Atomic Rex's leg. The saurian monster retaliated by slashing at its neck with his claws and decapitating the hooded head.

With half of his heads gone and massive amounts of blood being lost from various wounds, Tiamat tried to free himself from beneath the crushing weight of Atomic Rex. The dragon first attempted to throw Atomic Rex off of him by rolling to his side. When Atomic Rex felt the dragon's weight shifting beneath him, he lifted his leg and drove his clawed foot into the dragon's torso for a second time. With his claws embedded in the Tiamat's stomach, Atomic Rex pushed his foot forward and then pulled it up.

As Atomic Rex's foot lifted up from within Tiamat's body, it pulled most of the Dark One's intestines out with it. Tiamat's remaining heads all shot straight up into the air where they wailed like the sirens of myth for several seconds before they fell to the ground, devoid of any life.

Once Atomic Rex felt that Tiamat had finished struggling beneath him, the mutated dinosaur lifted his head into the sky and roared. Atomic Rex climbed off Tiamat with blood still oozing out of the wounds from his jugular. The kaiju took several off-balance steps and then he finally collapsed onto the ice. Atomic Rex closed his eyes and fell asleep which allowed his nuclear powers to focus on healing his badly damaged body.

Captain Travis flew over the remains of Tiamat and the resting Atomic Rex. He radioed back to Chimera Base, "General Parsons, Atomic Rex has slain Tiamat. I believe that he's resting now. It appears that the Arctic is safe for now."

Parsons' voice came back over the radio. "Excellent work, Captain. We are sending coordinates to the nearest base. You are to refuel there and then head home."

"Copy that, sir." When the coordinates for the refueling base reached Travis, he forwarded them to the rest of his squadron and then flew away from Arctic.

Several minutes after the jets had sped away, Cronus opened a portal above Tiamat's body and consumed the ancient dragon's lifeforce, adding the creature's power to his own. With the power of his fellow Dark Ones infused in his body, Cronus opened a portal to the Atlantic Ocean. He gazed down at the water. "I underestimated Atomic Rex's will power. I will never be able to control that creature, but there is still a beast whose power can be unleashed that is greater than Atomic Rex or Chimera. Once I locate and set him free, it will be the end of everything. Men, monsters, gods, only the creature will be left. We have feared him in the past as none of us possessed the power to stand against him. With your energy added to my own, I might possess the power to survive the creature's rampage across the planet long enough to absorb the lives of those he kills. Once I have absorbed enough life energy to surpass the creature's power, I shall slay him and take his strength as well." Cronus then stepped through his portal and began walking along the surface of the Atlantic Ocean.

CHAPTER 16

Boreal Forest, Ontario, Canada

The sun was setting as Luke and Diana finished setting up camp. They had flown to a nearby military base with Chimera following them at a much faster pace than he was able to while carrying Luke in his hand. After covering several hundred miles, Chimera was tired and in need of rest. While the Canadian government was fairly accommodating to having Chimera within their borders, both the base commander and Luke felt that it would be better for all parties if Chimera slept in the nearby woods instead of on the base.

Luke, of course, decided to camp out with Chimera as a precaution against the monster inadvertently causing damage to an area that he was unfamiliar with. Diana offered to accompany her friend so that he would not be alone with the fate of the world once more resting heavily on him. The two of them packed up two tents, amongst comments from several of the soldiers who were with them that only one of the tents would be set up, and headed out into the forest in a jeep with Chimera following them.

When they were several miles away from any populated area, they set camp. Once Chimera saw that Luke was resting, the exhausted monster wandered off into the woods and quickly fell asleep.

Luke and Diana could hear Chimera snoring through the woods as the last rays of the sun slid away. Once the sun had completely set, Diana built a fire that she and Luke sat around.

Diana could see that Luke was nearly as exhausted as Chimera, but she could also see that her friend needed to talk. "Parsons is still going with what the gods had suggested about Atomic Rex coming to North America?"

Luke nodded. "I don't know if Parsons believes the gods or not, but at the very least he thinks that Atomic Rex is too dangerous to run free. He figures that Atomic Rex and Chimera are bound to be on a collision course at some point and better to have it happen in an area with as few people as possible. Having Chimera take on Atomic Rex and hopefully send him to Asgard to either take out what's left of the gods, or have them send the monster after Cronus, is the best way to kill three birds with one stone."

Diana nodded. "We will reach the Hudson Bay tomorrow and the *Argo*'s sister ship, the *Hudson*. The *Hudson* will allow us to move Chimera to an intercept point for Atomic Rex fairly quickly."

Luke turned away from Diana and stared blankly at the fire.

Diana moved over next to Luke and placed her hand on his shoulder. "You miss Melissa and the girls, don't you?"

Luke smiled. "I am easy to read as an open book, I suppose." He shrugged. "I really hate downtime like this. At least when we are fighting monsters, I don't really have time to think about it. When we are trying to get to the next fight is when I miss them." He turned his head away from the fire. "It's not just that I miss them. It's that I feel like I am robbing them of time with me. I mean, what if I die while Chimera is fighting Atomic Rex? What if he walks across the world laying waste to it as he did his own and I am not there to protect my family? What if we stop Atomic Rex, but it still costs me my life and the girls never see me again? I have always told myself that when I died, if I did so with my girls around looking at me as if they were going to miss me but that they enjoyed our time together, then I would know I gave them all that I had. I want them to be sure that I loved them more than anything. That even when it didn't seem like it, they were my first priority." Luke began to tear up. "If I die in this battle, will they think that, or will they think their dad preferred to be out playing hero with his monster rather than spending time with them?" He shook his head. "When I first agreed to train Chimera, I honestly thought it would be a one-time thing. That we would fight the gods and it would be over. I didn't think that we would have to fight the Dark Ones, that monsters from parallel worlds could be an issue, and then there's Allison and Toombs still out there with twenty-some demi-gods and the brains to make a new monster." He held out his hands. "Is this going to be my life from now on? Leading Chimera into fight after fight until we come up against something that he cannot defeat? All at the expense of my relationship with my wife and daughters in an attempt to make the world safe when now it looks like it will never be safe?"

Diana leaned over and hugged her friend, and then she put her hands on his cheeks and looked him in the eyes. "I can understand your pain and fears. Please understand that while I understand them, I can assure you that they are groundless. You and I have been friends for two years now and the main thing you have learned from me is what good comic book stories are." She smiled which caused Luke to smile. "You have taught me so much more. You taught me about your vast knowledge about how to shape behaviors and how to set up a situation for the best possible outcome. You have taught me that being proactive and looking for ways to address a problem before it happens is the best way to deal with issues." Diana started to tear up as well. "You have shown me not only that there are still good men in the world, you have shown me what it means to be one of those men." She placed her forehead against Luke's forehead. "Before I met you, I would never have thought that I could be this close physically or emotionally to a man, without him thinking that I wanted more from him. I never would have thought I could feel so close to a member of the opposite sex without having sexual feelings toward him. The reason that we can be such good friends without any of that tension is because of the love that you have for your wife and kids." She pulled away from him. "That love and knowledge is why you are out here now. The best way to protect your family is by stopping something horrible from happening to them when you can. The girls and Melissa know this. They know how much you love them. They know that you are out here fighting for them. Most of all they know because you spend as much free time as you can with them. They know because you listen to them." She pulled her hands away from his face. "I am sure that they know this because it's the same things you do for me. I don't get to spend as much time with my best friend as I would like but when I do, you make sure it's worthwhile."

Luke reached out hugged Diana. "Thanks. I needed that." He pulled away and smiled. "You know, this whole saving the world thing takes its toll. Even the few perfect men like me are affected by it."

Diana punched him in the arm. "All right, don't let that all go to your head."

The two of them laughed. They didn't laugh at Diana's meager joke. It was more a laugh to release the stress and tension that was building inside of them from being on the front lines in war with gods and monsters.

Luke cracked his neck and rolled his shoulders. He then leaned back a little and smiled at Diana. "Enough about me sobbing and feeling sorry for myself. What's going on with you? Parsons mentioned something about getting a good Fantastic Four movie made so you could go on a date with a helicopter pilot?" Diana's face turned a bright shade of red and Luke laughed. "I am sure that he over exaggerated the story. So please fill me in on what really happened."

Diana smiled and shrugged. "No, that's a pretty spot on account of what happened."

Luke sat up in surprise and laughed. "Really! Now this is a story I need hear."

The Arctic

Darkness had fallen over the now refrozen Arctic and the slumbering kaiju. The lights from the Aurora Borealis cascaded over the unconscious form of Atomic Rex. The polar lights bathed the monster in their shimmering luminescence, giving his radioactive scales a neon appearance.

The monster had been asleep for roughly twenty hours when his eyes suddenly snapped open. Atomic Rex's amazing healing abilities had repaired all of the damage done to his body in his battle with Tiamat. The nuclear theropod stood and roared at the lights above him. He then turned and began walking south back to the closest thing this Earth had to his home. Atomic Rex began making his way back to North America.

Atomic Rex walked along the coastline for nearly an hour before he finally stepped into the cold waters of the Arctic Ocean. The kaiju slipped beneath the water and immediately picked up speed. The reptile's powerful lower body and streamlined form allowed him to move through water with much greater speed than he could on land. At the speed he was moving, Atomic Rex was less than twelve hours from making landfall in Northern Canada.

The Atlantic Ocean

Cronus had walked for hours before he found the spot that he was looking for. The mad titan stood on the surface of the ocean and he looked down through miles of water to see the seal that held that creature he was looking to free. Despite his arrogance and vastly increased power, Cronus stopped for a moment to reconsider what he was doing. Cronus ran his fingers through his beard as he considered if even he would be capable of surviving the wrath of the creature that he was about to unleash. The creature fed off life energy just as he did, but the beast would not be satisfied with the life force from this Earth or countless others. The monster would destroy every Earth that he could access. Once he had exhausted all of the life energy from the various Earths, he would seek other dimensions and other forms of life. Cronus knew that even if he was able to survive the monster's initial release, that at some point it would come after him.

When the beast was first located millennia ago, it took the combined power of Cronus, Surtr, Tiamat, Atlas, the Kraken, and countless other

Dark Ones and monsters to seal the beast away. Many of the Dark Ones and their monsters died in the war with the creature. It was the losses from the battle with the creature that made it possible for the gods to defeat the Dark Ones. Now as Cronus was considering releasing the creature from the cell he had sealed it in, he had to consider if he would be able to siphon enough life energy away from those the beast killed to challenge the monster at some point.

Cronus silently shook his head as convinced himself that he would be capable of meeting the creature one day and killing him. Cronus knelt down on the water and he used his mystical powers to reach deep into the ocean and below it.

At the bottom of the ocean, a colossal metal symbol that stretched for several miles began to glow a bright yellow as Cronus exerted his will upon it. Cronus continued to stretch his power down to the symbol, causing it grow brighter and finally to crack in several places. The seal that Cronus and his fellow Dark Ones had placed over the primordial beast was potent. Even with his enhanced powers, the titan knew that it would take him several hours to crack the seal and release the horror held within it.

CHAPTER 17

Boreal Forest Ontario Canada

It was five a.m. when Luke's cellphone woke him up. He rubbed his tired eyes and looked down at his phone to see that the call was coming from Parsons. Once he saw that it was Parsons who was calling him, any drowsiness that Luke was experiencing immediately faded away. He answered his phone as Diana was crawling out of her tent. Luke switched his phone to speaker. "Go ahead, Parsons, I have you on speaker with Diana."

Parsons' voice sounded even more ominous than usual. "Atomic Rex has left the Arctic. It seems that Zeus and Odin's predictions were correct. The kaiju is swimming across the Arctic Ocean and heading toward North America. We predict that he will make landfall on Baffin Island in roughly eighteen hours. If we can get Chimera onto the *Hudson* in an hour, we can intercept Atomic Rex on the northern part of the island where there are fewer civilians."

Luke started grabbing the essential items that he needed to bring back with him. "We will be there. Have some food ready for Chimera but not an overabundance of it. We don't want him heading into a fight like this on an empty stomach, but we don't want him sluggish either from an overly large meal."

"Copy that. The food will be ready."

Luke hung up his phone to see that Diana was already sitting behind the driver seat of the jeep they had driven out in. She yelled to Luke, "Leave the tents and other camping supplies! We can send someone out from the base to collect them! Call Chimera and let's get moving! If we have a chance to have Chimera fight that monster in a sparsely populated area, we have to take it!"

Luke grabbed his megaphone and left everything else. He ran over to the jeep and before climbing into it, he yelled into the megaphone, "Chimera, follow me." A flock of birds took flight from the trees as Chimera's stirrings shook the ground around him. The majestic kaiju rose out of the woods that he was sleeping in and towered above them as he reached his full height. Chimera stretched his arms out and roared, proclaiming to Luke and the world that he was awake and ready to do what was needed of him. Luke looked at Chimera and smiled. He then climbed into the car and said to Diana, "Let's go kick Atomic Rex's nuclear ass."

Diana smiled back at him and then she spun the jeep around and started head back to base with Chimera following behind them.

Arctic Ocean

Atomic Rex's mind was fixed on reaching the North America and in particular its East Coast. While the monster was keenly aware that this was not his Earth, he was still operating under the impression that the Americas would have ample food sources for him as they did on his planet. The monster also thought that the territory was still his and more or less devoid of the humans that he had run into on this planet. With his mind fixed on returning to what was as familiar to him as possible, the nuclear theropod continued his swim toward Canada.

Hudson Bay

Luke and Diana had managed to get Chimera to the *Hudson* in under forty-five minutes. They led Chimera onto the new ship where he found food waiting for him. Once Chimera was on board, Parsons immediately gave orders to set sail. As the ship was sailing across Hudson Bay, Luke and Diana were given a tour of the vessel by Parsons. Luke was glad to see that the *Hudson* was nearly an identical copy of the *Argos*. The *Hudson* was constructed with the *Argos* in mind to make it an easy transition for Chimera who was used to the older ship. While the ship's layout was replicated from the *Argos* to accommodate Chimera, Luke had to admit that he found it helpful as well to have the ship be a copy of the one he was used to.

Luke was not a soldier or sailor by trade. He was a teacher of students with autism and one thing that students with autism respond well to are familiar surroundings and minimal change. For years, Luke had kept the layout of his classroom the same with the exception of a few minor tweaks here and there. As time progressed, Luke found that he become as accustomed to needing things to remain as unchanged as his students did. So, for Luke, having a ship with the same bridge, communications room, and war room as the ship he was accustomed to were welcome benefits.

He was also pleased to see that Captain Brand was the captain of the *Hudson*. Given his familiarity with the *Argos*, Brand was the natural choice to command her sister ship. Accordingly, many of the sailors from the *Argos* were also reassigned to the *Hudson*. As Luke walked around the ship, he saw and was thanked by many of the sailors that he had met in Baltimore.

Parsons also had the helicopter squadron from Fort Hood transferred to the *Hudson*, as it was large enough to carry several helicopters and jets. After the impression they had made on Parsons during the battle with Atlas, the general felt that the squadron from Fort Hood would be perfect for his new flagship.

Diana was surprised and pleased to see Captain Pressley aboard the *Hudson*. She said hi to Pressley and then briefly introduced Luke to him. While Luke realized that Pressley was the man that Diana had a potential date with, none of them talked about it with a mission looming and a battle with Atomic Rex on the horizon.

The tour of the ship took an hour after which Parsons had Luke, Diana, Brand, and other key people on the ship meet in order to discuss how they were going to engage Atomic Rex. Parsons brought up a map of Baffin Island on the main screen and began to lay out his plan. "We are going to have the *Hudson* anchor near the port of Nanisivik. It's an abandoned mining town located in the northwest corner of the island which is in the process of being turned into a naval base. The plan is to have our helicopter squadron fly out and engage Atomic Rex before he makes landfall. From what we have seen from the kaiju so far, he is very aggressive and will pursue anything that attacks him. While the helicopters are engaging Atomic Rex, we will have Chimera head to shore where he will wait for the kaiju to make landfall. Additionally, we will also have our engineers set up our portal to Asgard there and activate it."

Parsons shifted his gaze toward Luke. "Luke, you will have to handle this battle differently than any other conflict that you and Chimera have been in. The radiation given off by Atomic Rex in his normal state is enough to kill anyone. If he unleashes the small-scale nuclear attack that he had displayed, it will give off enough radiation to kill any human within two miles of him, regardless of the protection we give them. Captain Pressley has volunteered to fly you to land where you will wait with Chimera for Atomic Rex. Once you see the kaiju approaching, direct Chimera to engage him and force him into the portal. Once you have given Chimera the directive, return to the helicopter, and Captain Pressley will fly you back to the *Hudson*."

Luke sighed. Parsons could see the disappointment and frustration on Luke's face. "Son, I know how much that monster means to you and how you feel responsible for him, but there is no way that you can be with him in this battle. You simply would not survive being that close to Atomic Rex regardless of if Chimera defeats him or not." Luke nodded as he knew that Parsons was right. As much as it pained Luke to admit it, there was nothing that he could do to help out Chimera in this fight.

With Luke accepting his reduced role in the mission and everyone else aware of their duties, Parsons brought the briefing to an end. "All right, we have roughly one hour until we reach the target. If we are successful in this mission, we will eliminate the threat posed by Atomic Rex and the Asgardians. If we are lucky, we may even take out the threat posed by Cronus as well. You are all dismissed."

Atlantic Ocean

The symbol that was holding the beast trapped beneath the ocean was starting to show cracks that spider-webbed across it under Cronus' assault. The cracks continued to grow and multiply until something from beneath the symbol burst free and shattered it. A second after the symbol shattered, something that was massive beyond description shot up toward the surface. The amount of water displaced from the beast rising up from the depths sent tsunamis heading out in every direction toward three of the Earth's continents.

Cronus flew up into the air to the very stratosphere nearly twenty miles above the earth. Cronus was skyrocketing upward when he looked down to see the face of Jormungand the World Serpent coming towards him!

Jormungand's face resembled that of constrictor snake such as a python or anaconda with the notable difference that it was two miles long. Myth had exaggerated Jormungand's length to be equal to the circumference of the planet. The mistake made by god and human alike was a simple one. Jormungand's body was not as long as the Earth's circumference. The beast's length was equal to the extent of the earth's stratosphere. The creature's height when fully extended was slightly over twenty-seven miles long. At that length, if Jormungand was to lift his head from the ground to its fullest extent, he would reach a height that would almost place it in space. It was this feat of nearly being able to reach the vacuum of space while still on Earth that earned Jormungand the title World Serpent.

When Cronus had flown as high as he could prior to reaching space, the titan halted his progress and focused all of his newly acquired might into forming a shield around himself. Cronus strained his new powers to the limit to form a translucent bubble of pure energy around his body and then he waited. A few seconds after Cronus had created the force field, Jormungand's head appeared next to him. The World Serpent unleashed a hiss that shook the sky when he saw the being that had imprisoned him so long ago. Jormungand then unleashed a blast of energy that enveloped the titan.

When the blast hit Cronus' shield, the Dark One felt as if he were trying to hold back the power of a supernova. The titan quickly realized that Jormungand's attack was not a quick burst but rather a sustained beam that was wearing his defenses thin. Cronus clenched his fists and gritted his teeth when he saw cracks forming in his force field. Seeking a way to escape from the monster he had freed, the titan diverted a small portion of his power to creating a portal back to his own dimension behind him. His force field was on the verge of collapsing when he jumped into the portal. The titan landed in his own dimension as Jormungand's blast tore through what remained of his defensive bubble.

The World Serpent looked through the portal at Cronus. Jormungand was fully capable of following the titan into his own dimension and destroying him, but the massive snake decided that revenge was his to take at any time he pleased. The monster laid back down into the water, generating another barrage of tsunamis, and then he began heading toward North America. From his own dimension, Cronus watched as Jormungand swam away. The titan breathed a sigh of relief. He realized that he was not ready to face the World Serpent, but his newly acquired powers had brought him closer to Jormungand's level than he had been during their last encounter. As the pilot fish swam beneath the great white shark and devoured the scraps that fell out his mouth, so would Cronus follow Jormungand's path of death from his own dimension, swallowing up some of the life energy from the creatures the World Serpent slew.

Cronus knew that both the gods and the humans would need to try to fight back against Jormungand. He hoped that between the extra power he gained in the serpent's wake and the energy Jormungand expelled fighting the humans, gods, and monsters, he would be able to attack the serpent when it was weak and slay him. If was able to slay Jormungand and absorb his life energy, Cronus would become the most powerful being in any dimensions across the multiverse.

Baffin Island

Luke grabbed his megaphone and ran out to Pressley's helicopter which was preparing for take-off. Luke climbed into the vehicle and strapped himself into the seat near the open side door. Pressley took off into the air and flew to the back of the *Hudson*. Once the helicopter was positioned in the back of the *Hudson*, a huge door opened up to reveal Chimera. The monster didn't need Luke to prompt him to enter the water. The kaiju had been out of his natural element for too long and was anxious to swim in the cool waters of Hudson Bay. Chimera walked to the opening of his hold and slid into the water.

Luke let the monster swim several laps around the ship in order to get his body lose and his blood pumping for the upcoming battle. Luke saw another helicopter take off from the deck of the *Hudson* and head for the island. He guessed that it was the helicopter which was carrying the trans-dimensional portal that Chimera was going to try and force Atomic Rex through.

The former teacher shifted his neck from side to side, causing it to crack a little. Luke was always nervous before leading Chimera into a battle, but this time, he was even more nervous than usual. While Luke was truly happy that he would not be almost under foot of two monsters as they clashed, he felt a little guilty about it. Luke knew that he was asking Chimera to put his life on the line and part of him felt that if he was going ask the kaiju to do that then he should be willing to do the same. If at all possible, Luke would have been on the ground with Chimera, but there was simply nothing he could do about it. Atomic Rex's body was giving off incredible amounts of radiation and it was more than any human could stand. Chimera's body would be able to withstand the radiation at least to the extent that he would have a fighting chance against Atomic Rex.

Once he felt that Chimera had enough exercise and the engineers had enough time to construct the portal, he called out over his megaphone, "Chimera, follow me."

The monster spun around in the water and followed his trainer. As they were making their way toward the island, Luke tried to take his mind off his apprehension over the upcoming battle by pressing Pressley about his date with Diana. "So, I hear that thanks to Grimm coming to life and defeating Atlas, you have a date with Diana?"

Pressley laughed. "Yes. As I understand it, you are her best friend and big-brother type. Are you going to give me the lecture about how I should treat her like a lady or else you are going to sic your monster on me?"

This time, it was Luke who laughed. "The wrath of Chimera is nothing compared to what Diana will do to you if you piss her off! Seriously though, she is a great girl. Just relax and have fun."

Pressley shrugged. "She is certainly unique. I mean, who else has the ability to have the highest-ranking general in the US Army pressure a movie studio into making a good Fantastic Four movie?"

Luke smiled. "Only Diana Cain." The two men shared a laugh and then Luke noticed they were over the island. He watched as Chimera stepped ashore and then his tone changed when he saw a half-dozen helicopters take off from the deck of the *Hudson*. He pointed at the ascending helicopters. "Is that the squadron that will be engaging Atomic Rex and leading him to us?"

Pressley nodded. "Yes, they have him on radar." He looked down at the crew who were working to put the portal together. "Those guys better hurry up. It won't be long now."

Atomic Rex was swimming along the surface of the water as he was approaching land. The monster planned to swim around Baffin Island and then cross Hudson Bay on his way to the Northeastern United States. The monster was starting to swim around the island when he saw the helicopters coming toward him. The kaiju let loose a small roar when he saw smaller shapes with smoke trails behind them detach from the helicopters and streak toward him. The missiles exploded against the face and head of Atomic Rex. The kaiju roared in anger at the small machines that were attacking him and changed his course to intercept them. The nuclear theropod followed them toward the island and when he lifted his head out of the water, Atomic Rex could smell another kaiju. The saurian beast roared out a challenge to this creature that had dared to enter his territory and who was also a possible food source. Atomic Rex took several steps on land and then he saw the awesome form of Chimera standing there with the helicopter flying around him. Atomic Rex recognized Chimera as the monster that Cronus had tricked him into thinking had grabbed him and brought him to this Earth. Atomic Rex roared at Chimera and then he charged the man-made monster.

The group working to set up the portal made the last connections mere seconds after Atomic Rex had roared. The two pillars were up and through them, Luke could see Asgard. While the portal was only forty feet tall, Luke knew from experience that it was capable of transporting a kaiju through it. He had once taken Chimera through a portal of the same dimensions in order to rescue his wife from Asgard.

The men who were working on the portal ran to their helicopter and took off. Pressley turned around and yelled to Luke, "Give your monster directions quickly! We need to get out of here! The radiation readings coming off Atomic Rex are off the charts!"

Luke grabbed his megaphone and walked to the open door of the hovering helicopter. He had been working with Chimera on being able to process multiple step commands. Still, getting Chimera to understand that he wanted the monster to push Atomic Rex through the portal rather than to try and kill him was something Luke was not sure that Chimera was able to comprehend. Luke took a deep breath and yelled, "Chimera, look at me!" The monster's head turned away from the approaching Atomic Rex and toward his trainer. Luke first pointed at Atomic Rex, and then at the portal. He yelled, "Push through there!"

As Luke was saying "there," Pressley was flying back toward the ship. Luke watched as Chimera threw his hands out at his sides, roared, and then ran toward Atomic Rex. Luke could tell that Chimera that was slightly larger and heavier than Atomic Rex just by looking at them. He hoped that Chimera's size would make the difference in the fight. The monsters were just about to slam into each other when a bolt of lightning streaked down in front of the helicopter as it hovered over the deck of the *Hudson*. For a brief moment, Luke thought that Zeus was finally playing his hand but when he looked out his window, he saw the thirty-foot-tall form of Thor standing on the deck of the *Hudson*. Pressley quickly landed his helicopter on the ship. Luke climbed out of it while dozens of soldiers and sailors surrounded the thunder god. Parsons and Diana walked out on deck and Thor looked directly at them. "You must return my belt to me! A horror has been unleashed that is beyond comprehension! If I do not stop this beast, it will destroy not only this Earth but all of the Earths in every conceivable dimension." Thor shook his head. "The battle between the two beasts on the island is a secondary matter at this point! The End of Days are here!"

Parsons looked over at Diana. "What's he talking about?"

Diana looked down at her tablet. "We have reports of tsunamis wrecking coastal areas along the US, Europe, and Northern Africa." She shifted the view on her screen. "We have a visual of something in the Atlantic, but it's too big for me to…" Diana stopped talking and then she gasped. Her face turned a pale white as she looked at Parsons. "It's Jormungand! Cronus has freed Jormungand!" She looked back at her screen. "Parsons, we are talking about a kaiju that is over twenty-five miles long according to our satellites!"

Atomic Rex and Chimera crashed into each other with the force of opposing hurricanes. The monsters bit and clawed at each other as they grappled for position. Being the thicker and heavier of the two monsters, Chimera was able to wrap his arms around Atomic Rex. The hybrid monster shifted Atomic Rex slightly to his right and then he shifted the saurian kaiju hard to his left, throwing the reptilian beast to the ground.

Atomic Rex rolled with the momentum of the throw as soon as he hit the ground. The nuclear theropod sprang to his feet and then leapt at Chimera. While Chimera was heavier and stronger than Atomic Rex, the saurian monster was by far the more agile of the two monsters. Atomic Rex clamped his jaws shut around the upper half of Chimera's right arm and used his claws to tear gashes into the hybrid monster's back and chest.

Chimera responded by landing three right-hook punches to Atomic Rex's ribs and a chop to the back of the monster's neck that forced him to release his bite. Chimera then used his right arm to hit Atomic Rex with an uppercut that snapped his jaws shut and forced his head back. Atomic Rex stumbled backward from the blow and he took a step toward the portal. Seeing an opportunity to force Atomic Rex through the portal, Chimera lowered his head and drove it into the reptile's chest, causing him to take another step toward Asgard.

The hybrid monster tried to land another punch, but Atomic Rex ducked the blow and slid under it. He then moved behind Chimera and sprang onto the hybrid's back. Atomic Rex dug the claws on his feet into Chimera's lower back and the claws on his hands into Chimera's shoulders. The nuclear theropod then bit down on the back of Chimera's neck.

Back on the deck of the *Hudson*, Thor was still screaming. "Mortals, are you deaf and dumb? For the sake of all life in existence, bring me my belt so that I may battle Jormungand! It is our destiny to die fighting each other, but I will not be able to slay him without my belt!"

The fearless general Parsons walked directly up to Thor. "We don't have your belt! I suggest that you worry about saving your city. Any minute now, either Atomic Rex or Chimera will be going through the portal to Asgard with the intent to destroy it. Unless, of course, if you can send them to wherever Cronus is hiding."

Thor shrugged. "My forces are prepared to send either your behemoth or the leviathan to do battle with Cronus, but without my belt of power, it matters not. Jormungand will destroy this Earth and every other Earth then he will turn to Asgard and we cannot stop him."

Everyone on deck was quiet for a moment before Diana screamed, "Wait! There might be a way to give us a shot at defeating Jormungand!" She looked at Thor. "You teleported here, right? Just like Zeus?"

Thor nodded. "Aye, fair one. All thunder gods are able to teleport."

Diana smiled. "All right, here is what I propose."

Atomic Rex was having difficulty biting through Chimera's thick mane in order to reach his spine. Chimera reached behind him with both hands and grabbed Atomic Rex by the neck and shoulder. He then pulled as hard as he could while ducking down at the same time. The maneuver allowed Chimera to slam Atomic Rex onto the ground back first. Atomic Rex stood up only to have Chimera spin around and strike him in the side with his thick tail, knocking the nuclear theropod down once more.

Atomic Rex looked up to see Chimera above him with his fist clenched. The hybrid threw his punch at the saurian kaiju, but Atomic Rex shifted his body to the right in order to avoid the blow. Chimera's hand slammed into the ground and it caused him to lose his balance. Chimera was trying to steady himself when Atomic Rex sprang back to his feet and wrapped his arms around Chimera's chest. The saurian monster bit into Chimera's right shoulder, causing even more blood to flow down the hybrid's back. Atomic Rex then stepped forward and in a display of his own considerable strength, he threw Chimera to the ground.

The nuclear theropod leapt onto the downed Chimera's torso. Atomic Rex then opened his jaws wide to tear out Chimera's throat but before he could do so, Chimera swatted the reptile off his chest. Atomic Rex stumbled off Chimera and then fell onto the ground. Both monsters stood up at the same time and then they stared at each other. Chimera threw his arms out again and roared. In response to Chimera's roar, Atomic Rex's scales began to glow a bright blue color.

On the deck of the *Hudson*, Parsons was shaking his head. "I am sorry, Diana, but we can't trust the gods! They have already proven that when Odin tried to take over Atomic Rex! Why should I trust his son now?"

Diana threw her hands into the air. "Because we have no other choice!" She pointed to the island and the clashing monsters. "Look at the way those two are going against each other! No matter which one of them wins, the other is going to be in too a bad shape to fight something like Jormungand ! Let Thor help force Atomic Rex through the portal.

Then he can take Luke and Pressley in the helicopter, and Chimera to engage Jormungand! It's the only hope we have! Jormungand will reach the US in less than an hour and we don't have anything even remotely capable of stopping him! Legend says that Thor is supposed to stop Jormungand but without his belt, Thor's only hope of stopping Jormungand is with Chimera's help!"

Parsons gritted his teeth. "Fine, let's go with your plan." Thor nodded at Diana and then he flew toward Baffin and the clashing monsters. Parsons yelled at Luke and Pressley, "Get back in the air. You two need to be ready to teleport, helicopter and all, as soon as Thor and Chimera force, Atomic Rex into that portal! Once you get to wherever Jormungand is, radio in your position. Your helicopter likely won't have enough fuel to return to shore, but we will send the nearest vessel out to retrieve you. If you need to utilize the life raft, make damn sure that you have the beacon on it!"

Atomic Rex lifted his leg into the air and then he slammed it into the ground, unleashing his Atomic Wave. A blue dome of pure radiation shot out from Atomic Rex and stuck Chimera. The hybrid monster had never felt pain or power to the levels that the Atomic Wave hit him with. Chimera could feel the outer layer of skin on the front part of his body being burned to a crisp. The sheer force of the blast him was enough to send Chimera flying backward several hundred feet before he landed on his back.

Chimera looked up from the ground to see Atomic Rex coming toward him. The hybrid turned his head in Atomic Rex's direction and then he fired a tightly focused sonic blast at him. Atomic Rex's arms shot out to their full extent, his eyes rolled into the back of his head, and his tongue slid out his mouth as a result of his central nervous system being disabled. The nuclear theropod took a step backward and then he fell to the ground.

Chimera forced himself to stand. He then started walking over toward Atomic Rex. Chimera stood over Atomic Rex and he delivered two thunderous blows to the saurian kaiju's head that drove it into the ground. Chimera was about to throw another punch when Atomic Rex slashed Chimera across the stomach with his clawed toes, forcing the hybrid to take a step back. The nuclear theropod quickly stood and slashed Chimera twice across the face with his clawed hands. He then wrapped his arms around Chimera and tossed him back to the ground.

Atomic Rex loomed over the downed Chimera. He was preparing to go for the hybrid's throat again when lightning began to reign down on him from the sky. Bolt after bolt of electricity struck Atomic Rex, forcing the monster to back away from Chimera and toward the portal. Chimera regained his feet and hit Atomic Rex with another sonar blast that disoriented the monster. Chimera suddenly detected a familiar and hated scent to his left. He looked over to see Thor standing next to him and making the same gesture Luke had made to push Atomic Rex through the portal. Thor then stepped forward and threw his hammer at Atomic Rex. The weapon struck Atomic Rex in the chest and caused him to take another step toward the portal.

Atomic Rex roared in anger at this new creature that had attacked him. The kaiju could sense that this new attacker was similar to the second being who had tried to control him. The one-eyed giant he had slain when they battled in the woods. The monster roared a challenge at this attacker. Atomic Rex was now determined to destroy this giant just as he had the larger one-eyed giant.

Chimera was unsure of why Thor was helping him, but the kaiju decided to accept the god's assistance, since he had given the same gesture toward Atomic Rex as Luke. Chimera could see that Atomic Rex was starting to regain his senses, so he charged at the mutant dinosaur. Chimera hit Atomic Rex with two punches that caused the nuclear theropod to move closer to the portal with each blow.

Atomic Rex ducked a third blow then he slashed Chimera across the face with his left claw. The saurian monster head was moving forward to bite Chimera when he was struck in the jaw by Thor's hammer. The blow stunned Atomic Rex. With his opponent stunned, Chimera lowered his head and rammed it into Atomic Rex's chest, knocking him through the portal.

Chimera roared triumphantly as Pressley was flying his helicopter back toward the island. Chimera looked at the helicopter to see Luke sitting inside of it. Chimera heard Luke yelling, "Thor, now! Teleport us now!" There was a bright flash of lightning and then the helicopter, Thor, and Chimera disappeared.

CHAPTER 18

Atlantic Ocean

Chimera dropped down in the middle of the Atlantic Ocean roughly two hundred miles off the US East Coast. The monster was surprised to find himself suddenly moved from the dark skies of Baffin Island to a sunny day in the ocean. The hybrid instinctively sent out a sonar pulse to determine what was around him. The monster was confused when the pulse bounced back, indicating that an incredibly huge object was heading his way. Chimera sent out a second pulse which yielded the same result.

Chimera swam to the surface of the water and he looked in the direction the pulse indicated that the object was coming from. Chimera saw a humongous swell of water moving his direction. In the middle of the water swell, Chimera could see the face of a snake that was many times larger than his entire body.

Chimera heard Luke's voice shouting at him from above. The kaiju shifted his eyes skyward to see Luke in a helicopter with Thor floating beside him. Luke pointed at the quickly approaching swell of water and yelled, "Chimera, attack!" Chimera roared in response to his trainer's command and then started swimming toward the oncoming Jormungand.

When Thor saw Chimera charging the World Serpent, he screamed, "Truly, the behemoth is fearless!" The thunder god then lifted his hammer above his head, "Hear me, Jormungand, I may not be at my strongest, but I am far from powerless!" Large dark clouds began to gather above Thor's hammer. Once the sky was completely blanketed with storm clouds, Thor began to swirl his hammer around above head. The movement from Thor's hammer caused lightning to dance across the dark clouds. Thor then screamed and pointed his hammer at Jormungand which caused dozens of lightning bolts to streak down at the giant snake.

Hundreds of thousands of volts of electricity struck Jormungand, but the World Serpent was unaffected by the attack. The look of confidence on Thor's face disappeared after his most powerful attack failed to harm his enemy.

Chimera had closed roughly half the distance between himself and Jormungand when he popped his head above water. The monster fired one of his tightly focused sonar blasts at Jormungand in hopes of disrupting the serpent's central nervous system. Chimera saw Jormungand shake his head but otherwise, the snake was unaffected by the sonar blast.

Pressley looked back at Luke. "Permission to attack Jormungand, sir?"

Luke was surprised that the pilot was asking his permission, but he guessed that Pressley was just following the procedures of his military training. Luke nodded. "Hell yes! Hit him with everything you can!"

Pressley flew toward Jormungand. The massive snake was swimming along the surface of the water and his mile wide and nearly thirty-mile-long body presented the pilot with an easy target. Pressley flew his helicopter over Jormungand's body, attacking it with bullets, bombs, and missiles. The section of Jormungand's body that Pressley hit became an inferno of explosions but as with Thor and Chimera's attacks, Pressley's assault had no effect on the monster. Pressley shook his head. "What in the hell do we do now? Call Parsons for a nuke strike?"

Luke looked down to see Chimera swimming toward a beast that made the hybrid monster look like an insect. Luke had worked with Chimera long enough to know that the monster was not only brave but also intelligent. Luke was certain that Chimera was fully aware that he was not a match physically for Jormungand. Luke was certain that since Chimera was still swimming toward Jormungand, he had some kind of a plan to attack the serpent. Luke shook his head as he responded to Pressley, "No, we trust in Chimera."

Chimera took a long breath and then dove deep into the ocean. The kaiju looked up to see the incomprehensible form of Jormungand swimming above him. The World Serpent was so large that it did not even bother to acknowledge Chimera as it swam over him. Once Jormungand's head was past him, Chimera swam back toward the body of the beast. As large as Chimera was, even he was caught in the wake of the serpent and dragged along in the current he was creating. Chimera tumbled over several times in the water before he was able to extend the claws in his right hand and dig them into Jormungand's hide. Chimera's claws were unable to hurt the colossal snake, but they did afford the kaiju a hold on the serpent. Chimera then unsheathed the claws in his left hand and drove them into Jormungand as well. Chimera roared and then began to use his claws as hand holds to pull himself up the side Jormungand's body. When Chimera broke the surface of the water, even his immense strength was tested by the volume of water sliding alongside Jormungand's body. The pressure generated by Jormungand moving through the ocean was almost enough to force the monster off the snake. Chimera pressed his body close to Jormungand's scales and then he continued to climb the side of the monster until he reached its back.

Pressley was doing his best to keep pace with Jormungand, but the snake was pulling away from him. Thor was flying beside them and doing his best to keep a barrage of ineffective lightning bolts focused on the serpent. Luke was watching Jormungand closely, looking for any sign of Chimera. Luke was starting to think that Chimera had either been swallowed whole by the beast or was simply unable to keep up with its speed. Luke's eyes were scanning up and down the body of the serpent, which was so long that it literally extended past the horizon, when he thought he saw some kind of gray bump on Jormungand's back. Luke quickly searched under his seat until he found a pair of binoculars. He looked through the binoculars to see that the gray lump was indeed Chimera.

Luke yelled to Pressley, "It's Chimera! I can see him through the binoculars!" Despite the severity of the situation, Luke laughed. "I never would have thought that I would need binoculars to see something as big as Chimera."

Pressley refocused Luke on the mission. "What's he doing? Does it look like he's hurting that snake?"

Luke no longer needed the binoculars. The speed at which at Jormungand was moving had nearly brought the part of his body that Chimera was on to the helicopter. Luke watched as Chimera pulled one of his claws out of Jormungand's back, reached forward, and then dug it into another part of the snake. Luke shrugged. "It looks like he's trying to climb the snake's body to reach his head. It kind of reminds me of the second Wolverine movie that I watched with Diana. Where he was using his claws to climb along the top of a moving train."

Chimera shot by the helicopter and Pressley laughed. "She made you made you watch Wolverine Origins before she let you watch The Wolverine and Logan?"

Luke shrugged. "She said watching the first one would help me appreciate how much better the next two movies are."

Pressley smiled. "If the world doesn't end, I am definitely taking her on that date."

Luke laughed. "Even when she is not here, she finds a way to lighten up the apocalypse."

Pressley shrugged. "We could sure use her now. We have about thirty-five minutes left until we run out of fuel and we are still several hours away from shore."

Luke took a deep breath. "Okay, what do we do?"

Pressley pointed to the back of the helicopter. "There is a life raft with a beacon on it in the back of the chopper. Grab it and walk to the side of the helicopter. I am going to fly us low above the water and away from Jormungand's wake so that we don't get pulled along by it. Then we are going to inflate the raft and jump into the water. I'll rig the chopper to fly away from us so that it doesn't crash on top of us."

Luke nodded. "What about help? Parsons said that they would be sending help."

Pressley shook his head. "I sent out a call for help, but no one is coming for us until Jormungand is dead. If Chimera can't stop him, you and I will be floating together in the middle of the ocean while he destroys the rest of the world."

Luke's voice suddenly sounded very confident. "Captain, you can book that date with Diana. Chimera is going to kill Jormungand."

When Thor saw Chimera clinging to Jormungand's back, he yelled, "Aye, monster, let us meet Jormungand in close combat as the Norns have decreed!" Thor then shot past Pressley's helicopter and disappeared over the horizon. The Asgardian flew over Jormungand's head and then turned around. Thor screamed, "Now, monster! Face me and face your death!" Thor descended and landed on top of Jormungand's head. The god lifted his hammer above his head and yelled, "Lightning, heed thy master, and help me to slay this monster!" Four bolts of lightning streaked out of the sky and struck Thor's Hammer. The hammer took on a bright blue glow and Thor brought it down with all of his incredible might into the World Serpent's skull. When the mystical hammer hit Jormungand's skull, there was a loud crashing sound similar to a bomb exploding.

Thor fell to his knees exhausted. To the thunder god's astonishment, his attack once more had no effect on the beast. Jormungand simply shook his head and tossed Thor into the air. Before the Asgardian could attain flight under his own power, Jormungand's head shot out of the water and swallowed him whole. With his ancient adversary now digesting within his stomach, Jormungand continued his journey to shore.

Hand hold by hand hold, Chimera continued to claw his way up the body of the serpent, moving ever closer to the beast's head. The climb was exhausting as the wind, water, and sheer strength of Jormungand were working against him. Chimera's muscles were starting to become fatigued, but the kaiju's will drove him forward. Chimera could sense that Jormungand was death incarnate. He knew that if the monster reached land, he would kill those whom he considered to be part of his family. Aside from Chimera's intelligence, and the bonding Luke had worked on with him over the years, Chimera was also partly comprised of the DNA of a lion and a gorilla. Both animals are social creatures and in both of their social structures, it is the responsibility of the alpha male to protect his family. Chimera considered Luke, Melissa, Suzie, Sally, Diana, and even Parsons to all be a part of his family and he was determined to protect them from the huge monster he was currently riding.

After nearly exhausting himself, Chimera had finally reached the top of Jormungand's head. Chimera continued to climb until he was directly over the serpent's right eye. Chimera then looked down into an iris that was three times the size of his entire body. Jormungand's eye shifted up to see Chimera roaring at him. Chimera took the type of deep breath that allowed him to stay underwater for over an hour. He then slid down onto Jormungand's eye and began tearing into it.

Jormungand violently shook his head as he tried to remove Chimera from the eye he had blinded but rather than being flung off the eye, Chimera forced his way into it. Once he was firmly in Jormungand's eye socket, Chimera continued to rip and tear apart everything that he saw. Jormungand continued to shake his head in an attempt to force Chimera out of his eye. Chimera was tossed around inside of the World Serpent's skull, but he refused to allow himself to be thrown out of it.

Chimera was falling down when he dug his claws into Jormungand's optic nerve to steady himself. The monster felt everything around him shake as Jormungand writhed in pain from the damage being done inside of his head. Just as he had pulled himself along Jormungand's body with his claws, Chimera used the same method to pull himself along Jormungand's optic nerve.

Chimera continued moving along the optic nerve until he reached a brain that was nearly a mile in circumference. Chimera attacked the soft gray matter with the fury of an angered silverback gorilla. The hybrid bit, clawed, and kicked at Jormungand's brain until he felt that the serpent had stopped moving. Once he was sure that Jormungand was dead, Chimera crawled back out along the eye socket he had hollowed out. Chimera emerged from Jormungand's destroyed eye socket covered in blood and brains. The kaiju looked at the dead form of the World Serpent he was standing on and then beat his chest in triumph. Chimera scanned the sky for the helicopter that was carrying Luke. When he was unable to find it, the monster dove into the water and began swimming back out to sea.

Luke and Pressley were sitting in their inflatable raft watching Jormungand's seemingly endless body move past them in the distance. They became concerned when what they could see of Jormungand's body began to shake and convulse.

Pressley pointed at the snake's body. "Is it under attack? I don't think as big and as fast as it is that it could have reached land yet."

Luke shrugged. "Chimera must have gotten to the point where he thought he could attack the monster."

Pressley's eyes went wide. "Whatever's causing it to move like that, it's trouble for us." The pilot pointed at a series of massive waves that were rolling toward their tiny raft. Pressley shouted, "Wrap your arms in the chord on the side of the raft. We need to hold onto it. No matter what, the raft will float to the surface, but if we lose hold of it, we're dead!"

Luke did as Pressley said. When the wave first rolled under the raft, Luke felt himself being propelled upward. He remembered thinking that as a child his parents had taken him to the top of the Empire State Building. The sensation he experienced when going up the elevator to the top of legendary building was the same feeling that he had now. The next sensation that Luke felt was as if he was dropped off the world's largest roller coaster as the raft slid down the back of the wave. When it reached the bottom of the wave, Luke felt the pull that Pressley had warned him of. Luke felt like his arms were being pulled out his sockets as the wave rolled away and pulled the raft with it. Luke's arms ached, and he was panting when the wave's pull on the raft finally subsided. The trainer breathed a sigh of relief and then he gasped when the sky suddenly disappeared from view as a second wave rolled toward the tiny raft.

Luke managed to hold on through three more waves before the ocean finally leveled out. Luke rolled over and moaned as Pressley pulled himself up to a sitting position.

The pilot smiled. "We made it. We survived the first set of waves!"

Luke's face went pale. "The first set?"

Pressley nodded. "Yes, every time that snake writhes like that, we can expect more waves."

Luke peeked over the side of the raft and took a look at Jormungand's body. He smiled. "He's not moving. He's not even swimming forward. I think he's dead." Luke pumped his fist in the air and shouted, "I think that Chimera killed him!"

Pressley smiled. "You're right! I think he's dead! What about Chimera? What happened to him?"

As if in response to Pressley's question, Chimera burst out of the water alongside of Jormungand's body. Luke cheered and pointed to his monster. The former teacher yelled, "I told you he would do it! I told you Chimera would kill that snake!" Chimera leapt out of the water twice more before he reached the raft and began to circle it. Luke leaned over and shouted, "Good boy, Chimera! Good boy! It will be all that you can eat when we get home!"

Pressley looked out at the circling Chimera. "Why is he circling us like that?"

Luke smiled. "He is protecting us. There isn't a creature in this world or any other that will dare attack us. All we have to do now is wait for our ride home."

Pressley was staring at something in the distance with a perplexed look on his face. Luke tapped the pilot's shoulder to get his attention. "Do you see something out there? Is it a ship coming for us?"

Pressley shook his head. "It's the weirdest thing. For a minute, I thought I saw a blonde supermodel in a bikini standing on top of the water." The pilot shrugged. "Must have been a mirage."

Luke looked out over the water. "Maybe a mirage or maybe you really did see what you thought."

CHAPTER 19

The Space Between Dimensions

Atomic Rex found himself falling through seemingly nothingness once more. The monster was experiencing the same sensation of disorientation that he had experienced when he had first been pulled from his Earth and placed on this strange new Earth. The falling sensation came to a sudden stop which slammed Atomic Rex into the ground stomach first.

The nuclear theropod looked up to see a strange city sprawling before him with the sun shining brightly upon it. Standing in front of the city were people like the humans whom he had seen before, with the exception that these people were each thirty feet tall. The people were all holding weapons, including swords, axes, spears, and bows.

The saurian monster roared at the people gathered before him. The kaiju was angered by the constant shifting between worlds that he was being subjected to. Atomic Rex could once more sense that the people standing before him were like the one-eyed giant and the warrior that had attacked him during his battle with Chimera.

Drool dripped out of Atomic Rex's mouth as he stared at the people who had once more moved him against his will. The kaiju roared at the people who he was certain were going to attack him or try to invade his mind as the others had. Atomic Rex was moving toward the strange warriors and their city when one of the crowd yelled, "Heimdallr, send him to Cronus before lays waste Asgard!"

A blonde warrior stepped forward and tossed a spear that landed at Atomic Rex's feet. The mutated dinosaur looked down at the spear which suddenly exploded in a flash of bright white light. Atomic Rex roared in anger as he was once more falling between dimensions. The monster was again shown a kaleidoscope of parallel worlds. He saw images of a strange bipedal monster with a hard caprice and orange sacks bulging out of its body moving toward a city. A vision of giant robotic cowboy fighting a demon and of a massive lion composed of flames fighting a shapeless horror.

When Atomic Rex suddenly stopped moving, he was not slammed to the ground as he had been previously. He simply stopped moving. The monster looked down at his feet to see nothing but pitch-black darkness.

155

He looked up and the only light that he was able to see was a bright red spinning vortex that was nearby. The vortex cast off a blood-red glow that partially lit up the seemingly endless darkness that enveloped Atomic Rex. The monster took a few steps toward the light when he was hit with an overwhelming sensation. Atomic Rex sniffed the air in an attempt to locate the prey that had eluded him for so long. The monster could sense that whatever force it was that had taken from his home, put him on the strange Earth, and tried to control his mind was here with him.

The new sense that the kaiju had gained since absorbing the Phoenix allowed him to detect the trans-dimensional beings that hailed from this dimension. Atomic Rex looked directly at the swirling red portal and roared. The nuclear theropod started walking toward the portal when a gigantic humanoid figure stepped out from behind it.

Cronus tossed his robes aside so that he was only in his loin cloth. The titan's muscles were rippling across his body. At his full height, Cronus was nearly fifty taller than Atomic Rex. Cronus shook his head as he laughed at the monster which had invaded his domain. "I must admit, beast; you have proven to be far more powerful and intelligent than I had ever imagined. I took you from your Earth to act as my puppet and you resisted my commands. Odin then had the foresight to send the Phoenix into battle with you, knowing that you would absorb its power. He hoped to control you as well, but with the enhanced powers of the Phoenix imbued into your body, you were not only able to resist him, but you actually slew the god king."

Atomic Rex could not understand what Cronus was saying. All that the kaiju knew was that the titan had tried to manipulate him and that alone was enough reason for Atomic Rex to destroy him. Atomic Rex charged at Cronus who stood his ground. Atomic Rex had almost reached Cronus when the Dark One swung out his hand and knocked the kaiju to the ground as he screamed. "I was not finished speaking, beast!" Atomic Rex was attempting to stand up when Cronus punched him the jaw and drove the monster's face back into the ground. Atomic Rex was lying flat on his stomach when Cronus kicked him in the ribs and sent the saurian creature flying through the air. Atomic Rex crashed back into the ground as Cronus continued his speech. "Surtr and Tiamat tried to warn me. They said that your power may rival even our own. They were correct, your power is indeed great; it was great enough to slay even Tiamat himself. While I was unable to use you to slay the humans so that I could absorb their life energy, your actions have made me even more powerful than I ever could have dreamt!"

Atomic Rex stood up and he once again charged Cronus. The titan tried to swat the mutant dinosaur aside as he done previously, but this time Atomic Rex was anticipating the move. Atomic Rex stopped short of Cronus' reach and when the titan swung at him, the nuclear theropod shifted his head, avoiding the blow. In a flash, Atomic Rex's jaws shot forward and closed around the Titan's fist. Cronus screamed in a mixture of anger and pain. His eyes began to glow even a brighter red as trails of crimson smoke rose out of them. The titan then fired a bolt of energy out of the fist Atomic Rex was biting and directly down the monster's throat. The blast scorched Atomic Rex's throat and sent the kaiju stumbling backward. Atomic Rex was shaking his head in an attempt to stop the burning sensation to his throat when Cronus stepped forward and delivered a roundhouse punch to the monster's ribs that buckled his knees. Cronus then scooped up Atomic Rex, lifted him in the air, and slammed him to the ground.

The titan loomed over Atomic Rex and stomped on the kaiju's head as he screamed. "Curse you, monster! You have caused me much trouble, but my moment of triumph is at hand and you shall listen to how I attained my greatness before you die! You killed Tiamat and Chimera killed Surtr, allowing me to triple my power by absorbing theirs! You then slayed my most powerful opponent in Odin. With the power I took from my brothers, I freed the World Serpent who killed Thor and is now battling Chimera. One of them will die and I will take their life energy. I shall then kill you and take your power as well. With you power added to my own, I shall crush the winner of Chimera and the World Serpent's battle! Then Zeus and his pathetic gods will flee before me. Soon, I shall extinguish not only all life on this earth but every Earth!"

Unbeknownst to the titan or the monster, a third individual slipped through the portal that Cronus had been watching. The slender figure shifted back into the darkness and watched the battle away from the eyes of the two combatants.

After several more stomps, Atomic Rex was bleeding from his mouth and nose. Cronus turned away from the monster and started walking back to the portal smiling. "I can sense it! Chimera has slain The World Serpent!" Cronus stood before the portal and he spread his arms above them, "Now, with the power of Jormungand, all reality shall fall to me!"

Atomic Rex forced his beaten body to stand. The monster used what remained of his strength to leap onto Cronus back. Atomic Rex bit down hard into Cronus' shoulder and dug his claws into the titan's side.

Cronus grunted in pain as he mocked the monster. "Do you truly think that you still possess the strength to challenge me?" The Dark One was reaching to grab Atomic Rex when he suddenly felt a blistering heat on his back. Atomic Rex dug his teeth farther into Cronus' shoulder and then he unleashed his Atomic Wave on the titan. Cronus was at ground zero of the wave as it unleashed its fury. The titan fell to one knee with Atomic Rex still on his back, as a blue dome of nuclear energy cascading out from him. When the wave ended, Atomic Rex was still latched onto Cronus' back. The titan's back was raw where the wave had made initial impact and strands of smoke were rising off it.

The Dark One started to stand as he sneered. "You have used your most powerful attack and still—" Cronus' thought was cut short by a second Atomic Wave striking him. This time, the wave threw Cronus to the ground face first. The titan screamed as the wave filleted the remaining flesh on his back and arms. Cronus bellowed in anger and placed his hands under his body to push himself back up when a third Atomic Wave slammed him back to the ground and burned the muscles on his back to the bone, and peeled the remaining hair off the giant's head.

Cronus moaned in pain as the third wave died off. He lifted his head off the ground and he said, "How? How can you have enough power to unleash three attacks like that in such rapid succession?" Cronus' answer came in the form of a fourth Atomic Wave that slammed his face back into the ground and singed his now exposed spine. The titan screamed in anguish as his exposed nerves were assaulted with nuclear energy.

The Dark One shook his head in disbelief as he realized that since absorbing the power of the Phoenix, Atomic Rex was now powered by nuclear fusion as opposed to fission. With this power under his command, that beast now had unlimited energy and the ability to create as many Atomic Waves as he wished. Blood spit out of Cronus mouth as he whispered, "I bragged of my power, but it is you that has become invincible." Cronus looked toward the portal for an escape, but he knew that his death imminent. A fifth Atomic Wave shattered the Titan's spine and burned off any flesh that remained on the back of his legs. The blast also managed to scalp what little hair was left on Cronus head, leaving nothing but the exposed back of his skull.

The Dark One could feel Atomic Rex preparing to unleash another blast when he saw Allison step out from next to the portal wearing Thor's belt. The belt had dramatically increased the nymph's size and power, making her nearly the same size of Cronus. The titan screamed at her, "You! You have the power to transport me away from here! Save me and I shall grant you power beyond your dreams!"

Allison smiled and shook her head at the titan as Atomic Rex unleashed another Atomic Wave. Cronus screamed in both pain and disbelief as his body was disintegrated. With the Dark One eliminated, Atomic Rex roared at the black nothingness that surrounded him. The monster turned toward Allison and she took a step back. "No, monster, you have nothing to fear from me. You have proven too dangerous to be kept around." She placed her hand on Thor's belt and drew extra energy from it. "I think it's time that we sent you home. You have cleared the board of enough game pieces for me."

A portal opened beneath Atomic Rex that sent him tumbling through multiple realities. The monster saw all forms of other monsters as he fell. When the beast finally struck the ground, he shook his head and sniffed the air. Atomic Rex immediately knew that he had been returned to his Earth. The monster roared once at his victory over the creatures of the other Earth and then he let his concerns over them slip from his mind. Atomic Rex was hungry and his only current concern was hunting.

With Atomic Rex gone, Allison walked back over to Cronus' portal. She looked into it and said, "A quick trip to Russia and then back to the Congo. It's time to start tying up loose ends."

EPILOGUE

Chimera Base

Luke and Pressley had drifted for nearly ten hours before a rescue plane was finally able to locate them. The two men were flown home where they were greeted by Parsons, Diana, and Luke's family. As Luke stepped off the plane, his two daughters came running toward him. Luke felt an overwhelming sense of joy and pride at seeing his girls. They sprinted up to him and hugged him. Suzie yelled, "Daddy, Chimera beat up the devil, and a Godzilla dinosaur, and a big, big snake, bigger than the moon to save the world!"

Suzie nudged her sister. "He knows, and I bet Daddy helped Chimera out a little. Didn't you, Daddy?"

Luke smiled. "I helped out a little."

Melissa walked over to them. "I think Daddy probably helped out a lot and he is just acting shy in front of you two."

Diana walked over toward Pressley. "It could be awhile before Parsons gets the Fantastic Four movie made, so how about you come over to my house tonight and we watch the most recent movie about the FF?"

Pressley's face contorted. "We both thought that movie was terrible. Why would we want to watch that?"

Diana grinned. "Well, if we decide the movie is no good, we can always think of something else to occupy our time."

Pressley shook his head and smiled. "Then I am totally in for watching the Fantastic Four with you tonight."

After giving Luke a few moments with his family, Parsons walked over to Luke. "Damn fine work again, son. I still find it hard to believe what you get Chimera to do."

Luke shrugged. "I just encourage him. He does all of the hard work. What about Atomic Rex and Cronus? Are they still a threat?"

Parsons nodded, "We saw through the portal that the Asgardians sent Atomic Rex to battle Cronus. We have no way of finding out the outcome of the battle but there have been no reports of Atomic Rex or any other monsters. Hopefully, the monster and the titan destroyed each other."

Melissa placed her hand on Parsons' shoulder. "General, can I ask what you plan to do with the body of a twenty-some-mile-long snake?"

Parsons shrugged. "Luckily, most of it is in the ocean. So, we are hoping that it's partially eaten by sharks, fish, and orcas. We will cut up as much of it as we can as well. Some of it we will study and some of it we will tow to the Arctic where it will keep from decaying as fast."

A loud roar boomed from outside the base. Everyone looked to the side of the base that was closest to the ocean to see Chimera walking toward them. The monster gingerly walked onto the base, which brought a cheer from Sally. "Daddy, look! Chimera has learned how to walk when he is around buildings just like you were trying to teach him!"

Luke laughed. "I guess he has." Realizing that he left his megaphone on the plane that flew him back to land, he cupped his hands and yelled, "Good boy, Chimera!"

The monster grunted and then walked over to the hangar that held his food. Luke yelled over to the soldiers who were manning the hangar, "Open it up, boys, he's earned it!"

The soldiers obeyed and opened up the top of the hangar to reveal Chimera's food cubes. The kaiju slowly sat down and began eating his reward. Parsons turned back to Luke, Pressley, and Diana. "You have all done more than anyone could have asked. Enjoy some time off."

Parsons was turning to walk away when Luke grabbed him. "Parsons, for a second out there, Pressley thought that he saw a blonde supermodel standing on the water watching Chimera and that big snake fight." Luke shrugged. "It could have been Allison."

Parsons shook his head. "Possibly, but that little vixen keeps herself well hidden. I have people all over the world looking for her and we can't find a thing. We do have a report of Toombs being in Russia and of kaiju attack that recently took place there. It doesn't seem to be related to the Dark Ones. It's possible Toombs may have created a new hybrid with Allison's help. Whatever Allison is planning, we will have to wait until she plays her hand to act. Which is exactly why you should enjoy some time with your family now."

Luke nodded and started walking back to his beloved wife and kids as a soldier ran to Parsons with reports of giant insects and lizards appearing in the Sahara Desert. Luke grabbed Melissa, hugged her, and said, "I know that it scares you when I am out there with Chimera fighting all of those monsters, but I did it for you and the girls. I don't want you to think I feel the need to save the planet to prove myself." He began to tear up. "When I am out there, I try to think about saving you and the kids. The hell with the planet; you three are my world."

Melissa kissed him as Sally and Suzie hugged his legs. "We know, and that's why we are so proud of you."

The Congo

Allison appeared in the front of the cave and the children who now appeared to be closer to thirteen than ten came running up to her. Allison opened her arms to them and yelled, "Today, my children! Today, is the day that you leave the cave and walk in the sunlight! Today, is the day that you meet your father!"

The children all screamed with joy as for the first time in their lives they ran out of the cave. For the demi-gods, the act of leaving the cave was akin to a second birth. They all looked up at the bright blue sky above them and opened their arms. Many of them ran into the jungle and jumped into a nearby river. The kids were laughing and having fun when a storm cloud suddenly appeared overhead. The cloud landed in front of the cave as thunder and lightning shot out from it. The cloud dissipated as quickly as it had formed to reveal Zeus.

The god king was staring in disbelief at the demigods that were running around. When they saw him, the demi-gods began to walk over to the Olympian. He shook his head. "My children? You live? I thought that the nymph had slain you all!"

The children were glaring at Zeus as Allison stepped out of the cave. She put Thor's belt around her waist and grew to a height of two hundred feet tall. She smiled. "Yes, children, this is your father. The god who sired you to serve as his slaves. Just as he treated me and your uncle as slaves for thousands of years."

The children were closing in on Zeus as he stared at Allison. "Thor's belt. Do you think the belt will increase your power enough to challenge me? For taking these children and disobeying me, I shall break you! Then I shall return you to your former role in my harem!"

Allison smiled and laughed as she mocked Zeus. "My former lord, I know that your powers are not what they used to be after Chimera destroyed your throne. Still, even with the belt, your power may be greater than mine. The belt is currently only serving to deter you from attacking me while we test your strength, as well as that of our children." She looked at the gathered demi-gods and said, "Now, children, attack the one who abandoned us to a cave! Who sought to bend us to his will! Who created you and tossed you aside like garbage!"

The demi-gods fell on Zeus, striking him with blows powerful enough to shatter boulders. The god king was caught off guard and was knocked to the ground. The children continued to strike Zeus until they were suddenly cast off by a flash of lightning. The children were laying around Zeus as electricity danced across his eyes. "Enough, wench! Do not doubt that I still have the power to humble you and destroy these bastards! Did you truly think these halflings could defeat me?'

The giant Allison smiled and shook her head. "No, as I said, this was simply a test. Thank you for showing me that our children are not yet ready to face Chimera." The ground shook as a thundering impact echoed through the jungle. Zeus began to look around nervously. When another impact tremor shook the ground, the god king created a storm cloud around himself. He was shocked when the cloud faded away. He looked up to see Allison holding her hand out above him. She smiled. "One thing that this belt does give me the power to do is to prevent you from teleporting away from here." She smiled. "Your time has come, mighty Zeus. The Dark Ones have fallen and now the last of the god kings shall fall as well."

A roar ripped through the air as several trees were crushed. Zeus turned around to see a giant horn piercing through trees and in front of it was Jonathan Toombs. The giant horn came out of the woods to show the massive face of a rhinoceros. The monster walked out of the jungle on four muscular and feline-like legs. As the beast continued to emerge from the jungle, the porcupine-like spikes on its back became visible. Toombs pointed at Zeus and the kaiju stepped forward. Zeus turned to run only to find that he was surrounded by the demi-gods. The god's eyes went wide as the monster lowered his head and drove his horn through his midsection.

Blood spurted out of Zeus' mouth as the monster moved his head up and down, causing the god to slide down the colossal horn. Allison removed Thor's belt and shrunk back down to her normal height. She walked up to the dying Zeus, grabbed his bloody chin, and turned his head toward her. She sneered. "How does it feel, god king, to be penetrated as you penetrated me so many times? How does it feel to know that your concubine, one of the humans you sought to exterminate, and the bastard children you have tossed aside have ended you?" She patted the monster's blood-covered horn and said, "This monster will ravage you as you ravaged me and then he will do the same to this world." She looked at the beast and smiled. "Ravager. That will be a fine name for my monster."

Zeus' eyes closed as Allison laughed at him. When the god was finally dead, Ravager shook his head and sent Zeus' corpse flying. Toombs walked over to the nymph whom he worshipped. "When do we make ourselves known to Parsons, my queen?"

She looked over at the demigods. "In a year's time, our children shall be ready to challenge Chimera. Until then, take the monster to

Antarctica and keep him hidden while I search for the final weapon we need to ensure our victory." Allison smiled, "Chimera is not the first god slayer." She turned and looked at the demi-gods and Ravager. "When the time comes, an army of demi-gods, your newest monster, and the weapon I unearth shall crush Chimera. Then I shall rule over this world!"

Japan
Atomic Rex's World

Chris and Kate Myers were sitting in the cockpit of the Steel Samurai as it floated over the Japanese Islands. They were looking down at a massive kaiju that was making its way into the ocean. Kate shook her head. "It's just like when Atomic Rex ran out of food in the US and we had to draw him to South America. That thing has eaten up its food supply and it's looking for new hunting grounds. It's going to cross the ocean and head toward our settlement."

Chris grabbed his wife's hand. "That thing killed every kaiju in Asia. It might be the most powerful kaiju that we have ever seen."

Kate shrugged. "I know. It's clear what we have to do. It won't be like the other times we tried something like this. It won't be drawing multiple monsters into confrontations. It will just be leading that monster and Atomic Rex against each other. The winner will have South America." She placed her head on her husband's shoulder. "I know the kid's mech is finally ready, but are they?"

Chris smiled. "They take after their mom. They're ready for anything."

THE END

CHECK OUT OTHER GREAT KAIJU NOVELS

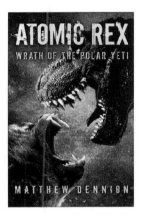

ATOMIC REX: WRATH OF THE POLAR YETI
by Matthew Dennion

It has been fifteen years since Captain Chris Myers used his giant mech to draw the kaiju of North America into each other's territory to have them destroy each other. Once all of the kaiju had battled to the death only Atomic Rex was left standing. In Antarctica, the kaiju known as Armorsaur has entered the frozen valley of the yetis and attacked them. Devouring all but one alpha male yeti who was exposed to the kaiju's blood and left dying in the snow. The yeti awoke to find himself transformed into a kaiju with an obsession to destroy Armorsaur. Chris and Kate are forced to protect the people of their settlement by drawing Atomic Rex into South America where he will battle the kaiju there to usurp their territory and claim their hunting grounds as his own. As Atomic Rex enters South America from the north the enraged Polar Yeti enters the continent from the south. The two most powerful kaiju in the world will battle their way through a multitude of giant monsters as they are set on a collision course with each other!

KAIJU CORPS
by Matthew Dennion

They are four soldiers who were genetically created to be mankind's last line of defense against potential world ending threats. They are soldiers who can transform themselves into gigantic monsters. They are the Kaiju Corps and they are facing a threat that is beyond the scope of even their fantastic abilities.

CHECK OUT OTHER GREAT KAIJU NOVELS

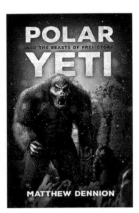

POLAR YETI AND THE BEASTS O PREHISTORY
by Matthew Dennion

A team from Princeton University searching for a lost tribe in Antartica discover a hidden valley filled with wooly mammoths, saber toothed tigers and other Ice Age beasts. Seizing the opportunity of a lifetime, the team set up camp to study the amazing creatures. But there is something else that lives in the Valley. Something terrifying. Something beyond imagination. POLAR YETI!

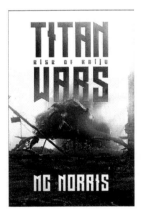

TITAN WARS
by M.C. Norris

Millions of microscopic alien life forms escape a sample canister of water from the frigid depths of outer space. Invisible to the naked eye, a menacing menagerie of more than seventy deadly species react to Earth's warm and fertile seas by launching into metabolic overdrive. Waves of gargantuan abominations begin to rise from the sea, transforming our world into a zoo without cages, where humans plunge to the bottom of the food chain.

In dire need of a zookeeper, the Allied Navy turns to "Psyjack," a bickering geek squad with an outrageous plan to hack into the minds of the megafauna with some reengineered neurosurgical technology. The young gamers hope to level the uneven playing field by fighting monsters with monsters, but they couldn't have anticipated how deadly their technology could be, if it ever fell into the wrong hands ...

CHECK OUT OTHER GREAT KAIJU NOVELS

KAIJU SPAWN
by David Robbins
& Eric S Brown

Wally didn't believe it was really the end of the world until he saw the Kaiju with his own eyes. The great beasts rose from the Earth's oceans, laying waste to civilization. Now Wally must fight his way across the Kaiju ravaged wasteland of modern day America in search of his daughter. He is the only hope she has left . . . and the clock is ticking.

From authors David Robbins (Endworld) and Eric S Brown (Kaiju Apocalypse), Kaiju Spawn is an action packed, horror tale of desperate determination and the battle to overcome impossible odds.

KUA MAU
by Mark Onspaugh

The Spider Islands. A mysterious ship has completed a treacherous journey to this hidden island chain. Their mission: to capture the legendary monster, Kua'Mau. Thinking they are successful, they sail back to the United States, where the terrifying creature will be displayed at a new luxury casino in Las Vegas. But the crew has made a horrible mistake - they did not trap Kua'Mau, they took her offspring. Now hot on their heels comes a living nightmare, a two hundred foot, one hundred ton tentacled horror, Kua'Mau, Kaiju Mother of Wrath, who will stop at nothing to safeguard her young. As she tears across California heading towards Vegas, she leaves a monumental body-count in her wake, and not even the U. S. military or private black ops can stop this city-crushing, havoc-wreaking monstrous mother of all Kaiju as she seeks her revenge.

Printed in Great Britain
by Amazon